DAVINA BELL

The
END
of the
WORLD is
BIGGER
than
LOVE

D0556377

TEXT PUBLISHING MELBOURNE AUSTRALIA

This book was written on the lands of the Wardandi and Wurundjeri Peoples—land that has never been ceded. The author acknowledges the Traditional Owners and pays her respect to their elders, past and present.

textpublishing.com.au

The Text Publishing Company
Swann House, 22 William Street, Melbourne Victoria 3000, Australia

The Text Publishing Company (UK) Ltd
130 Wood Street, London EC2V 6DL, United Kingdom

Published by The Text Publishing Company, 2020
Reprinted 2021 (twice)

Book design by Imogen Stubbs
Cover illustration by Kate Forrester
Typeset by J&M Typesetting

Printed and bound in Australia by Griffin Press, part of Ovato, an accredited ISO/NZS 14001:2004 Environmental Management System printer.

ISBN: 9781922268822 (paperback)
ISBN: 9781925923353 (ebook)

A catalogue record for this book is available from the National Library of Australia.

Department of
Local Government, Sport
and Cultural Industries
GOVERNMENT OF
WESTERN AUSTRALIA

This book was written with the support of a grant from the Western Australian Department of Local Government, Sport and Cultural Industries.

Davina Bell is an award-winning author of books for young readers of many ages. She writes picture books (including *All the Ways to be Smart* and *Under the Love Umbrella*), junior fiction (*Lemonade Jones*) and middle-grade fiction (the Corner Park Clubhouse series). Davina lives in Melbourne, where she works as a children's book publisher. davinabell.com

To the memory of my mother.

The ending is not the story.

The End of the World Is Bigger than Love

'In the midst of winter, I found there was,
within me, an invincible summer.'

Albert Camus

Summer

The first thing you need to know is that my name is Summer and my sister's name is Winter and I know—it's ridiculous, right? But that's the kind of dude our dad was, and it probably wouldn't surprise you to learn that he devoted a lot of his life to studying axolotls, which are those disgusting Mexican walking fish, and that's why he was taken away by a bunch of guys dressed like ninjas. At least, that's what we thought till we figured out what really happened, though now I wonder why we didn't cotton on earlier. Probably because we were busy reading.

You might be thinking, where was our mother? Surely she could have put her foot down, unless she was in some post-birthing medical haze and was all, like, YES! to giving her identical twin daughters matching trans-seasonal names. Well, sure, maybe she would have, if she hadn't died with Winter still inside her, all curled up like a little fist and just wanting to hang around where it was dark and quiet. I was out by then, so I probably saw it go down. But do you want to know something creepy? The doc didn't even know Winter was coming—total surprise, like when you open the front door and there's a guy there in a gorilla suit and he's singing you happy birthday.

Did you know that once they used to do some kind of weird X-ray scan on pregnant ladies to show that sort of stuff—straight onto their skin? It's gross to think about now, I know, but at least it would have given our mother the chance to up her bootie-knitting rate. And it wouldn't have taken them until after she was gone to figure out that Winter was still in there, rapidly forming that part of her that likes to wander off in golden fields, trying not to hurt daisies as she picks them while I'm left all alone, going out of my mind with no one to talk to. That happened a lot once we got to the island. We were literally stuck by ourselves on a piece of land the size of a spitball. Oh, and we lived in the shell of a church. Not even joking. Our dad was there at the start, but then…you know. Just over a year later there was the whole ninja thing.

After Pops (our dad) was taken away, we kept things going, like we had when he was still around. So if he ever came back one mid-morning, say, strolling in with his hands in his pockets, he'd see us pretty much where he left us, sitting on those big old wooden pews in the sunshine, reading through the set of our mother's classics with the patterned covers and arguing about Jane Eyre, who I called Jane Airhead but who of course Winter really liked. Winter really likes everyone—she even felt sorry for that guy we saw kicking a dog on an excursion to the Refuse and Recycling Centre.

But you wouldn't understand all that, not yet, because I haven't explained anything properly. Not Bartleby, the big old ruin of a church with half the roof busted in. How it became our home because Pops had to take us on the run and find somewhere to hide away until all his troubles blew over, though at the time he still insisted that the remote island's unique ecosystem was needed to further his axolotl breeding program.

I know it's hard to believe now that nobody goes anywhere ever, but we had been before, to the island at the top of the world. It was one long summer holidays while Pops was away on axolotl business, and we were seven and had just learned to cartwheel with our legs straight. We sailed there from another, bigger island with my grandfather—right across the ocean, skipping over the waves in a proud little yacht, not even the tiniest bit afraid of being shot down by a plane.

It was like a dreamscape from a book, that island—like a diorama made by the only kid in the whole school who really has a future in Art. The mountain sat at the back, huge and majestic, white-peaked, and, boy, was it *high*. Every time I looked up at it, I felt that shiver you get when you hear the roar of a lion, even through the TV. The next layer was the green plush of the forest on the right, the red rocks of the headland on the left. Then came the church, with the bell tower and the moat, and alongside it the sweet burble of the river that came down the slope, all melted snow, so icy and clear you could see your feet turning blue as you slipped round on the rocks trying to cross to the meadow on the other side, where a tiny white shack sat on grass so bright it glowed green. If there had been anyone else on that island, we could have rented that lawn out for barefoot bowling, but it was just us—that was kind of the point. In front of the grass was the sand, fine as flour, and the little jaggedy cove, the shape of a bite mark chomped into the shore, which was where our grandpa pulled up the boat that first day.

The whole place smelled like honeydew melon and sheets dried hot in the sun, and as we climbed out of the boat, Winter said, 'Let's never leave,' and I added, 'Except to get nachos,' but even then I didn't really mean it.

Our grandpa's name was Walter, and we called him that. He didn't say much except with his eyes, and Winter was mad for him. 'This is paradise,' he said with his eyes as he introduced us to the island, and truly it was. I don't even have the vocab for that kind of beautiful and I'm basically fluent in three languages.

'What's on the other side of the mountain?' I asked Walter one afternoon, when the sun bounced off the water so strongly that it burned my nose.

'The end of the world,' he said, scrubbing at the hull of his boat.

'Can I go there?' I asked.

'Nope,' he said, not in a mean way, but so I knew not to ask why.

'What's this island called?' I said.

'The island,' said Walter. 'You sure ask a lot of questions.'

'You bet,' I said happily. 'And look at this cartwheel.'

3

For weeks we stayed in that wooden shack, so close to the beach that the sand blew in and got caught in the cracks of the floorboards, no matter how many times Winter swept up, hoping that Walter would notice.

Walter slept under the table that summer, so that we could have the bed. He braided Winter's hair to distract her when she found an octopus washed up on the shore, rotting purple, and our hair isn't that easy to plait on account of being so curly. He planted things— saplings, I think, that he'd brought across in paper sacks. I guess they were the fruit trees we ate from, years later. Did he bring them there for future us? Was the island actually his?

His boat was pulled up right outside the window, like a friendly dragon keeping watch outside a cave. In my mind, half the summer was spent scrubbing that boat, preparing for the journey home. Our grandpa was a thorough guy. He was a doctor once, Pops told us. He studied AIDS, which used to be a kind of virus, and you probably remember the hoopla when they found the cure—an injection quicker than a bee sting. Boy, was that a happy day across the planet. We weren't that old, Winter and I, but I remember watching it on TV, the cities wrapped in ropes of white garlands that fluttered merrily as if they were hanging there to say 'You see? There's still hope for the future.' But honestly? Hope had been fading for ages by then.

And after that summer on the island, we never saw Walter again.

Winter

They sat by my bed. Adjusted my drip. White walls, white sheets, white masks on their faces. A curtain that was always closed.

They watched me pretend to sleep sitting up.

When I had grown thicker, they asked questions I couldn't answer. Not even on paper.

They gave me one sheet. They said, 'Write what you cannot say. Write it down. Like it's all just a story. Write it here. Write it down.'

But Summer had made me hold that story inside so long. Now it sits in my throat, a dry cough. It won't come out. There is nowhere to start.

The next day, they came with this notebook, a sun on its cover. 'Write your happiest memory. A toy. A pet.'

And so.

Summer

Five years later, after Japan, after Egypt, after Turkey, Japan again, we returned to the island with Pops. What a time. If you've ever sunk a seaplane deliberately in the middle of the night, you'll know what I'm saying here.

Pops's work had dragged us all kinds of everywhere over the years, and it sounds disgustingly smug but by then we'd seen enough places in the world to realise that Bartleby was pretty dang beautiful, and not just as far as remote abandoned churches go. Sure, it wasn't anything like ending up in India, say, where even the smog haze felt electric, and currents of spicy smells ran under everything, and the people made rainbow tides. But in India, trying to watch all the coloured saris was like trying to see all the specks of a cloud of confetti at once (FYI—impossible), and the cows were so bony that even as I was saying to Winter, 'Look at those tough old horns, they're as strong as marble coathangers,' one died right in front of her and she had to go and lay her cheek against it until the owner lashed at her legs with a big jerky piece of bamboo. Above all, the island felt safe, safe, safe, and though the shack was gone, returning still felt like coming home.

The first thing we did that first day when the sun came up—even before we unpacked—was plant parsley, because did you know that parsley has the most calcium of any food ever? So I guess Pops always knew we'd stay a while if he was thinking about our growing bones, because it's not like we had cows or goats or camels or any other kind of friendly, milk-giving mammal arriving anytime soon, and the last thing we needed was to grow up all soft-boned and bent over. It was going to be hard enough getting boyfriends in the future.

The second thing we did was realise that sea water had ruined our sourdough cultures, which are those weird, alive yeast things that you bake bread from, and maybe it was because we'd been awake for thirty-six hours straight, but Winter *really* cried. And if I'm totally honest, which I'm trying to be, I cried too, because hot bread—proper leavened bread—risen and baked over some kind of fire, well, is there anything better?

And Pops did what he always did when we cried: mutter something about needing to work, and put his hands in his pockets, and back out of the room quickly, though to his credit he came back a moment later with a box of books and slit it open before scuttling away. And what was the first one, just shining on out at us? It was *To Kill a Mockingbird*, and though everyone thinks it's their favourite, we felt an especial connection, Winter and I, because we'd lost our mother, just like dear little Scout and handsome, moody Jem, and we were also often left alone. And I'm not saying our father was Atticus Finch or anything, but not everyone was that crash-hot on Pops, so when the townspeople turn against Atticus and want to bash his hat off, we could kind of relate.

We lay under an almond tree in the sun, and I read it aloud until we may as well have been in the mossy balm of southern Alabama and that hot, salty mash of good versus evil, and eventually we drifted to sleep. When we woke up, the sky was pretty and the breeze was chilly and we agreed that if we were Harper Lee, we wouldn't ever have written another book either, because nothing can be more perfect than perfect, and that's how we felt about *Mockingbird*. And wasn't that a scandal, when it turned out that the long-lost prequel was actually written by her lawyer with help from dear Harper's personal diaries that the lawyer had swooped from the back of a garage and gone through with a highlighter.

As the last of the sun hit the bricks of the bell tower, and gulls wheeled and the ocean murmured, we jumped up and did split leaps over the sand and yelled, 'Pork!' as we threw our ruined sourdough to the birds, and suddenly life didn't seem so bad.

We spent the next few days tracing over our summer with Walter, dragging our toes through the sand to draw an outline where the white house used to be. We were so into it that we almost forgot our twelfth birthday. If I squinted, sometimes I thought I could see us cartwheeling along the shore in the sunshine, the sea behind us breaking out in a rash of diamonds.

Winter

Our Pet

His name was Pete.

He was my mother's dog. A springer spaniel, white and brown. His smile belonged on a birthday card.

Summer taught him to stand like a man. On his back legs, he could foxtrot to music. He waited for us by the big school gates. Like a nursery rhyme.

Then my mother died. We were eleven.

Pete started snapping.

First just at flies. Pond fish in a park.

Then the hem of a little girl's dress.

A baby's sunhat.

My father's calf.

We came to the island with chickens for eggs. Their blood crusted brown on his lips.

On windy nights, he howled. He threw himself at walls, at the stained-glass windows of our small church. He was sick with love that had nowhere to go.

'Did you know glass is actually a slow-flowing liquid?' Summer said once as his rope lead burned in my palms. She was pretending not to notice him. When Summer pretended, I almost believed.

Not long before the boy showed up, Pete started to circle Summer.

He walked around her in slow, smooth circles. He purred like a motor. His teeth glowed.

Eventually we ate that dog. Summer said it wasn't dog meat, but I knew.

I pushed the plate away with my eyes. I shook as she gnawed, her thumbs slick with grease right up to the joint.

'Eat,' Summer said. And then, '*Eat*. There's nothing else left.'

I wanted to try.

Even for Summer, I couldn't.

The boy and I, we had watched her kill Pete. As she hacked off his leg, Summer frowned like she did when we pulled Christmas crackers.

The boy held my hand. At least, that's how I remember it.

We were down in the moat. We often were. By then, we were one and the same. Or maybe just mingled together. Sand from two beaches on the point where they meet.

But all that came after. I will go back.

Summer

You might be wondering right about now how we managed, two tweenaged girls all alone, not connected to anyone anyhow, gadgets or otherwise, and in a church to boot, not, like, a laser-tag arena or a mall after closing time, or any other place you might imagine being locked in if you had to write an essay about it for school.

Well, we had the mountain, which was like a grandfather clock, or maybe even a grandfather, ancient and solid and friendly. Its party-hat peak nudging the clouds, making heaven feel closer and everything somehow less lonely. There was the sea, which, if you've been there—and who hasn't?—you'd know is a big old twinkly sheet of kindness that makes everything else seem pretty irrelevant, especially you.

Then don't forget about all the books, my mother's books, all those juicy classics, and there were so many of those that by the time we got to the end of her collection, we were excited again about the ones from the beginning. Like the first day of school after the summer holidays when you can't wait to get there and see if your friends have new haircuts. Winter loved to be read to, though often I had to skim the parts that I knew she couldn't handle, like Beth from *Little Women* dying, and any scene in *Pride and Prejudice* that featured Mary, the loser brainiac sister who everyone in her family picked on.

'Poor Mary,' she'd say, her eyes full of everything. 'They all make fun of her. But she's still a person. I wish I could tell her.'

'Don't be a feather,' I would say. 'She probably went off with her big old brain and cured cancer and laughed all the way to Baby Dior, where she bought a zillion-dollar cape for the little girl she had with a handsome professor.'

'She'd never have believed a professor could love her,' Winter insisted. 'I know.'

Pops started working all day and all night and we were alone most of the time, left to wander and Self-Educate. All the normal things in life fell away like those big old rocks, the Twelve Apostles, which crumple into the sea one by one at random moments—suddenly there and then not. I wonder if any more of them have done that lately, because of course I wouldn't know. We didn't have the internet (don't get me started) and we couldn't duck out to get a newspaper on account of there being no newspapers by then. No shops, no buildings, no civilisation—just us in that big old church.

Autumn came, and then winter, and then the apple trees were smug with fruit, and it was summer again. Gradually the days just seemed to smudge into each other, because it's not like Pops took weekends off from his homemade laboratory, which was really just the part up above the church at the back where the choir would have sung—I don't know the exact word for it and Winter isn't here to ask, and I want to say vestibule but I know it's wrong.

Even though it was all kinds of crumbly, Bartleby was so beautiful that some days, with the sky peeking in and the ivy vines climbing up the inside walls, my throat would close up. I haven't even got to the stained-glass windows or the baby grand piano with the honeysuckle growing out the top or the cool moat around the edge that somehow always left our hair soft after swimming in it. The church was so big that even though Winter and I were basically jocks, we couldn't have thrown a football from the back to the altar, and the roof was so high that, at the start, it felt like someone was sitting up there in the rafters, watching us mooch around and reading the thoughts floating up from my skull. And, sure, we'd been in churches before, but at first camping there seemed kind of wrong and, like, unholy, if you get what I mean? Eventually, though, I made my peace with whoever might have been peeping down at me, and once we strung up some golden fairy lights and hooked them to the generator and made little nooks for sleeping and reading and a sort of ping-pong table, and we figured out how to fly a kite out through the (very large) hole in the roof, it felt cosy, like one of those self-sufficient caravans that the Famous Five used to get around in on their summer hols. From up in the bell tower, with its four stone arches, you could look out in every direction, like you were in the crow's nest of a tall ship.

When the ninjas came and ransacked that church—turned over every tin, ran up and down the bell tower, flicked through each page of my mother's books till they were satisfied there was nothing to steal but our dad—Winter wanted to go with them. Of course she did. Winter would walk into a fire for anyone, and, boy, she's lucky it was just us, that we didn't have some evil older brother who liked pulling legs off insects, because her whole daisy-picking-earth-child thing would have got her completely pummelled. It was bad enough to see her climb out of the piano that day in her lemon-and-white-striped dress, no shoes, and hold out her hands, twisted politely together so they could snap the cuffs straight onto them and Pops wouldn't have to leave alone.

Weird thing was, they didn't want her, those guys, so I've never felt too bad that I didn't come out from where I was hiding under the ivy, all gallant and feisty, to hold her back. I just stayed where I was, my feet tucked up, hanging from strands that were as thick as old sailing ropes, and watched them wave her away, barely looking at her, even though she was beautiful. I know that's a big-headed thing to say given that we're identical, split from the same zygote and all, right? And get this: there wasn't a freckle or a birthmark or a knobbled bone or a narrow, forceps-squished face that set us apart—physically, at least. Nothing except for the wisp of a scar on the bridge of her nose, which I secretly wished I had too. We used to push our palms and the soles of our feet together just to see, and even the white specks in our nails grew out at identical rates, and our eyelashes fell out on the same days, and you're thinking, *As if*, and believe me, I KNOW. It wasn't normal, whatever that is. And that's not even the weirdest part of this story, which takes a lot of twists, let me tell you.

But, yes, even with her home haircut, Winter was time-stoppingly beautiful, and maybe never more than when they led Pops out through the big arch that must once have been home to a huge church door, and she was just standing there, her wrists still twined together, her head tilted to the side like a dog's when it hears a strange noise. I knew we would never see him again; he would die with his secrets sealed up in his mind—except the ones he'd left with us.

I could say that I'd never loved Winter more than at that moment, too, but that would be another lie because the day I loved her most was the last day I ever saw her. The day we came down from the top of Our Mountain. And I guess this is the story of how we got up there, and why, when all I wanted after Pops left was for everything to stand still. For it just to be us forever and always, with Winter safe and close enough to loop my thoughts around her like a lasso made of light.

And this probably isn't a Spoiler Alert but, FYI, everything changes, and by everything, I guess I mean everyone, and by everyone, well, I guess you get who I mean, and maybe that's why only one of us really survived.

Winter

He arrived late in our second spring on the island. By then we were alone. He walked out of the forest, and slowly.

He never said where he came from. I didn't ask. I think I knew.

He was a boy, mostly.

He was wild, but not wolf-wild or fox-wild.

I made him a nook. I fetched water in a cup.

His hair stuck up. His skin glowed brown. He was shaking. He was tall. He needed something. Maybe me.

You might be trying to figure out what we ate on that island, or perhaps you're just thinking that it was soylent, which was that liquid food/sludge that most of the world was surviving on by then, but you'd be wrong and here's why. Out the back of the church was a hall so crumbled and cave-like, I wouldn't have been surprised if we'd walked in one day and knocked ourselves out on a low-hanging stalactite. That's where Pops had built a Great Wall of Canned Food, and that sounds sort of gross, but it was good stuff, which wouldn't have surprised you if you'd met our dad, who liked fancy things. There was a stack of some kind of French chestnut cream in posh jars, and there were sliced Mexican chillies, like floating green wheels with spokes, and these tartan tins of Scottish Christmas shortbread in the shape of highland terriers, which is what we'd eat as a treat if we were up to date with our reading, which mostly we were. I know you're thinking we were pretty tame, but you try being wild when you're *in* the wild—it seems pretty stupid.

It was actually kind of spooky out the back of that Emporium, so big and echoey, all flickering shadows, so we didn't go too often. When we did, we just grabbed things blind and stuffed them in a huge sack in that way you do when you actually just want to get the hell away, which was maybe why we became so good at adjusting to unusual flavour combinations that we could have seriously *killed* on one of those cooking show competitions they had before everything on TV was just calming shots of tropical island scenery on a loop, and warbly panpipe music.

And, sure, out in the forest there was many a tasty bird, a woodlands animal, and if you knew how to start a proper fire (which, FYI, we did), there was wood galore and you could skewer those into some tidy kebabs to barbecue al fresco. But as if Winter would have been okay with munching on a teeny squirrel or a gosh-darn bluebird, and besides, the effort factor was high because the axe was pretty blunt, and I had tried a bunch of things, but I just couldn't seem to sharpen it. Back then I wouldn't even have dreamed of unsheathing The Knife. The motor blades on our father's massive generator had cracked almost as soon as he left, and of course we had no idea about how to fix that kind of thing, so we just packed away the kettle and the fairy lights, and said goodbye to all our appliances. Instead we hung our clothes on the generator to dry when we washed them in the moat with hotel hand soaps, which we seemed to have about a zillion of, and got by on kerosene lamps and sleeping huddled up in winter.

Truth be told, we got seriously loved up on the whole Playing House thing, hauling buckets of water from the river, scrubbing our clothes on stones. We'd read enough *Little House on the Prairie* for that to seem dreamy, all the baking and foraging and darning and living in semi-rags, dresses made from T-shirts and shoes made from bits of old tyres because our feet were growing fast, and wearing nine jumpers on top of each other for warmth, and tapping sap from weeping trees and taping up twigs to make scratchy brooms and the satisfaction of finishing complicated quilting patterns using cut-up priest dresses, which I want to call tussocks but I'm pretty sure that's wrong. From where I am now I can see that all that homemaking was probably to do with controlling things that felt out of control. Being our own mothers, or something, like, psychological. But at the time it just seemed really nice compared to the last few months of our old life: all those midnight bolts to the door of a waiting black car with tinted windows, rolling into it while it was half taking off to a weird abandoned airstrip where a plane with a sharp little nose would always be waiting, its propeller already ticking like a sped-up heart.

Sure, from time to time, Winter would get all mopey—would ask stupid questions, would open the curtains that we had agreed to keep shut.

'Why doesn't Walter come to find us?' she asked one hot evening. We were lying on our backs in the moat, its surface rippling with echoes of stars, our bodies white whispers below. 'Why has he never come?'

'We've been a lot of places, Winter. And it's not like he could just email.' I trailed my fingers through the water. Together, apart, together, apart. 'How would he even know we were here?' I said, not wanting to really get into the whole Walter thing.

'But if he loved us,' said Winter, standing up and squeezing out her ponytail, 'couldn't he tell?'

'Oh, sure,' I said. 'He put a tracking device on the back of one of the unicorns we flew here on.'

'I always knew where Mama was,' she insisted. 'I could tell. Even in Tokyo—'

In one motion I flipped myself over and slapped her so hard, the sound made us wince, made us deaf, and my hand burned raw, and I couldn't catch my breath, my chest was that tight with fury.

Her dog started to bark so loud, it was like a saw in my ear. 'Shut UP,' I yelled, and flicked water at him. He stumbled back in shock and whimpered.

Winter didn't cry. She just sank down and put her face in the water, maybe because some part of her was dripping blood—the corner of an eye, a nostril.

She stayed like that for ages, long after my hand stopped stinging. By the time she lifted her head back up, my collarbones ached with regret. And sure, I'll bet now you're thinking, *Hoo boy, that Summer is a real psycho*. But I wasn't—not usually. I just loved Winter with everything in me—till sometimes I sprang leaks and it burst out of me.

'Why does everyone who loves us always leave?' she asked, and I swear she was asking the stars—that she was no longer talking to me at all.

'*I'm* still here,' I said.

She looked over at me, and even through the gloom I could see that her lip was split and blood was trickling down her chin, down her neck—that when she licked her lips, she would taste it.

'Just so you know,' I said coolly as I pulled myself up out of the water and onto the flagstones that bordered the church. 'Pops told me never to tell you, but Walter died. He was captured. Ages ago.'

It wasn't even true—well, it might have been by then. Who knew? But it was worth it to see her cry all the tears I never could, her big eyes leaking and gorgeous.

Winter

At first, the boy slept, hot and turning. He glowed like old fire.

Summer said not to go near him. That it might be catching. That it might be a trick. He would crack us in half, mess us up in nasty ways.

She was sure of so many things. Each of them like a pin in a board, trapping me under, a fluttering scrap.

She said we didn't know what the world out there had become. We had been alone there so long on that tiny island, in that tiny church.

But in the night, I couldn't bear it.

My chest beat like wings.

I went to him with a wet rag.

His lips were cracked deep. They ran with blood. His tongue was a white sea-sponge in his mouth.

He didn't say anything—not for days. Until his fever broke, he just looked.

His eyes were all of the world. I wanted to stand on the feeling they gave me, so no one could see it.

They made me want to be alone for the first time ever.

Not alone by myself. But alone without Summer.

Alone with that boy, under the moon.

Stroking his hands.

Forever.

Sure, after our father left, we probably should have scratched the days into the bedpost in neat stacks of five and counted them up to keep track like they would have in an Enid Blyton novel. But we didn't really have beds, just piles of communion cushions made into a sort of cosy nest, and who could bring themselves to scratch things into a pew? Well, maybe plenty of people, but not me, and totally, completely, definitely not Winter. And besides, we knew what season it was on account of the weather, and I don't think we really believed we'd be there that long. Who can imagine forever?

We tried it once. We were down on the edge of the sea, which, kid you not, was a swimming pool's length away from the church with only that green lawn between. That's where we were lying, looking up, talking about infinity, and, yes, we were nerds, so it's lucky we were diving prodigies, or we probably would have been called a lot worse than freaks. But other kids seemed to respect the fact that even when we were standing on our hands ten metres up on a big old plank, we weren't even the tiniest bit scared to bend our elbows and push off and pike and twist and tuck before cutting the water like neat blades and leaving behind only the tiniest ring of bubbles, like a goldfish makes when it blurps. I don't mean to be immodest here, but in the minds of everyone who's anyone in the diving world, we had pretty much won the Olympic gold medals in synchronised diving for the next zillion years with perfect tens in both categories (three and ten metres). To tell you the truth, it was getting a little boring. Like someone giving you a perky round of applause every time you breathe.

'You can't tell me you can visualise infinity,' I said to Winter that day on the lawn, the sunshine finally warm again—our second spring on the island. We were looking up at the clouds, which were racing away as if they had somewhere good to get to, perhaps a cloud ball, which is something Winter would have loved to imagine, and I'll keep that stored up to tell her when she gets to this place I'm in now.

I looked up at those clouds and I said to her, 'Nothing goes on forever.'

'It does, doesn't it,' said Winter happily and closed her eyes so her eyelids would get sunned too, because heaven forbid you should neglect your eyelids or anything else that might need the sweet and inextinguishable rays of your compassion. That's why Pops and I would privately roll our eyes at old Winter, and say to each other with only our minds, 'What a sap, am I right?'

'It's nice, isn't it,' Winter said then, 'not knowing what day of the week it is.'

I said, 'Don't be stupid, it's—'

And when I said, 'Saturday' and she said, 'Wednesday?', something inside me went cold, because Winter was ridiculously clever, and I wasn't, like, totally stupid either. But before I had the chance to go into full hiding-my-breakdown mode, Winter said, 'Summer, what's that moving?'

Well, it was a plump brown bear waddling out of the trees at the bottom of Our Mountain.

Except there weren't any bears on that island.

So what was he really?

Winter

'Look at that moon,' I said to the boy, hot-sick in his blankets. 'You wouldn't want to miss all those moons we've got coming. And the sunsets. It's worth staying just for those, isn't it? All peaches and orange and berry and plum. We grow those things here—all of them. We have trees. We make jam in late summer. If you stick around, we'll put it on a scone for you. We don't have cream or butter. But if the scone's hot, you hardly notice that it's a bit floury.

'I was reading, just today, a quote about suns. Well, it was about Islamic women in extremist regimes. Saying how they're like suns trapped behind walls. Isn't that sad to think of? A thousand splendid suns all tucked away, blazing into nothing.

'But then I thought…I still think, well, we're those suns, aren't we? Tucked away in here all day. Like we're locked in a big cell. We're suns, too—at least, a little. Summer would never admit it. And I know we're lucky to still be alive and it's safe here. But sometimes it feels so small, this church. Like a jar. And I look out at the sea and I think…Well, I guess I don't know what I'm saying, just rambling. I'm out of practice. Usually I only have Pete to talk to.

'I checked your back, by the way. And it's fine—no bruises, no lumps, and your skin is still brown. I hope you don't mind. You know how it is with The Greying. Summer says that everyone would know now—everyone everywhere.

'If I just keep talking and you just keep breathing, that's a fair deal, isn't it. In and out, just like that. You should be proud, how well you're doing. I'm proud of you and I don't even know you. I'll be here—every night, I'll be here. You just sleep.'

Summer

We wrapped him up, that bear, as if he were a loaf of still-warm sourdough bread in a brown paper bag. For the first few hours, tight in his blanket, he shook like he was sitting on top of a dryer. He must have been scared, not cold, because it was spring then, and the sun was still rising and setting, rising and setting, like a super-reliable yo-yo, and the days were clean and blossom-warm.

Boy, was that bear *cute*. He was small and soft like...well, like a teddy, and that's how he got his name. Edward. I had to grit my teeth a lot when he was lying in my arms and looking into my eyes as if I and only I were Love. Sure, he wasn't quite a baby, but something in us must have wished he was, because we carried him round on one hip, even though it hurt our backs. I swear if we'd had access to a bonnet, he would've been getting around in that daily. I talked to him, that bear. I purred, 'there there,' and crooned and asked him questions that I answered myself and said the kind of rhymes I imagine a mother would murmur, though how would I really know? Never had one. But if there's one thing I can tell you, it's that a heck of a lot of things rhyme with 'bear', and it was nice to chat with someone after all this time—maybe a year?—of just us and old Bartleby. How was I to know what would happen after that?

I rocked him and swayed and walked around and, using all my might, lifted him up under his arms so we were face to face, and I rubbed our noses together, and kissed the flat little patch of fur between his eyes. You pretty much get the whole gooey picture, and if you're thinking, *Um, hello, wild animal?!* then you're smarter than we were, and we once tied for first place in an International Maths Olympiad, I kid you not.

Winter didn't talk to him—not even a whisper. She just held him on her lap, quiet and tender, and sat by the stained-glass window and looked out, not down, and she didn't tuck the sheet in or fuss about, blowing raspberries onto his pudgy beachball of a tummy. As I watched her, I felt impatient to have him back in my arms—could feel the weight of him there already—and those hours waiting for my turn were complete torture, like when a cake's in the oven and the crust is baked but you know the middle is still runny and you just want to pull it out and stick a spoon in anyway.

But on Winter's lap, that's where he stopped shaking, and I swear to you that he yawned and stretched out his arms and smiled at her, and shook his head back and forth as if to say, 'What the heck have I just been doing? Fool!' Winter lowered him to the floor and off he went, loping in a happy kind of hop down the aisle, like he was fizzed up on communion wine. As we chased him around the church, we were laughing. He was so quick and funny and nosy and sweet, and here's a word that people don't get to use enough: gambolling.

After about an hour, he needed an actual nap like a real baby, and he tucked himself under the altar, coiled up like Pete would sleep each night in the crook of Winter's knees.

We watched that bear for ages, not saying anything, both just deep in loving him, and maybe it wasn't even him—maybe it was the idea that something else was out there in the world.

At first, it didn't occur to me to do anything but love him till it hurt, so that's what we did.

Winter

I went to that boy. Night after night. Pete came, too.

Gradually he cooled down.

At first, his throat was too tight for talking. But some nights he winked. The flutter of his eyelid on the skin of my heart.

Eventually he croaked out his name. It sank into me like a cutter through dough.

In the mornings, Summer felt my yawns as if they were hers. 'I am warning you, Winter,' she said. 'You don't know where he's from or what he wants or how he even got onto this island. What if he's actually some kind of kinky murderer who's going to stuff us into a rubbish bin and pour acid on us so that our bones melt? Or if he's been sent to steal all of Pops's stuff, like those—'

'He's not,' I said quickly. 'He hasn't. I just know.'

'Your problem,' she said, 'is that you always believe the best in people. It's like a disease with you.' She clicked her tongue. 'Not everyone is sweetness and light and floral aprons. Just look at your dog,' she added. 'He looks harmless enough and yesterday he tried to chew off my face.'

'He's not *my* dog,' I said.

But Summer wouldn't hear that. There was so much she wouldn't hear, so much that I wasn't allowed to say. I had stopped trying—my voice wasn't loud enough. 'Please let the boy stay,' I said. 'Just till he's better?'

'Or dies,' said Summer, and thought for a while. 'Well, just don't think I'm helping you dig a grave, because remember the blisters I got when we buried the guinea pig? I couldn't hang from the monkey bars for ages after that.'

'Thank you!' I said. I curled my arms around her neck. Even her neck felt stronger than mine. I didn't even mind the lie about the guinea pig. The hole we dug was so much bigger than that.

'Just remember the rules,' Summer warned. 'Don't you even *think* about mentioning what's in the bell tower.'

'I won't,' I said. I never break the rules. Or at least I never did.

His name was Edward Ashby, in case you were wondering.

Do you know—have you ever even thought—how handy a bear actually is to have around? Even a little-ish one, or one that starts off little, makes a great table on a hot summer's night, when you want to pretend you're a just-married couple at a resort in Bermuda and you eat dinner down on the sand with a white bit of cloth over the bear's back and an altar candle on that flat part on top of its head, though this comes with a warning that crabs come out at night, and boy, do they *nip*.

If you have even the most basic supplies, like the end of a bell tower rope, you can make a bear cub its own cute harness and attach it to a little cart, and it can jog alongside you, right up to the base of Our Mountain, with enough books and apples and thermos tea to last until sunset. You could get through two *Harry Potter*s before you had to wind things up and sit on its back and ride down the mountain, talking deep about whether you're a Ron or a Hermione or a Harry or a Hedwig the owl.

That delicious summer with the bear ended in a confetti-pop of magic and long days out and about, and silky, salty morning swims before the sand blew up all gritty. Lunches in the meadow, plush with flowers—purple ones, mostly, but not just purple how you're seeing it in your mind right now, I'm talking so many shades of purple that some are shaking hands with blue and some are sidling up to hot pink and the rest are having a good old time with whites and greys and browny-blacks.

And the smell, well, it was like your mum's high-end perfume and a Christmas tree (a real one) and a florist's shop and an ice-cream parlour and a pile of grass clippings dumped next to a swimming pool on a sunny day and the cool stone foyer of a posh hotel; it was all of those things together. The smell—that's what I remember when I think about those long, lazy days when we were three together: Winter, the bear and me.

I had folded an old altar cloth into a sling and strapped Edward onto Winter's back, all snug, and as a Surprise, I'd cut off a couple of squares and made us headscarves so we could play out that scene from *The Sound of Music* where they get those rocking curtain clothes and go all loose and crazy in Vienna, singing about deer. That was Winter's favourite, and I know sometimes I could be a little, you know, bossy, but shoot me cold if I didn't try every nanosecond to make her happy—if every titchy thing I made us do wasn't to keep her true heart beating on just the way it did. And considering we'd had to stop wearing underwear a while back because we were pretty low on the old textiles, I think you'll probably get what a Sacrifice (capital S) that Von Trapp headscarf really was.

That was the day we taught Edward to roll down the hill, that funny old bear, and to turn in circles looking at the sky until he was fall-down dizzy. We taught him to stand up on his hind legs and hold the end of our skipping rope so that we could skip without having to tie the other end to an organ pipe or the stone font where Pops told us that babies were dunked in water, back when churches were still used for holy things. And even though it took some doing, eventually that bear could arc the rope around with the best of them, so that it flicked white against that blue, blue sky, and swoosh it so it nearly touched the ground but didn't. Blow me down if it wasn't nice to have him around, sort of festive, like gelato, or a new nun/nanny who makes you realise you've been living your life answering to a whistle when you could have been wearing curtains and choreographing marionette shows.

And I guess I figured that if we stayed there, playing grown-ups, maybe we could stay kids forever. I'm not talking in a Peter Pan way (because, honestly? I think that guy had Issues). *Summer*, you are thinking, *fourteen is not a kid*. Fourteen can hold a machine gun on its shoulder, a baby in its insides. But to me, we were very much Not Yet Adults, in spite of what was going on under our shirts. I guess I just mean I wanted to be wrapped up safe in the way we knew the world, and the way the world knew us.

Winter

When he first got out of bed, I was standing in the doorway.

'Hey,' he whispered.

Pete was tucked at my side. I was holding him back with all of my thoughts. Earlier he had snapped at Summer's Achilles. Gnashed the air so hard he cracked off a tooth.

'Here, boy,' Edward croaked, and Pete went.

'You're a good guy,' he said, and Pete sat.

I couldn't believe it.

The boy said, 'Fancy a run?' and Pete wagged his whole self. And to me he said, 'Come with?'

I said, 'I don't know how to run.' And I didn't.

'You don't know how to walk?' He smiled. The gloss of his eyes was silver. 'You don't know how to breathe? Because that's all it is: fast walking, deep breathing.'

He wore my father's old pyjama pants. He ran his hand through his hair.

I said, 'We never did sports.'

He cupped his palm on Pete's head, patient and gentle.

Pete rolled over. He waved his paws around.

'He can foxtrot,' I said. I don't know why I told him. I knew Summer would hate it. I swallowed. 'I'll come.'

But after three steps, Edward fell down, still fever-weak and shaky. A mauve egg popped up on his forehead.

I had to call Summer to help lift him. I didn't know if she would.

'Your skeleton must weigh a *lot*, because there's not much else left of you,' she said from under his arm.

'It's my brains,' said Edward. 'They're huge.'

'You'll fit in well here, then,' Summer said back. 'Sudoku at seven.'

And after that we never spoke about him leaving. Not once.

The days got longer. Edward got stronger.

He caught things. In his hands, in nets. He dug around and pulled things up.

He loved to carve. He loved to fix.

We found coffee at the back of the church hall. He made it with condensed milk. Each morning, we combed through our dreams as we drank it. Summer lived to talk about her dreams.

She stood on his shoulders to clean the stained glass.

Pete grinned by his side wherever he went.

Picking mulberries, still warm from the sun. Riddles as the sky went dark. My stomach hurt. I had swallowed a star.

'Here's one,' said Summer up the plum tree one sunset. 'What is greater than God, more evil than the devil, the poor have it, the rich need it, and if you eat it you'll die?'

'Hmm.' He chewed awhile. Even the way he ate plums was something. 'Tricky one, Surf.'

'Surf?' said Summer.

'Summer's a name for a surfer girl, don't you think? All blonde and tanned and with a cute nose.'

'A cute *nose*? A surfer *girl*?' Summer rippled. 'You have some seriously outdated conceptions of gender.'

'You have a cute nose,' said Edward. 'Oh, wait—sorry, that's your sister. My bad.'

Summer threw a plum at him. It hit him in the temple.

'Easy,' he said as he rubbed his head.

'*You're* easy,' said Summer.

'Your mother's easy,' said Edward, without thinking.

There was silence.

'Sorry,' he said awkwardly. 'I didn't mean it. Guess I'm just used to being around dudes. We say things like that. Your mother...' He swallowed. 'Is she…I guess she's not around?'

I should have known we would get here sometime. In my mind, I saw Summer and me on opposite banks of a pounding river. Between us raged our different truths. They clashed into foam.

'She died when we were born,' said Summer brusquely. 'We don't discuss it. And FYI, our dad was taken by ninjas.'

'It wasn't ninjas,' I said quietly.

But Summer ignored me. 'The answer is nothing, by the way.'

'How do you mean?' Edward asked her.

'The riddle. Think about it.'

Winter got it in her head to take the bear for a visit to the forest so it wouldn't forget its roots, which—as you can imagine—I thought was completely ridiculous. 'He's not a Chinese orphan living in America,' I told her. 'It's not like he needs to go to Mandarin School on Saturday afternoons and learn one of those complicated string instruments to keep in touch with his culture. Besides, that forest is creepy. Remember the snake?'

And, of course, though she'd been all gung-ho for it, that was enough to put Winter off, because in our first autumn we had found a snake in there, and I kid you not when I say that it had swallowed a human arm—you could see it through the skin, like the hand was wearing a snakeskin glove. If you think we'd gone more than a few steps into the forest since then, you have a banana for a brain, because even a basketful of fresh mushrooms plucked from the earth wasn't worth accidentally picking up a stray finger or stepping over a log onto, like, a head with those white, staring eyes you always see in zombie movies at sleepovers, not that we really ever went to that many, because here's the thing about being a twin: people kind of assume you don't need other friends, and they're sort of right.

Try not to get too judgey, but I didn't even like Winter wearing headphones to watch plane movies—I just didn't want there ever to be anything between us, for our worlds not to be in perfect sync. And, sure, in hindsight some people could say I was a little controlling, but Winter was the best part of me, and who wouldn't want to keep that part safe behind glass and shiny for always, especially when nobody else was going to do it?

When The Greying started, we were in Tokyo. I would set my alarm each night just to check Winter's back as she slept. I tried to hoik up her nightie without waking her to see if she'd caught it but, boy, does she sleep light. 'Am I dreaming?' she would murmur, or she'd whisper to herself, 'Peter Pan, Peter Pan, Peter Pan.' Who knows what that guy had to do with the whole global pandemic, but some nights, as I lay awake watching to make sure she breathed, I would imagine him flying up onto our windowsill to keep me company, and, truth be told, it helped a little.

'Dude,' I would whisper to Imaginary Pan, 'you know you'll have to grow up sometime, right? It's, like, science.'

'You sound just like Wendy,' he would whisper back, rolling his eyes. 'Girls suck so bad.'

'Good luck finding a girlfriend with that attitude,' I said.

'That's a bit presumptuous, don't you think?' said Pan, all snooty. 'Because FYI, I think I'm actually gay.'

'You're a pretty sharp dresser,' I told him. 'Makes sense.'

'Not all gay males are stylish. You're making assumptions,' he told me. 'Again.'

When things got REALLY bad and we left Tokyo for the island, I stopped watching over Winter as she slept. Pops had brought us here to get away from the evils of the world, so I never worried about The Greying following, trailing behind us like a mournful, ashy ghost. It faded away from my thoughts, along with the internet, and dairy products, and sunscreen, and diving training, and hair dryers, and streetlights, and all the other parts of our lives that had once seemed Essential (capital E) but now felt kind of irrelevant. It stopped occurring to me to cut rectangles in the backs of Pops's old sports T-shirts, which we rumbled around in, thinking they made pretty great mini dresses.

And, sure, some nights I would wake and get all existential: I'd start wondering if we were already sleeping in the building we'd die in, or if we had died already and this was Purgatory, or some kind of big old holding pen where we'd dwell forever in limbo. Generally,

35

though, I thought we were happy in our dreamy, slightly feral alone-
ness, half in love with reading the classics out loud to each other and
perfecting our fire-making skills.

But only a few months before that bear showed up, I was tucked
up in the bell tower at sunset, writing a poem about a particularly
melancholy goose who gets left behind when his chums fly south
for the winter, and it sort of makes me cringe now to think about
it, that clunky rhyme, the whole autobiographical angle. I'd been at
it all afternoon, deep in my own genius, and now the sun was
plunging down through the sky. The sea was milky in the dying
winter's light, and I had my back to the warm stone wall, wrestling
with the final stanza as the world burned gently orange around me.
Metaphorically speaking.

Three times that afternoon Winter had called up from the bottom
of the stairs to offer me snacks and encouragement. She never came
up to the bell tower. Most things to do with Pops spooked her right
out, and the three things that were left there, out of sight if you
weren't used to looking, were so close to his heart they were
practically ventricles. I had sent her away, all sniffy. 'Real artists
starve for their craft,' I called. 'But when I'm finished, can you make
that dehydrated beef bourguignon?'

When it got too dark to see the page, and I closed my notebook,
and looked out through the west arch at the sea, there she was, where
the waves slid up on the shore: not heating our dinner on the camp
stove, but struggling with the weight of a full backpack as she tried
to pull herself up onto what seemed to be a sort of homemade raft.

I stood up and leaned right out over the stone balustrade, and
when I squinted I could see that it was plastic barrels, tied together—
some of the empty barrels of fuel that Pops had brought with us to
power up the generator, which we hadn't been able to use for ages.
On days when it was super hot, we'd take the empty ones up the
mountain, launch them on the river, curl our tummies over the

36

warm, yellow plastic that smelled like a baby doll we'd once had. We'd ride them back down, our arms outstretched so that we could hold pinkie fingers as we floated.

But now, as she tried again and again, unsuccessfully, to jump up onto her raft, Winter clearly wasn't waiting for me to join her on a nautical adventure. The big backpack was dragging her down pretty hard. It must have been heavy and that's when I realised: Winter wasn't just planning a short picnic with the dolphins.

You know that feeling when your head goes hot hot hot at the same time as your insides turn to ice, and you sweat right at your hairline while your stomach clenches up, like it wants to turn inside out? That—that's the feeling I got when it dawned on me that Winter was running away, or trying to. That however you tried to look at it, she was running away from me.

Just when I could hardly see her through the gloom, Winter gave up. She pulled the raft onto the sand and looked around to make sure nobody was watching, nobody as in me, and I bet you're thinking that this is the moment when I stormed down the 362 steps of the bell tower and out onto the beach to confront her, waving my arms, all bold and loud and mad.

But I didn't.

My legs were shaking too much to move anywhere, and as she dragged the raft across the lawn and scampered off to stash her supplies, I sank to my knees, closed my eyes. And when I came down and Winter was serving up a dish of steaming dehydrated French beef stew for me to eat by starlight, I didn't say anything at all. I didn't ask where she thought she was going, or why. Was I frightened of the answers, or did I know them already? I just said, 'The way you make this—it's so good,' and tried not to throw up as she beamed at me proudly.

I'm not sure why I was so shaken, so surprised, because after Pops left us, I was the one who wanted to hang around when Winter had begged, over and over, to do the one thing we could that would allow us to leave. 'There's nobody here to take care of us,' she wept. 'Nobody knows that we've even survived. *Please*, Summer? Please can we just go?'

'*I'm* still here,' I'd say sourly. 'I can take care of us. And it's not so bad, just you and me. Besides, Pops wanted us to stay. We're doing this for him.' I would turn my face away from her fear and her red-rimmed eyes.

So after Edward arrived and I saw how much Winter loved him, how much he adored her—that's when I could finally relax a little, because now she had something to stay around for. Like a mound for her to stick a flagpole in and claim her place in the world. Eventually I stopped getting edgy every time she left the room, and when he would pad after her, I'd try not to mind that he'd left me behind. When he was around, she seemed to forget that there was even a way we could escape from here at all. And after a while Winter overcame her squeamishness and took the bear to the forest so he could put his paws in piles of leaf litter and commune with the spirits of his forebears, or whatever she thought he was doing in the forest. If only I had gone along with them—well, you'll see.

Winter

'What's with all the reading, anyway?' Edward asked one night. He was lighting the fire.

We were reading in the pews, Summer and I, our feet sole to sole. Summer liked them that way, all lined up. We had two copies of *Gone with the Wind*. I read faster, but I waited at the end of each page. I knew she liked us to turn them together. It gave me a chance to watch how he moved. Smooth somehow.

'It's kind of, you know…passive,' he said. 'Wouldn't you rather be up and doing something than sitting round like this, flicking pages with your thumb?'

'*Passive*?' bristled Summer. '*Flicking*? You think ingesting deep truths about the human condition to better understand humanity is passive? That's the most meat-heady thing you've said yet, and that includes your views on soft-plastic recycling. Did you miss the memo? Reading is the new social media—people are crazy for it. Have you ever even finished a book?'

He sat back on his knees. He ran his hands through his hair. His jawbone popped out as he clenched his teeth.

'You can't read,' I realised, and wished I hadn't. When I looked up, I could see the part of him that could fight off a wolf. Something hard passed over his face.

'Winter can teach you,' Summer said breezily. 'No probs at all. We were at a camp in South Sudan once and, I kid you not, she taught a bunch of kids their ABCs, and they couldn't even speak English to start off with. We ended up taking turns to read them *Anne of Green Gables* out loud, and they lapped it up like a bowl of melted ice cream. Boy, those kids were *tall*. Taller than you, even. Maybe.'

How I loved Summer then, her straightness. It wasn't always easy to love her that true.

'I can teach you,' I said. 'If you want to learn. I can help.'

'Can't,' he said, and his voice was husky. 'I've tried before.'

'But you can speak,' I said. 'You can see. That's all it is: words and looking.'

Edward looked up at me and winked.

'And Winter is *patient*,' said Summer. 'Heaps more than me. Even if you're a total cheese brain, she'll get you there in the end. She could teach an Eskimo to rollerblade.'

'I don't think you're allowed to say Eskimo anymore.' I felt shy. 'I think it's Inuit.' I turned to Edward. 'You're teaching me to run, remember?'

'Vaguely,' he said.

'WHAT? Winter can't run.' Summer frowned at me. 'Why would you even want to? And where?'

'In the forest,' I whispered.

'Well, that's the most idiotic thing I ever—'

Pete woofed, and raised his eyebrows.

Summer clicked her tongue and turned back to Edward. 'Just say yes already. I know a book you'd go totally nuts for.'

Edward smiled. 'I guess it's time I understood humanity a little better.'

Summer

Us and Edward and the beach at sunset, right where it rubbed shoulders with the meadow, and that feeling like the one you get from a movie where there's a bunch of kids in a performing arts school and they all understand The Pressure of Being an Artist, and they walk along in a row with their arms around each other's shoulders, boys and girls, like it isn't awkward—like it's actual, deep, respectful, abiding love that will last way after the applause at the end of the end-of-year show, where they are hoping to attract talent agents, even though you and I both know that eventually they'll be going up against each other in auditions.

There was Winter, turning cartwheels on the sand with her toes pointed, and me talking about rodeos, and the bear trying to nibble the waves, not understanding the fundamentals of solids and liquids and gas, and us laughing at his sweet pudgy face, biting down on our teeth because we could have squeezed his skull till his eyeballs popped out, that's how much we loved him.

And then the BOOM, which was the crash of a plane hitting the base of Our Mountain, and the hum and the silence, which was the propeller slowing and me freezing up and Winter running across the grass towards the wreck, and the bear following, so that I had to sprint not to be left behind as they circled the oozing smoke, like it wasn't about to pop in a giant orange cotton-wool fireball.

'Get away!' I screamed, still running. 'Get away NOW— Winter—GET—A—WAY.'

But I knew that while there was a chance of a chance of a pilot trapped inside, Winter would be there, thrusting her fist through the window without even so much as a tea towel wrapped around it, and it was useless to wish otherwise. I could almost feel the heat from the explosion that was going to rip her into fragments so small, I'd have to sweep them up with a paintbrush. You can imagine my relief when the bear overtook her, bounded past and leapt onto the creased-up wing, stretched to full height as if he wasn't a bear but a volunteer firefighter crossed with a superhero. And in a movement that was graceful and frightening both together, he flexed his arms and bent and ripped off the pilot-side window, just like that, as if he were lifting a tray from an oven.

By then I'd reached Winter and was pulling her back and away, and her elbows were pummelling my ribs, pow pow pow, like tennis balls being served straight at me by a tall Russian dude, and we were both shouting 'No!' but for different reasons. It was only when she kicked her heel back into my kneecap that I let her go, more in surprise than pain. Turns out I wasn't the only one in for a surprise, because by the time Winter had climbed up next to Edward on the wing, he had leaned back from the cockpit and had his head on one side, scratching it, all confused, because there wasn't anyone in that plane—the pilot's seat was empty. The whole plane was empty.

As Winter ran her hands over the dashboard, I said, 'It's a—'

'I know what it is,' she said sharply, and that's when I knew just how top-of-the-roller-coaster frightened she was.

And so, yes, I admit it might have been overkill when I said, 'They're coming. They know what's here.'

Winter

It wasn't the alphabet he had trouble with.

It wasn't the sounds or the letters.

It was holding the words in his head as he ran along the lines. They were like train carriages, uncoupled.

I started with joining two at a time. I wrote them down big: *I see. You are. We feel. I wish.*

'What do you wish?' Edward asked.

I looked over at Summer, who was darning.

I looked up into Edward's eyes. I saw my reflection—a tiny me, twice.

'I wish…I wish that my mother hadn't died the way she did,' I said.

I saw Summer freeze.

Edward nodded, but he didn't ask for anything more.

And I didn't regret it. I took the pen. 'Try this one,' I said.

'*Right now*,' he read eventually.

And then there was a roar. A crash that shook my skull.

BANG went the mountain.

Up swirled the flowers.

His hand on my arm.

Down fell my heart.

After that, the planes came more regularly—not crashing, just circling like lost, dreamy albatross. But I convinced Winter they were just drones sent to take pictures. 'It's just part of a standard government mapping procedure,' I said.

'Which government?' asked Winter.

'Oh, shut up,' I said crossly. 'You don't always have to know everything.'

'I thought they were banned, the drones,' said Winter. 'After that horrible thing with the acid and—'

'I said, shut *up*.'

We hadn't found any explosives attached to the plane that had crashed on our grass. The empty cockpit reminded me of those driverless cars that were popular for a while, until the prank where hackers all around the world drove them into frozen yoghurt shops remotely at the same time, like some sick flash mob, and all those people died—kids still clutching their fro-yos, sticky and melting and pure.

But how long till anyone dropped by in person to check the whole scene out? Gradually the background mosquito-whine of the planes became the soundtrack to something—the return of some kind of uneasiness that we'd thought we could finally stop running from.

Thank goodness for Edward, that bundle of golden happiness. We just had to look at him and we were beaming—could waste half a day folding newspaper hats and trying to get him to wear them, weaving him meadow-flower garlands, giving him foil packets of black-pepper-and-lime-flavoured cashews and watching him try to pop them open.

I wanted to teach him things, fill him up with the goodness and light that I wished somebody would pour into me, like lamp oil. And I'd tried not to mind at the start, but now whenever Winter took him anywhere alone, I would pace and ache and act all aloof, like I didn't care, while I fretted a thousand frets. Basically, I acted fourteen and in love, which is what I was. Or were we fifteen now? It felt strange not to know.

'Let's take him up to the bell tower,' I said to Winter one evening, betting she'd say no and I would have him to myself. 'We can show him the sun setting over the sea. We want to cultivate an artistic sensibility in this guy, am I right? Painters love sunsets.'

'I don't think he can see that far,' she said doubtfully, but of course that's not the reason why she wouldn't come.

'Suit yourself.' And to Edward I said, 'Come on, you big potato. Let's go and get you a poet's soul.'

Lucky for me he was tuckered out by the time we reached the top, had hardly made it up all 362 steps, or he could have caused all kinds of problems if he'd really been sniffing around.

Though it was tricky now the bear had got so plump, I scooped that rascally guy up in my arms and nuzzled him, did the thing where we rubbed our noses like Eskimos (Inuits?), swung him high over my head and turned him upside down so his fur flipped and he looked like a baby with a comb-over, all serious eyes and plump belly, and I seem to remember he had fat rolls on his thighs but maybe that's just wishful thinking. I'd pretty much forgotten the sunset by then; it wasn't nearly as eye-popping and spectacular as my love for Edward. As I'd tried to tell Winter, I could practically see my feelings for him streaking across the sky like the northern lights. But I knew, I just knew, that she thought she loved him more. Not that it was a competition or anything, but you try being a twin—it's hard not to always be measuring yourself.

'Now, usually you're not allowed up here, you scamp,' I said to the cub as I spun him around. 'And if someone comes, no matter how official they seem, they're not allowed either, okay? Not terrorists, not tech dudes in baseball caps, and not *you* ever again, you roly-poly dream. Ooooh! I could eat you up. This is where the SECRETS are, and you're Just. Too. Silly. To understand those.'

I wasn't actually joking about any of that, and maybe that bear could understand more than I thought, because I swear he frowned then and wriggled free of my arms, dropped to the ground and ambled over to the north arch to take a peek out at the world.

'Careful, sport,' I said to Edward. 'Watch yourself up here.' Just like Pops had said to me a hundred times—a thousand.

If you didn't know what was in the bell tower, right now you'd probably be thinking something like, *Oh, how nice of that nerdy dad to keep his daughters so safe on that beautiful island at the end of the world! How smart to find it, so far away from everything rotting and tortured and dark.* And, hoo boy, I feel as if it's my duty to point out that it's not as simple as it seems, but is anything?

What you should actually be asking as you read my very neat, small, tidy writing (which, can I say, is not easy to execute when you're left-handed) is some kind of version of this: what did their dad do that was so bad that he had to drag his charming pair of daughters to camp out like fugitives at the ends of the earth?

And, well, I guess it was sort of bad, though he was actually trying to do something boomingly, globally, totally GOOD, at least to start with. But things don't always turn out how you want them to—ask most people here, I bet, not that I've seen any since I arrived.

So—it came out later—my dad wasn't studying axolotls at all. He was the guy who figured out how to put free wi-fi in the takeaway coffee cups that nobody was using anymore on account of the role of disposable packaging in environmental carnage and also because they didn't want everyone else to think they were arseholes. By then the shame factor around single-use objects was *high*. This was around

46

the time that the phone companies got everyone hooked on looking at the internet on their mobiles approximately a zillion times per day as if they seriously couldn't help themselves, and then jacked the prices right up so that—no jokes—people started getting bills that meant they had to sell their houses and move into the weird white tent cities that sprang up around the edges of the actual cities like inside-out bread crusts. You probably remember what went down then—all the kinds of things that happen when people feel desperate and hard done by. Black markets, hostages, dodgy deals, you know how it goes. For about a year, the world was data-starved and mean with it. People were on fire with jealousy, which was fitting, given that huge stripes of the planet were on fire too.

So when Pops figured out how to pick up internet via the little fibres in cardboard, and people, with some light googling, could tap into the networks that were still around (government ones, mostly, and rich people's), boy, was he a hero for three hot seconds. He was on about twenty-four thousand podcasts and even a TV talk show. Once Winter and I found a clip but we couldn't watch past the theme music because it was the one with the host who makes everyone dance along to the opening credits. We shrieked and slammed the laptop shut. Let's just say Pops might have been one smart dude, but he did not have an innate sense of rhythm.

With so many users back online, Big Tech made waterfalls of money again, and they loved Pops's socks right off. They offered him a high-powered job on a top-secret project that was called—I kid you not—Operation Freedom. They wanted him to figure out if the internet could travel through sound waves in water so that it could be literally everywhere twenty-four seven. Turns out it can, even through puddles and taps, and because water is most places, that meant, with the help of some wires and magnets, free internet access for most everybody, coffee cups or not. Except, I guess, for desert nomads, but are they really busting to do internet banking?

You can see how it's not a completely stupid idea and would have made things more democratic and egalitarian and all that rumble, and because Pops is an A-plus genius, he got it done. We were four when Operation Freedom launched. If you look hard enough, there's a photo of Winter high up on our father's shoulders on the day they metaphorically flicked that switch. He's shaking hands with a guy in a baseball cap—you know the guy I mean. Winter isn't looking at him, that guy, which is kind of funny, given that he was so famous. Her hands are buried deep in Pops's curls, her head tilted back, eyes closed to the sun and smiling. But perhaps Pops knew what was coming, because his eyes are scrunched with worry behind the dark frames of his glasses and if you look really carefully, his left hand is gripping Winter's tiny thigh so hard that it looks like he's sinking his fingers into pizza dough.

Winter

'Why would he come here?' asked Edward as we lifted the pilot out
of the carcase of the plane.

His face dripped from every hole. His chest pooled blood until
it didn't. Summer dropped his feet. She went to throw up. Pete
circled. His eyes rolled. He barked till his voice was a scrape. When
Summer dragged him away, he nipped the webbing of her fingers.
But she didn't let go.

That pilot wasn't much older than us. Next to Edward, he seemed
small.

'Do you think he was lost?' Edward asked.

'No,' I said firmly. Because he wasn't. There was every reason for
him to come.

Edward buried the corpse so I didn't have to watch. I didn't tell
him that we had done it before.

After a couple of years, Pops quit that job at Operation Freedom, though the guy with the baseball cap begged him to stay. Pops told us it was time to return to his true love: herpetology, which is the study of amphibians, and includes, more specifically, neotenic salamanders. He told us it's what he'd dreamed about his whole childhood, the big weirdo, out walking on the moor, where he grew up, and that all the tech stuff had just been a diversion on the way to him finding his bliss. We never thought to question that story, though I guess we were only six.

This was about the time when Winter and I started to travel with Pops round the world, but not to the south of France or the Italian lakes or Whistler or the Amazon or any of those usual holiday destinations. I'm talking some weird places, like Guatemala and Burkina Faso and Myanmar and French Guiana and Sierra Leone, and if you have to look a couple of those up, don't feel bad, I did too. It's pretty sad to think of that year we spent on the banks of sludgy brown rivers and slim, hungry creeks, peering over the edge and looking our hardest for Mexican walking fish, which is why we thought we were there—to help Pops make breakthroughs in the fascinating world of axolotls. Sometimes I worried that Winter would strain something in her big doe eyes, she searched so hard with everything in her.

The joke was on us, in the end, because it turns out there are no axolotls in the Nile or the Ganges, just a lot of funeral pyres, which are basically dead people bobbing around like floating candles in the bath.

Then we moved to Tokyo, where the only salamanders are in tanks, and we hardly saw Pops at all. He spent most of his time in his lab, 'writing up his findings', apart from a few random trips that he dragged us on. We never left the hotels, where he met people in dark corners of lobbies while we mostly hung out at the pool. We assumed they were other amphibian experts, but of course they weren't. Some were from Big Tech and some were from the Resistance, and to cut a long story short (which is, quite frankly, difficult for me), it all grew into something bigger and Pops was right at the centre, like the faux-yolk in a Cadbury Crème Egg, which wasn't a good place for him to be, already half mad with regrets.

That's how we ended up flying here, Pops at the controls of a seaplane that he seemed to be driving straight into Our Mountain, and truly? In that moment, as the rockface rushed towards us, after everything that had happened, I didn't even blame him. I just reached for Winter's hand and closed my eyes as she whispered to herself beside me, and waited for the brutal, life-ending slam that never came.

Now, looking out at Our Mountain from the bell tower, I shuddered at that memory, and I picked up the bear to squeeze it away. 'Come on, Edward,' I said to that imp of a cub as I gripped him tighter. 'You're out of bounds, and you're never to come up here again without us. And if we're all up here together and I'm pulling something out of the wall, well, then you know we've reached the moment where shit's about to get real.'

The bear looked up at me, looked over at the wall. I squeezed him tighter. And then, I swear to you, he looked me in the eye before he reached up with his gorgeous little paw and scraped his claws down my face, so hard that it acid-burned and blood pearled up straight away, and I screamed and I dropped him.

'Hey!' I yelled, my hand to my cheek. 'That's not nice. You come back here and say sorry.'

But the bear just sniffed at the south-arch wall until I started after him, and then he ran, ran, ran, scrambling down the stairs, all 362 of them, while I burbled down after him, feeling raw and cross and mean.

Winter

I had to stop. My throat burned. My legs just wouldn't.

Pete bounded ahead. He looked the way Summer did when she played charades—like someone doing just what they were born to do. I crouched on the forest floor.

'No way.' Edward laughed, doubling back. 'That's, like, less than a minute you lasted.' He held out his hands.

I shook my head.

'Sure you can,' he said. 'You can walk. You can breathe.'

'Hardly.' But I gave him my palms. His hands felt big but soft, like my father's driving gloves. We started again.

'The trick is to set a goal, like that giant tree up yonder, and then distract yourself till you get there.'

'How?' I wondered who still said 'up yonder'. 'I'm dying.'

'I'll say. Do you come this way often?'

'No. The forest is creepy. And once…we found…a dead person…' I puffed. 'Why have we stopped?'

'We reached the tree. Dead how?'

I stood with my hands on my knees. My ribs hurt with breathing. If I gasped a little, I didn't have to answer. 'Are we reading tonight?' I asked when I could again. 'We could go to that bit of the forest with the tree stumps to sit on. I could tell Summer that I'm counting tins in the Emporium. She hates it back there. And you could be fixing something.'

'Some kind of dirty secret, am I?' Edward was smiling so it didn't sound mean.

'I just…Summer doesn't like to feel left out, that's all. And I don't like to make her sad.'

'Well, if you can make it back to the start of the path without stopping, you've got yourself a deal. But don't think I'll enjoy it. 'Cept the part that means sitting down next to you.

'Speaking of dead guys. That pilot...' he said as we turned around. 'What was the deal with that? You girls haven't mentioned it since. Isn't that kind of weird?'

'We did,' I panted. 'Summer described her dream funeral, remember?'

'Yeah, that was morbid. The girl has issues,' said Edward. 'Just tell me where he came from. I know that you know. I've got, like, intuition. Don't laugh—for a guy I'm pretty sensitive.'

Perhaps it was because it had been so long. Or because Summer was the one who always told our story. Perhaps I wanted his hand on my head, fingers on my sorrow. Perhaps that is why I told him so much.

Summer

By the time I got to the bottom of the bell tower, Edward was sitting at Winter's feet where she stood dusting the altar. His back was against her shins, his chin up and his eyes closed.

'He scratched me—on purpose!' I told her. 'See? We need to punish him, that little monster.'

Winter looked horrified, and I waited for her to rip a strip from her shirt to wipe the blood off my face in that gentle dab she does so well for injured things.

But she didn't. She bent down to rub his head, that bear. 'Don't call him that,' she said. 'I'm sure he didn't mean to. He's just a baby. He doesn't know any better.'

'He dang well does,' I said darkly. 'I'm putting up a gate so he can't get back up those stairs and TBH he should go sit in the corner to think about what he's done.'

As I stalked out the back door to find Pops's building stuff, I heard her whisper to him, all tender. I couldn't make out the words, but they made me want to hammer things hard.

Everything went downhill swiftly after that. And, looking back, if I'm going to blame anyone, it isn't just Edward alone—it's also *Diary of a Young Girl* by Anne Frank, and here's why. I've told you enough by now that you could probably guess how Anne's story affected Winter. Every couple of years when she picked it off the shelf, I would groan on the inside and dredge my soul for arguments about why we should all Keep on Living in spite of all the injustice in the world. And I'd brace myself and dig out the hazelnut praline from the back of our Emporium and grab a couple of hankies we'd made from the raggedy old christening gowns we found in a chest.

Why she got it in her mind to read Anne Frank to the bear, I'll never know, because I was usually the one who read aloud and did all the voices, and besides, even though I was faster, Winter could still read so quickly in her head that it must have felt like she was tap-dancing in quicksand to say each word individually. But when she opened it up and said to Edward, 'This is our story,' I felt a little panic. Because I'd never thought that we were like Anne Frank, with her coffee-puddle eyes, locked in like a caged canary at an old person's home, death all around her and not quite knowing the point of it all but still trying to sing.

Anne was confused and Lonely (capital L) and she could have been caught any second, so no wonder she had to keep a journal and wax lyrical about all kinds of profound stuff. And, sure, we were alone, me and Winter, but we had each other and Freedom and no bickering, farting adults or sweaty adolescent boys playing with our heads like they were harp strings, and, yes, some mornings bugs flew into our tea and, truth be told, I would have liked some overhead lighting installed. But, hey, compared to what was going on out in the world, well, you've probably read all about that and so you'd have to agree that we had it pretty dang good. I know you're probably wondering if we even knew what was going on out there, and I guess the answer is that we knew enough.

'If you're introducing him to strong female characters, wouldn't he prefer Pippi Longstocking?' I asked Winter. 'There aren't any animals in Anne Frank.'

Winter just Looked at me (capital L) and if you think she's all windchimes and fairy floss, you've got her totally wrong because, believe me, Winter is boulder-stubborn. So Anne Frank it was, all day and all night.

Here's the kicker: the bear really liked that story. Sounds ridiculous, I know, but he sat there on Winter's lap, all innocently, and I swear that when he heard Anne's dreams about being in love with Peter Schiff and then eye-sexing with Peter van Daan, he blushed all rosy, and if you think that's impossible, well, you've never read Anne Frank to a bear—at least not all the way to the bits about the Peters.

When she got to the end, when the diary just stops, Winter wept, like I knew she would: deep throbbing sobs that shook her shoulders and also my core. 'Here,' I said, handing her a jar of hazelnut praline and a spoon. 'It's not so sad to end up a sunbeam in a zillion people's hearts. Anne would have liked that, I'll bet. And for real, I bet her spirit really dug floating out of the Secret Annexe after being cooped up there so long. I bet it went and got hot chips on the way to heaven.'

But that just made Winter cry harder, and scrunch her face into her knees, and nothing I said made any difference and I felt like I was throwing flour into the wind until Edward nosed his way into Winter's lap and started licking the tears right off her cheeks, and I could say that maybe he was just salt-deficient and acting on animal instincts to seek out sodium, but I don't think so, because by the time her face was wet with bear slobber, Winter had stopped her weeping. She scooped up that bear—at least, she tried to, but that was the second I realised the bear had Grown, and instead he tipped Winter backwards onto the floor, his paws on her shoulders, like those gold pins you stick in paper dolls to make their arms move, and he held her there, kissing her eyelids with love. And though she laughed and laughed, I didn't laugh, because I could see from the outside that Winter couldn't have pushed him away even if she'd wanted to. I thought about the scratch on my cheek that still hadn't healed. He wasn't a cub. Perhaps he never had been. He was almost a man of a bear now, and while I'd been busy worrying about old Anne Frank, Edward had got too strong.

Winter

'Do you remember...' I began as we kept jogging. 'Do you remember when the internet came back, through the water, and they started to use it for terrorism?'

'Those beheadings?' said Edward. 'The live hangings, and the stonings—all that?'

I nodded. It had started as a trickle. Prisoners decapitated on video. A beloved world leader lynched, his limbs torn off by two tanks rolling in opposite directions.

At the beginning, each piece of footage only lasted a few hours online before it got taken down.

But then there were more and more until every day a new one arrived. As soon as they were removed, someone else would repost them.

Soon they popped up in emails from banks and airlines. When people switched on their computers, they played automatically, until everyone was too afraid to shut down.

The images were embedded in games that taught children to read, flicking on screen when they reached the next level. A new war that was everywhere. Or a reminder that war had always been everywhere, but half the world had been ignoring it.

'Are you saying that your dad was one of those guys?'

'No! I mean, yes, but not how you're thinking. My father—he was a scientist. An inventor too. A zoologist mostly.'

'That's why he got taken away? For being some kind of renegade zookeeper? That's why they risked sending that pilot here?'

'A *zoologist*. He specialised in amphibians, and then saltwater reptiles. And from there, he sort of...got involved in things at the bottom of the ocean.'

'He was a scuba diver?'

I shook my head. 'Think about what else is under the sea.'

'Sand…crabs…shipwrecks…gold. He was a pirate! Hey, we're back at the start. Looks like I'm reading tonight after all.'

We slowed to a walk and found a tree stump to stretch on. Edward was serious about stretching.

'A lost city—whatcha call it, Atlantis? He found Atlantis?'

'Think about what we were just talking about,' I said. Hamstrings. Quads.

His expression changed. 'Oh. The internet. The thing with the cables. That wasn't…Was that *him*?'

I had said too much. Summer would know it. She would see— could see all of it. How these days my heart was tennis-ball bright.

'I need to go and cut fruit with Summer,' I said as I shook out my legs, one then the other. 'For the jam.'

Edward looked up to the sky and smiled. 'You girls. Such closed books, for all of that reading. Go on, then, to your big peach emergency. Leave me here hanging with good old Pete. I'll make up my own version of how that story ends. Might read it to you some day.'

Before everything, when Summer and I still went to school, most people thought the internet was beamed by satellites. But it was really a web of thick cables dug into the seabeds. The Earth was wrapped in it, like a net. If an anchor ripped a cable out or a shark bit it, the system was set up to use another cable, another pathway.

'That's just the way it evolved,' our father told us once when we were playing under his desk. 'Impossible to destroy, unless millions of people around the world simultaneously take to it with axes, and even then parts of it would survive. So how else to shut it down? That's the trillion-dollar question. That's a whole life's work.'

'What's that got to do with axolotls?' I asked him.

'Everything,' he said. 'Everything.'

Summer

I woke up and they were gone, and I know I was sleepy—that I'd stayed up too late reading the sexy bits from *Forever*—but I wasn't so out of it that I could have missed a giant bear at the breakfast table, which is where he should have been, sitting there all politely while Winter made porridge on the fire pit, just like every other day. I went and did a lap of the moat, because sometimes Edward liked to float on his back there if the night had been hot. I checked the meadow, and even went up Our Mountain a little so I could see over the long, yellowing grass in case they were snuggled low in the flowers with their noses touching, or sitting on the rocks at the river bend. I even checked the Emporium, grabbed a jar of eggplant kasundi on the way through, and poked my head into all the weird priesty rooms out the back where Pops had stashed stuff, like bows and arrows. But there was nothing, nothing, nothing.

I started running, then—down to the sea, which was all cornflowers that morning, along the beach in one direction so fast I thought I was going to barf, and walked back heaving. But even though my legs were literally shaking, I started sprinting up the steps to the bell tower, all 362 of them, because I got it in my head they were there—that Winter had broken her promise and was showing Edward everything, and I didn't care that he was a bear—he was poking around places that he shouldn't. With every step I climbed, I got madder at him for taking Winter away to enjoy for himself. I got madder at Winter for betraying our little family. I got madder at myself for letting it happen, right under my gosh-darn nose. I tried to ask myself, I promise I did: are you sure you're not just jealous, Summer? Are you just making a big deal out of nothing because you feel like a third wheel on a bicycle built for two?

And, sure, maybe there was a bit of that, but there was something else about that bear—something that gave me feelings like the heavy air before a storm. So when I reached the top of the bell tower, I threw the door open so loudly it split when it hit the wall and bounced back against me, and my shin was bleeding and I was hopping and the worst part was that it was all for nothing, all 362 steps, because they weren't there. It was the same as it had been the day Pops got taken away and Winter and I had vowed to protect his secrets with our lives, and wrapped our pinkie fingers together and each kissed them after we'd said it, though in hindsight Lord knows what the kissing was supposed to achieve.

I knelt at the east arch, which looked out over Our Mountain, and ran my finger along my leg to scoop up the blood and licked it as I contemplated how different things seemed from up here, like in that old movie where the schoolboys stand on a desk to see things from another perspective and are so inspired by the whole caper that they cry out 'O Captain! My Captain!' as they jump off, and I think the name has something to do with Dead Guys Who Were Poets.

But I didn't want to shout 'O Captain! My Captain!', all triumphant and sentimental.

Suddenly I wanted to cry, because the forest was so dense, and the mountain so sharp and cold and bare-faced, and the whole place loomed harsh and unfriendly—hostile, even—and it suddenly seemed ludicrous that we could hope to survive alone for more than a heartbeat. Winter had been right all along—from the very beginning. We needed to go.

In that instant I realised I wasn't angry at the bear anymore. I was angry at our father for leaving us here—no, for taking us here in the first place, away from everything we knew, when we'd already lost so much. And, yes, I get it, the world was getting crazier by the minute, and we might have been dead by now if it wasn't for Bartleby. But I was starting to wonder quite seriously if it isn't kinder just to kill a bug with a flyswat rather than letting it suffocate in a jar with no holes in the lid, if you get my drift.

I had these types of thoughts from time to time, and that was usually when I would read aloud to Winter from *Little Women* and try to get myself in a more Jo March-ish frame of mind, because the last thing dear old Winter needed was me getting all dark and weepy when I was the strong one who was going to pull us through all this while whistling. But where was Winter now? She had either evaporated into a perfect cloud, or she was with Edward in the forest. She wasn't here to listen to me do all four March daughters' voices differently, and to swoon over Teddy, and to long for a Marmee of our own, and without her, what was the point of *Little Women*, or any of it?

Thankfully I didn't have to ponder that too long, because suddenly there was the bear, breaking out through the edge of the forest, and he was carrying Winter in his arms, and of course I immediately thought of Anne of Green Gables falling down the well, and assumed a broken ankle—at the very least twisted—and as I was running down the 362 steps, I was mentally bandaging it, elevating it, and wondering what on earth we could use as a substitute for ice, and then congratulating myself on thinking of the cold, dark, icy moat, and if you think this sounds like a mentally exhausting journey, try living it.

But when I got down to the bottom and raced outside, Winter was walking on her hands and Edward was holding her ankles, which were very much intact, and they were wheelbarrowing around the fruit trees. She so very much was NOT injured and my first-aid skills were so clearly not required that I couldn't help but feel a bit put out.

'Where the hell have you been?' I shouted—loud as I could. 'You didn't even leave a NOTE.'

Edward was so shocked by my yelling that he let go of Winter's feet, and she fell to the ground heavily, hitting her stomach in that way that knocks out your breath and leaves the top of your belly all tender, while he dropped down to all fours and hid his head between his front paws.

'You scared him,' she said crossly.

'You frightened me,' I said more crossly. 'Where have you even been?'

Winter went over to that stupid old bear and climbed onto his back and leaned forwards so that her cheek was against the plush spot just behind his ear. 'We went running in the forest,' she said. She looked up at me and her face softened and she smiled that twinkly, Winter-y smile that gives me the same feeling as looking very closely at the skin of a perfect peach. 'Summer, it was beautiful. Next time you have to come with us.'

'There's not going to be a next time,' I said swiftly.

But there was.

Soon they were always off in that dank, creepy forest, and even when they were here, right in front of me, they were far away, being something I wasn't, which was perfectly, viciously, so-sweetly in love. And if you think an animal can't be in love, haven't you ever had a dog and left it and come back and had it jump at you, as if the floor was sprung, and cover your face with epic amounts of lick-spit while its eyes were like, 'You are all things in the universe and I would run under an air-conditioning repair truck for you'? Edward had those eyes, and sometimes he'd nuzzle Winter's knees with his nose as they walked side by side, just saying, *Hey, I'm here and I love you, and I can't put my paw in the back of your jeans pocket, but in another life I would.* She would lie for hours with her head in his cross-legged lap as he stroked her hair, and before you get all het up about bears being able to sit with their legs crossed, I'm not kidding when I say Winter taught that bear to do yoga, and his dragon pose was really something to see.

This is the moment where I could have felt happy for Winter, could have walked alongside her and smiled as she skipped. I should have felt safe, deep in the little chains of love that joined us up in our amniotic fluid and have never since broken or rusted away. This is the moment when I could have thought, I have always been strong, I have always kept her safe, and perhaps now I've done such a good job I can brush my palms together and go rub on some coconut oil and bake while sun patterns dance on my eyelids, because she doesn't Need me (capital N), and that is a good thing.

But I couldn't. I couldn't stop watching the bear now, wondering about those claws: how long had it been since he had killed something large enough to quiet the parts of him that were Beast? Was there something in his eyes—something hungry? Was I wishing it there? I couldn't sit still with wondering.

Maybe it had to do with an article I once read about an ambulance officer who, on his days off, would pace the streets, just willing cars to smash into each other and flip over, glass shopping-centre roofs to clatter down, so that he could rush in there, brave and bold, and pull suffocating people from the shards and open up their throats with a pen. That was me, pacing by the stained glass, brooding on the organist's stool, swinging darkly on the vine ropes, guiding our kite out the hole in the roof, all the while hoping that Winter would run in, melting in tears, her heart broken so badly that only someone who knew every bit of it could ever superglue it back together. And maybe some part of me wanted to do both: the breaking and the sticking back together.

He'll be gone, I told myself. Come winter, he'll be gone, asleep and tucked in a cave somewhere. Because that's what bears did, hibernate, and even Winter couldn't mess with nature and the Way of Things, even though she was technically in love with a forest animal.

But here's the thing about love, which I figured out on a night when the moon was cream and round as a compass.

I'd woken up at some crazy hour craving salty peanuts, and on the way to find them, I tiptoed past the alcove where the stained glass made heart-squeezing kaleidoscopes. There was something tucked in there that from a distance could have been a lumpy sofa but was actually Edward on the floor with his giant arms snug around Winter, like two big old hairy seatbelts crossed over her heart. She was sleeping under those colours and under his chin, and seeing her there, well, it was as if she was walking beside me in the rain and not offering me even a scrap of umbrella, which might not mean a lot to you, but if you knew Winter, you'd know that it was everything.

And as much as I was starting to really hate that bear, I wanted to wake him and tell him—watch her. Don't let her give you her shoes—the soles of her feet get raw and she won't tell you. Don't let her pull out her eyelashes for you to wish on. Pretend you hate blackberry jam or she'll rip herself up on those brambles, trying to find enough ripe berries for another batch.

But do bears even have eyelashes? I didn't know, and I didn't want to wake her, and so I left them there, the moonlight straining in through the glass, and out by the moat I pondered how much bears love honey and the little pens of anti-bee-sting stuff we're supposed to stab into our thighs if we're stung, which we've never had to do, and would they even work after all these years, because do things like that expire?

I skimmed rocks and thought about Winnie the Pooh and Rupert and Corduroy and Paddington Bear and of course they were all boys and we'd loved them forever.

I thought about Winter's face when she had hazelnut praline, which she thinks I'm allergic to, which was a lie I told because watching the joy in her face as she eats it is like standing on top of a star. I thought of how I wished sometimes, when her hair was wet and matted, that she'd just duck her head under the gosh-darn umbrella. I thought about wanting when you don't quite know what you're wanting, and the things you can't have, and shouldn't.

And I threw a stone that wouldn't skip and I wished I could dive right in and get it back so I could do it again better, and that's when I realised that big thing about love that I mentioned before. It's this right here, and it's going to sound corny but I'll say it anyway: love is a place you can't follow. Maybe the only place, though there's always Death (capital D), but if Winter had been dying, at least I could have squeezed next to her on the hospital bed and clamped my arms around her shoulders and looked into her face and kissed it.

Even if I'd put a glass up to the wall of Winter and Edward's big love and listened, I probably wouldn't have heard anything anyway— just my big old heartbeat in my ears and maybe the sound of eyes closing happily. And, boy oh boy, I had never felt so very, completely, incredibly alone.

Winter

Part of me wanted Summer to know it, the forest.

As each week passed, I loved it more fiercely.

The scales of gold light that fell on the ground. The trees spaced just so you could swing round them, like lampposts. The wispy air, cool in your mouth, damp in your nose. How it all hung together, like the stripes of a rainbow.

But that part of me, the sharing part, got smaller as my lungs got stronger.

'What do you even talk about, anyway?' she would ask. 'What do you tell him? Is he trying to get into your pants, Winter? Do we have to have a talk about contraception methods?'

I laughed. I couldn't say he was already in my pants because he was already in my soul. Summer would have rolled her eyes but only to cover up the fact that, deep down, she loved all that stuff. It would hurt her to hear it.

'We talk about reading,' I told her. 'We go over what I teach him at night. And books. I'm telling him the plots of all the *Harry Potter*s.'

'Jeez,' said Summer. 'Scintillating. Wish I was along on that ride. How did he go with the rules of Quidditch?'

'He gets it,' I said. 'He gets everything. Come next time. Please? For me?'

But for the first time, I didn't mean it. And Summer could tell. I just knew.

On the back of the toilet door at our last school, there was a quote. In the top right-hand corner. The handwriting had beautiful loops. It said:

Sometimes a pop song can hurt more than the whole of Cambodia.

Though she hated graffiti, Summer loved that quote. She wrote it on her art folio in gold pen. She told my father she was going to get it tattooed. 'Down my backbone, Pops. Or would you prefer it across my knuckles?'

But I never believed it, that quote. Wherever I went, I could feel Cambodia inside me, pressing, and no pop song came close.

And then I found Edward. He pulled the world out of me. He pulled me out into the world. It didn't hurt how I expected.

Summer

Flashback! We were in Belarus at Christmas, seven years old, and, boy, was it *cold*—I'm talking the kind of cold where you touch your cheeks and it feels like your fingertips are patting the big old cushion of a leather sofa, you're that numb. That's why we were wearing those ridiculous peach knitted beanies with pompoms so large they were the size of cantaloupes, and Pops had on his brown Russian fur hat, and Winter was wearing the stripy mittens she was so proud of—she hadn't even taken them off to eat high tea at our ridiculously grand hotel.

It was the afternoon and already dark, which was blowing our seven-year-old minds, and the streetlights were big round balls of glow, the kind that form round fairies in cartoons. All around us, the drifts of snow glowed golden as tiny sand dunes, and flakes floated down, big and flat, like pressed pansies. Gomel, I think the town was called, and we couldn't get over how heart-crackingly pretty it was—all those old buildings with arched windows, painted mint green and yolk yellow and mauve and peach; fountains and statues and columns and domes. Curly gates, frills on the balconies, and a river, which was where we were walking, arms linked, in a little line, our little family. The iron park benches looked as if they'd been iced with wedding-cake icing, the snow was that thick. A sleigh went past with a powdery swish. 'See?' I said to Winter. 'I was right about wearing gumboots.'

'Such a know-it-all,' said Pops as we reached a street corner and he put out his arm to stop us from walking out into the traffic, even though we were totally old enough by then to figure that out for ourselves.

'But she does know it all,' said Winter loyally.

'Ha!' said Pops. 'You can cross now.'

We had been singing rounds of Christmas carols, and I have to admit I was pretty good at the harmonies, and Pops knew half the words in Latin, and I reckon we could have made enough busking to buy the extra-long string of fairy lights that we'd been coveting since the summertime, Winter and I, as part of our room redecoration project.

'Now let's do "O Come All Ye Faithful"!' I said.

Pops and Winter groaned because, yes, we had already done it three times already, but when I belted out the first line, they joined right in, and when we finished, down by the riverbank, people actually clapped through their mittens as I forced Winter to bow, even though she said it made her feel like a giant show-off.

We kept on walking along the river towards the biggest tree in the square. The one in Gomel was lit up more beautifully than any we'd seen, with a string of lights shaped like icicles threaded all the way through.

'Like those ones, Pops,' Winter said, pointing. 'For our room. As long as those, but with the really tiny, tiny globes.'

Pops grunted. 'I've just agreed to the rabbits. Isn't that enough for now?' He strode over to the tree to start reading as Winter reached for my hand before I could cross my arms and sulk.

The Resistance had set up these trees all over the world—there was one in every town. It was usually the widest tree, the one with the lowest hanging branches, and next to it there was always a huge basket of white baubles and a big dish of black texta markers. People would write messages on those baubles, and thoughts, and complaints, and quotes, and dreams, and they'd hang them up for everyone to read, or maybe leave them there for someone specific to find. Those pale little balls would stay there until Sunday night, when the tree would be cleared and the whole thing would start again. People took turns tending and clearing, as if they were word farmers. The trees were sort of like the internet in real life, which was kind of the point—to show it was possible to live entirely offline—and people really grew to love them fast. They were like solid, friendly scarecrows of hope when the world was starting to get really spinny and out of control.

We followed Pops over, and soon we were lost in that fascinating forest of #content, and we forgot it was cold enough to freeze a homemade blueberry yoghurt popsicle right out in the open. My favourites were the ones describing things that people used to post photos of—they had #pic in front of them.

#pic a really tall waterfall that catches the sunset and looks like it's made of cascading fire, running down the crack in a giant cliff.

#pic a tiny baby bat wearing a tiny nappy, hanging upside down from a guy's coat.

#pic a grumpy kid in a pram looking right at the camera and holding a white bauble that says #pic.

I pointed at one of those white balls of surprise that had a Martin Luther King quote. 'You don't have to see the whole staircase, just take the first step,' I read. 'See? That could apply to your ukulele practice. Just focus on getting the chords first, and the rest will—'

'Wasn't that man at our hotel?' Winter whispered, cutting me off, which she never did.

'Which man?' I asked sharply.

She cupped her palms together and lifted them to her mouth, pretending she was blowing on them to keep warm. Then she leaned a tiny bit to her left and flicked her fingers towards a really clean-cut dude in a hiking jacket and a wholesome-looking backpack with a Canadian flag stitched to the top. He was writing something on a bauble, sticking his tongue out a little to the side with concentration.

'That guy?' I whispered. 'He's, like, a forest ranger. No way he's the creepy type. Trust me.'

I turned and stared as the guy hung the bauble, tossed the marker back into the dish, and then put his thick black gloves into the pocket of his jacket and strode away.

'Pops?' I called. 'Winter thinks that guy was following us—the guy who just wrote that there.' I pointed, and Pops walked over, frowning, to pluck the bauble.

He read it. He pulled it close to his chest.

And then he didn't move, not for ages.

'What does it say?' I asked impatiently, reaching out. But he wouldn't give it to me.

My father sank to the ground, cross-legged, right in the snow.

'FYI, your jeans aren't waterproof,' I said. 'You're really going to regret that later.'

But he just closed his eyes. Those icicle lights must have been on a timed setting, because they started to blink, one at a time, as if a tiny squirrel were running along the light rope, turning on each one in turn with his nimble squirrelly feet.

'Um, do you need a hand?' I asked uncertainly when Pops still hadn't moved and it really was starting to get pretty chilly.

Winter knelt down opposite him and put her stripy hands on his knees. 'You don't have to see the whole staircase,' she said kindly, 'just take the first step.'

Pops looked up then, and he actually smiled, which was probably about as rare as that waterfall catching the sunset and looking like cascading fire.

He cleared his throat. 'So we're moving to Tokyo,' he said slowly. 'In the autumn. But first...How would you like to see Grandpa Walter?'

Winter clapped her hands with joy like the goofball she was, but I had other things on my mind. 'Hey, do you know what they're mad for in Tokyo, Pops? Fairy lights. Can't get enough of them. We'll fit right in.'

And you know what? We did. After that summer with Walter

on the island, we started our new life in Tokyo with suntans and full hearts. We loved our skyscraper school and the Harajuku girls, with their gelato-coloured hair and mint-green knee socks with bells on them, and that there was nothing you couldn't get from a vending machine. We loved everything manga and the maid cafes in Akihabara, where girls in aprons made us wear bunny ears and tickled our noses with feather dusters. We loved Minami Tatako.

Minami came into our class mid-term, which caused a little stir, like when you shake up salad dressing in a jar. There was something about Minami. And, I kid you not, it was the very next morning that, unbeknownst to each other, Winter and I came into the kitchen, ready for school, both with our hair parted just like Minami's, straight down the middle and silked flat against our skull, imagining that our eyes were big and round and dark and full of some kind of snow-kingdom magic, like hers seemed to be, and that we glided, not walked, as she'd done that first day.

Oh, you will have read about it in books—a magnetic personality, a hypnotic beauty—but all those words are just paper in the wind when there is someone you want to be and be around and be part of and never apart from, and that was Minami, and we both felt it, Winter and I. We couldn't look away and our ears were sore with straining across the classroom to hear if she spoke, because it didn't happen often, and her voice was gentle and her handwriting was thin-elegant perfect, and even though our school was an International School and we were used to all types of genius clowns blowing through, Minami was Something. She folded paper so crisply, the edges meeting perfectly every time, no overlap, which Winter particularly loved.

Minami wanted to be a vet when she grew up, but get this: she was actually a film star. Well, an actress, and that's what she was doing in Tokyo, because she was filming a scene from the movie adaptation of a famous book that we actually technically couldn't have loved more and had read approximately nine zillion times. Here's a hint: it was *Bridge to Terabithia*. After a few weeks of rehearsals, she even cut off her hair so she could be more like the girl in the story, who's an A-grade tomboy and doesn't give two hoots about hair styling. 'Isn't she brave?' Winter and I would say to each other as we brushed our teeth.

'Minami Fever', our father dubbed it, and for him to pick up on it, it must really have been a Thing, because he came in and out of his lab so rarely that it was like he was flipping a book with his thumb and the little cartoons at the bottom of the page were flicking fast to make a story, a life—our life, sped up and without the living in it.

I bet you're thinking that this story ends with us befriending Minami, and getting invited onto her film set, and going skiing with her and wishing we had her perfect white fur-lined ski outfit, and staying up all night calculating what love percentage our names made with every boy in our class, and laughing.

But in actual fact, though we longed for that more than anything, we never really even had a full conversation with her—neither of us. We just sort of looked at her from across the street, the classroom, the climbing gym, aching, and had an imaginary life where we were BFFs, us three, and she came over to stroke Scout and Jem, our pair of miniature lop-eared rabbits. Boy, were they ever soft. And the weird thing is that Winter and I never even discussed it, our love for Minami—we just Knew each other's hearts because they were basically two halves of a butterfly. At least they had been, right up until now.

Winter

Out by the dunes, I asked Edward when his birthday was. He said he didn't know. He said he'd never had one. He didn't need one. If you had good things, eventually you would only lose them.

The wind blew strong. We threw stones.

I said, 'I could be your birthday. If you wanted.'

Then I pulled down my hat.

He tilted it up.

His eyes were so brown. Suddenly I couldn't push my lips together.

He reached into my pockets and found my hands.

I'd left them there.

He pulled them out.

That night, I started to sew.

I found scraps. It was all we had.

I imagined that the thread was love.

It sounds silly now, I know.

I had made such a fuss at the start about not going with Winter and Edward to race around the forest—had made it clear I thought it was lame and pointless—that even if I'd wanted to, I couldn't have joined in now. I wouldn't have anyway, because I hated being bad at things—just ask the teacher at that puppeteering course we went to one holidays. I could tell that Winter was getting good and, sure, I could've caught up, but I didn't want to seem, like, desperate or anything, and, yep, I was proud and stubborn—tell me something I don't know.

So, as the start of autumn minced in, still warm and all crimson gold, it was just me alone, out pruning the graveyard roses with nail scissors and stacking firewood like an obsessive Norwegian, cursing their love as I slammed each log onto my very symmetrical pile. I thought dark thoughts about that bear as I was stewing approximately 1.4 million apples into some kind of watery sauce, wishing we had pastry for pie.

You've probably assumed by now that our wish list would be mighty long and I'll bet you're thinking up near the top would be 'ASAP rescue operation!' or 'engaging human company' or 'new books' or 'iPhone upgrade' or 'certainty about the future', and that's probably because I'm being shady on the details of what everything was like out there before we came to dear old Bartleby. If you'd seen what we'd seen, Winter and I, you'd be quite happy too, burrowed in with nothing that came from that world except a cathedral-sized room of high-end canned food that even included a case of that freeze-dried ice cream that astronauts eat.

And as for the future, well, I just imagined we'd grow old at dear Bartleby, like a pair of elegant maiden aunts, and delight in each other's company and the changing seasons, and as time went on, we'd get better at some things, like ping pong, and worse at others, like, I don't know, seeing and hearing. And though we wouldn't have done anything Grand (capital G) with our lives or had a job or gone to university, maybe we would have written some philosophical poetry with geese metaphors, or made meaningful sculptures out of driftwood, and some day when we were skeletons lying side by side with our knuckles in a jumbled-up pile, someone would find our stuff and shriek 'Genius!' and we'd be posthumously famous forever more, and enjoy it all from heaven while eating Bonne Maman jam from the jar with spoons.

I'd say about an eighth of our Great Wall of Canned Food was Bonne Maman, though truth be told it was less a wall than a cavern, and so of course I never much thought about it running out. We foraged things from nature, like mulberries, and dug up the potatoes that Pops had planted, and I guess we could have dried the spring grass and ground it up for flour or something like that if we'd got desperate, which we never were. So it wasn't until the day I suddenly got a hankering for some Italian nougat, which we inexplicably had in truckloads, and sprinted out the back to find some that—BANG!—it hit me, like when a cartoon villain stands on a rake and the handle flicks back hard and hits him in the face and there's a ring of stars round his head.

There wasn't any Italian nougat, or any kind of nougat at all. There were only four jars of French chestnut cream left. One box of parmesan twists. The macadamia and coconut muesli we had eaten every day since forever was down to one last row of shiny silver foil packets. The huge sack of lentils that Winter had once disappeared in during hide-and-seek was empty enough to kick under your bed if you had to clean up in a hurry. All that we seemed to have in any kind of abundance was a stash of some kind of meat paste that you could boil up, though who ever would because it was

Disgusting. Somehow we'd finished a zillion cans of Italian chickpeas and Spanish anchovies, which are pretty good sources of protein, FYI. I don't remember when we'd polished off the packets of peanut brittle, but apparently we had. Or someone had.

Perhaps you're thinking, *Well, they could probably forage and hunt and wear furs and streak mud on their faces and turn a little feral, and it would all be totally fine.* And as I walked out into the fuzzy autumn evening with that awful nervous stomach you get when you're about to give a book report for a book you haven't read because you thought the cover was lame, that's what I was telling myself, that it would all be totally fine. There was nothing so far that we hadn't been able to handle—we were like those tiny Chinese kids in fancy circuses who wear cute hats and start off juggling three balls and end up tricking with seventy-seven and never even drop one, while the audience goes, 'Awwww'. But then I remembered Winter's face when we'd gone to one of those expensive circuses, and I knew, I just knew that she was practically bleeding with how many hours those kids had to practise away from their families, maybe with someone who was brutally strict and made them do hundreds of push-ups, or who just wasn't very kind—who didn't occasionally say, 'Nice job!'—and the heaviness that went into bending their springy little bodies into those tricksy arches, and the lives they might have been rescued from, and all the things the money they sent back home could do, and all the things it couldn't.

I missed Winter.

I missed her wispy warmth, so close. With all that running, lately she'd become so pink, and brown, and freckled and light-haired and long-limbed and late-summer autumned. I could feel the earth coming off her like some weird radiant energy when she came back from the forest, all flushed, her feet hard-soled but not dry and scaly like in an advert for heel balm. And the bear, so tall and broad and solid, like a statue in bronze in a pretty town square that a million people had climbed on to have their photographs taken. 'Do you think he minds?' Winter would have asked me while everyone clambered on the back of that bear statue to selfie themselves into the big old cloud of Data that was just floating around us like invisible coats we didn't even realise we were wearing.

Or perhaps, now that she knew that bear—now that she knew something that wasn't the dull pulse of the world's pain—she wouldn't have said that at all. Maybe she would just have turned to look up at the day-hidden stars and smiled.

As I looked around me, despairing at the empty space where cans of sardines used to balance in delicate towers, I realised—duh! The solution was right in front of me. This right here was the way to Houdini us out of this bizarre love triangle without anybody getting hurt at all, how I could lasso Winter and draw her back in to me, like I was some kind of Wyoming cowgirl taming a brumby on a golden plain. We had to leave the bear behind or we would starve or end up eating each other's brains with spoons. We needed to leave and find someone—Walter, maybe—who would care that we were still alive. And possibly make us nachos.

Winter

'So what's up there?' Edward asked as we rounded the last bend, sprinting.

Today I hadn't needed to stop once, and we had run far. My feet were hard now. My heart was light and floaty, a rice-paper lantern. 'Up where?'

'In that tiny tower at the top of your church. We've never been up. Pretty view?'

'Not really,' I panted. 'It…it smells. Bad.' I pulled up to a stop. Wiped my forehead.

'I bet you can see the lights from up there.'

'What lights?'

Edward looked at me strangely as we walked the last stretch back to the moat. 'From the settlement,' he said. 'On the other side of the mountain.'

'What settlement?' I asked. 'There's nothing else on the island.'

'But Winter,' he said slowly. 'This isn't an island.'

'That bear has cleaned us out of all the Fortnum & Mason stuff—even the currant and rosemary jelly that was supposed to go with a rack of lamb,' I told Winter. 'In less than two seasons! We're down to those lentils with the sprouty bits and that weird beef drink in the jar. Either the bear has to leave or we will. We need to go up to the bell tower, I mean, and—'

'But that's enough, isn't it?' said Winter. 'For the winter. We like broth. And in the summer we can pick things again.'

I thought of me and the dribbly apple sauce and trying to chop up kindling alone with hand blisters that sang pain, and wishing I was Laura Ingalls Bloody Wilder with a dad in the woods with a big old gun, and then realising that was just what we did have, for a while, and it wasn't actually that good, and I said, 'You think?'

'Edward can have my half,' said Winter. 'More than my half. I don't need it.'

And I could have smashed her beautiful, rosy cheeks in, because of course I knew that stubborn expression—that if she wanted to she could totally become a breatharian and live off the full sweetness of air in a cave, draped in some kind of toga, and no one would be able to stop her.

I sighed. 'Don't be an idiot. A bear can't survive on broth and you can't survive on half-broth. We can't stay here, Winter. Besides, doesn't he need to go find a cosy spot in the forest to hibernate or whatever?'

'No,' she said quickly. 'He can sleep by the windows. With me.'

And I said, 'Winter. He is wild.'

And even as the words came out of my mouth, I knew the truth, which was that Winter was wild, too—that perhaps she always had been, and I had been trying to carry her around in a lunchbox, sort of against her will. I don't mean wild like smoking-behind-the-shed wild, or pleather-hot-pants-and-too-much-eyeliner-lip-synching-on-a-naughty-video wild. I mean, well, I guess I mean, ever so deeply free.

'We need to leave,' I said carefully, 'or we'll die. It's time to go up to the bell tower and get things happening. And you know Edward can't follow us there.'

'*Please*,' said Winter. 'Maybe he can catch enough food for winter. Maybe in the forest—the river…Some salmon. Please, Summer? Just give him a little while?'

And even though, let's face it, I had murdered that bear a thousand times in my mind—had smoked its hock into a fine pancetta—of course I couldn't say no, because Winter's head was tilted to the side, and her whole body was rigid with pleading. I looked at the scar across her nose that I didn't have, and I felt the boxer inside me put down her gloves.

'Two weeks,' I said with a sigh. 'Two weeks from today, and if we're not hot-smoking an entire winter's worth of salmon, we're climbing those stairs and we're gone.'

Winter

'I don't think your sister likes me,' said Edward. He was sitting on a tree stump, stringing pieces of wire across the hole in an old tin. 'And she *really* hates your dog. Maybe it's time we moved on, Pete and I.'

'Don't do that,' I said quickly. This was our favourite clearing. I leaned back against a tree. 'It's not safe out there. Besides, I need you. I mean, we need you. Both of us.'

He was making them shorter, tighter, those strings, so that he could pluck them. Like a guitar.

We were up to five words in a row with his reading. We'd got there last night.

I think I like you.

We are all safe here.

Please don't leave without goodbye.

He should have felt happy. But he looked sad.

'She does...' I said. 'She likes you. It's just...Summer is...'

'A big old liar? A total control freak? A thousand times a day, she lies—don't think I haven't noticed. A million times she tells you what to do. It's not healthy.'

I felt hard little kicks in my stomach. I couldn't agree but I couldn't disagree. I rubbed my feet against Pete's back. We had washed him in the moat with lavender shampoo, Edward and I. I didn't tell Summer. The shampoo was supposed to be for that day in the future when we would go up to the bell tower, ready to leave.

'Don't look like that, all cute and worried like a lost lamb,' said Edward. 'I know how you feel about her, and I like Surf—I really do. I'm just trying to understand the whole thing better, I guess. The way it works between you.'

'Summer finds it hard to trust people,' I said. 'She thinks she needs to keep me safe.'

Edward strummed all the strings at once. There were three so far. They sounded pretty. He reached for the next. 'And does she?'

I plucked at the grass and thought of all the things we had seen. I thought of the flash of bullets outside the window of our seaplane, how Summer had told me they were shooting stars. That I should wish. I thought how easily she had forgiven me when I still couldn't forgive myself.

'When you have seen a lot of things,' I said eventually, 'sometimes it is easier just pretending you haven't. That way, you can believe that bad things aren't still going to happen. At least, you can sometimes. Sometimes you need to pretend that you know how the story ends.' I looked up. 'Do you get what I mean?'

'Sure. But I'm here now,' Edward said. 'The past doesn't matter anymore. Nothing bad's going to happen while I'm with you. I'm like a one-man SWAT team. I'm like a force field.'

He sounded so sure. But that was just what our father had promised when we left Tokyo. So I didn't say anything back.

I thought about Summer. How hard it was to admit to myself that my feelings for her had changed.

It wasn't that I loved her less. It was realising that I could still love her from further away. Like you can love the house you grew up in from two cities west. From across the world.

'What's Summer's favourite song?' he asked when he'd fitted five strings. 'What kind of music does she like?'

'Summer loves Elvis,' I said. 'The slow ones. Sung slowly. "Can't Help Falling in Love"—that's her favourite.'

'Too easy,' he said. 'Give me a day. No—a week. Two weeks? Leave it with me.'

Summer

Winter woke me sometime in the space between midnight and dawn, when the world is otherworldly and your mind takes up all of the bedroom, not just your head, and your breath is a tiny thing. It was so lovely to see her there, so unexpected after all the hours I had spent like a rolled slab of dough with a cookie-cutter girl missing from the middle. In the wide moonlight, her teeth shone so that I could see that she was smiling as she said, 'Come with me.'

And even though I knew that wherever she took me, that bear would be there too—even though I knew that and I couldn't think how to warn her about him, and even though, whatever I said, she would never believe me—I followed her out across the moat and through the orchard and over the cold night dunes. Edward was waiting on the beach, standing up on his hind legs and gazing out at the water with a kind of sea-captain longing. By now he was so tall that we came only part-way past his knees and when he dropped back down to all fours, Winter had to take a run-up to vault onto the solid rug of his back. They both turned to look at me and it was so deeply annoying to know that I couldn't do what Winter had just done, that it was only because of all her running muscles that she could jump so high. I kicked at the sand and looked out at the crinkled desert of moon-hit sea and sulked.

Then the bear lay down, flattened his belly against the sand and put his head on his paws, just looking at me and waggling his big old ears, and Winter held out her hands, even though she knew I'd only pull her off if I took them, and the breeze was running through her hair like kind fingers, and the rocks in the distance shone like basking whales. I swallowed my pride and went over and took fists of his fur and pulled myself up onto his back. I even tried not to yank it too hard. Nestled in behind Winter as the bear stood, I may as well have been five years old and riding Tanka, that fat old brown pony with the snowy mane who came each year to the Scandinavian Christmas Bazaar, except it was always me up front, every time, his plaited reins through my fingers and my heels kicking, crying out 'Yeeha!' and Winter behind me, worried that two was too much for a pony, trying to make herself feather light and her bones small.

Edward's back swayed as he sloshed into the sea and though I guess I should have been wondering if bears can even swim, I was really just half drunk on being so close to Winter, feeling her heart beat through the back of her ribs. I put my arms around her waist and my cheek against the wing of her shoulderblade and my lips against the sharp angle of bone, and at that second, the bear's feet lifted off the bottom of the ocean and I opened my eyes to see that as he paddled, all around him, in the webs of his fur, little beads of phosphorescence clung and sparkled—so many that, in their eerie glow, I could see a turtle pass beneath us, could make out his pinprick nostrils and his prehistoric beak and his grumpy little brow with those eyes that said, 'I s'pose you really *have* to be here?'

Winter said, 'Watch this!' and kicked her foot through the sea so that water showered down in a spray of emerald phosphorescence, and I felt my stomach slam up against itself, not because it was so sublime, because it was, but because she knew how to flick her toes like that, just so, which meant that she'd been here before, perhaps a heap of times, and as we glided, ringed with light, parallel with the shore, rising up and down as the ocean shrugged beneath us, I was sad with love that had nowhere to go.

Winter turned her head to me and I wondered if she could feel it—if somehow she knew what was boiling inside my heart.

'Isn't it like we're on Aslan's back,' she said loudly, 'just flying?'

There was nothing and no one Winter loved more than Aslan, that wise old papa lion from *The Lion, the Witch and the Wardrobe* who's one part Jesus and one part love and one part brute animal and one part all the world's wisdom in a pelt. How many hours Winter had wept for him, vowed to live her life as a tribute to him and the Good (capital G) he represented; how she had put all her longings onto him for the things we didn't have. I felt sorry for the bear, then, because I knew what I was going to do—the only thing I could do in the face of that love, which towered over me like a cliff and cast a grave-cold shadow so big it had its own postcode.

I couldn't wait two weeks. Could hardly wait a hot second.

I squeezed my arms tighter around Winter, trying not to bend her ribs with all the sorries I felt for what would come next. And all the ones that I didn't.

Winter

Edward didn't let us outside all afternoon. Not till after the sun had gone down.

'Stay in here and read something,' he said. 'Isn't that what you do all day anyway?'

'Are you trying to curtail our fundamental liberties?' Summer demanded. 'Are you threatening our right to freedom of movement?'

'Go write a poem about it,' said Edward. 'If you keep the lines short, I might even read it.'

She didn't. She climbed up on the bookshelf that Edward had made for my mother's books. She pulled down *The Secret Garden* for me and *Oliver Twist* for her. 'These are both narratives of oppression, so that's fitting,' she said. 'What's he doing out there, anyway?'

'I don't know,' I said. 'It's a surprise.'

'As if,' said Summer. Her voice had a sharpness to it that I hated. 'Don't you two tell each other everything now?'

I looked down at the book—at dear Mary Lennox. I ran my fingers over the title and thought. How sour she was at the start, and how creamy at the end.

People change, she whispered to me from the cover. *And that's not a bad thing.*

So instead of feeling the sad sorry that I'd left Summer out, instead of all the apologies to make it better, I told the truth. 'I tell him the things you won't listen to. We talk about the things you won't talk about.'

Summer didn't respond. She opened *Oliver Twist*. She started reading furiously.

The last of the sunlight came sideways through the windows. Everything glowed and flickered, but inside, I felt calm.

And something else—something unfamiliar. I felt strong and tall. Like a lion. Like a bear.

We read in silence, but not the silence we were used to. Outside there were scrapes and knocks. When the light got low, I lit a lamp.

'I bet you think he's Dickon,' Summer said viciously as I sat back down.

Dickon is the Yorkshire boy in *The Secret Garden* who teaches Mary Lennox about hope, and nature, and love. 'What a babe,' Summer would always say when we reached the part where he rescues the secret garden.

'You know,' I said quietly, 'I hadn't thought about it. But you're right. He's a lot like Dickon.'

'Seasons!' Edward called. 'Get out here!'

We didn't look at each other as we walked outside.

At first I couldn't see anything. When you haven't had it for so long, electric light is blinding. And it seemed to be flashing all around us, little balls of it. There was loud whirring. When my eyes adjusted, I saw that it was my father's old generator, put back together. Something smelled incredibly good in a fire-y, charcoal-y, smoke-house-y way.

And then it started—the song.

It was the tin guitar. But because of the fairy lights that were strung up over the moat and the table with the white cloth and some kind of roasted meat and some kind of flowers in a jam jar, and the stars and the moon, it sounded like an enchanted harp.

I didn't recognise the tune at first. Just that it was beautiful.

But gradually it rearranged itself in my mind.

Then Edward began to sing and I knew for sure. It was a song my father had sung to my mother in a time so long ago, I wasn't sure it had really happened.

It was slow, slow Elvis, and next to me Summer was crying.

Maybe I felt guilty for what I hadn't even done to the bear yet—
maybe that's why I picked a fight. And if you think it would be
impossible to pick a fight with peaceful, sweet little Winter, well,
you're so almost very right, and, sure, I could blame the hunger that
bumps along behind two meals a day of beef broth and minimal
snacks. But by now Winter was hardly eating anything—was giving
it all to that stupid bear—and you didn't see *her* picking at my scabs
with the filthy point of an old compass.

'Winter,' I said, when she ran back in the door, panting and pink,
forest-glowing, her hair spritzing out at the sides. 'Don't you think
it's sort of kind of weird that a bear just arrived here—out of
nowhere, I mean?'

'No?' said Winter, putting her hands on her knees to catch her
breath. 'There are other animals here.'

And she was right, there were—bunnies and foxes and squirrels
and geese and all kinds of birds, which had been so scared of us at
the start that for ages we hadn't been able to coax them back to their
own nests, they were that shy, and it had taken Winter's patience
and sugar water and days.

'But there are lots of all those—you can see how they'd breed.
How does just a single baby bear end up here? Isn't that, well, odd?
Sort of...*suspicious*?'

Winter was quiet, and I knew that type of quiet; that was fright
quiet, shutting-up-shop quiet. That was Pops-is-yelling quiet, and
bullets-on-the-side-of-the-plane quiet. And you'll think I'm a total
brute, but I liked it—I liked that I could make her feel that way, and
so I went on.

'Have you actually even checked his fur—you know, for bugs?'

'He doesn't have bugs—he's clean. He doesn't even smell bad.'

'I mean electronic bugs. You know, like in spy movies. Listening devices or whatever. Or some kind of bomb. He has a lot of fur. It would be easy to strap a bomb on him—a mini one. Like a suicide bomber crossed with that dog they sent into space. The Russian one.'

And you probably won't even get how cruel that was, because when Winter learned about Laika and how they'd sent her up to float around the stars as an experiment in the early spaceship days, that she had died alone in that floating cage, Winter had practically ripped her own heart out of her chest with sadness. She had even written a gosh-darn poem about it, and it won an award in a country we weren't even living in, but our teacher had sent it off along with the kittens she'd given birth to when she read it.

'Stop it,' whispered Winter, and she looked at me with eyes that said, *Why are you doing this to me?* And I liked that even more.

'Pretty clever, wouldn't it be, to make an animal swallow something with a timing device, or one of those cameras that can see through skin. They'd learn a lot about what's in the bell tower that way.'

'He doesn't know about the bell tower,' Winter whispered. 'I promise.'

But she said it a little too quickly—only a nanosecond, or something like that, but if anyone had an Olympic-grade timer that could detect those teeny fractions of Winter, it was me, and suddenly I wasn't just trying to poke a stick in a bee's nest, I was actually, genuinely angry, because we'd made a promise to our father that we'd never, ever, in a thousand years, on pain of death, with a knife at our throat, with acid being poured into our eyeballs, with our feet pressed up against a barbecue—well, you get the picture. We'd promised never to tell anyone what was up there, because the contents of the bell tower were worth more than our lives, and I know you'll think I'm being dramatic and all, but I'm not exaggerating when I say that what was up there was Everything. It was the future of the whole world. If the wrong people got it, well...

'You know what your problem is?' I said coolly, much more coolly than I felt, which was molten. I looked her right in the eyes—right in her pink-cheeked, loved-up, gentle face—and I whispered, *'You're a slut.'*

Winter stepped back as if I had slapped her with a palm full of thumbtacks. She even put her hand up to her cheek to soothe the sting, like the illustration on the cover of some kind of dime-store romance novel, and I hated her even more because she looked so ridiculously beautiful as she did it.

'Don't use that word,' she said. 'And besides, I haven't done anything. We haven't done anything. And even if we had...If we had, that's okay too.'

'That bear couldn't care less about you,' I spat. 'And you think it's love, I can tell, but he's a goddamn *animal*.'

'You're just jealous,' Winter said in a low voice. 'You're jealous. You're jealous. You're jealous. You're—'

Winter

We were often in the moat, Edward and I, through long afternoons, the water silky dark. We could signal each other under the surface, away from the blade of Summer's gaze. With our fingers we spun a new language between us. As our third winter approached, it wasn't warm. But the river ran too fast to bathe in. I still wasn't the strongest swimmer.

'You're getting too scrawny—that's the problem,' said Edward. 'You can't float if you've got no body fat. That's just science, right there. You've got to eat more.'

But there wasn't really more. Every day there was less. Soon there would be none. The generator was already almost out of fuel for stewing apples. Boiling broth. Edward hadn't caught a fish in weeks.

'It's like they're in hiding,' he said, pushing off from the edge of the moat and gliding to the other side. 'It's like they're gangsters who've been tipped off before a drug bust, and they're just trying to keep a low profile.'

'You sound like Summer,' I said. I was trying to float on my back, hipbones to the sky like he'd taught me.

'When was the last time she even spoke?' said Edward. 'She's like a ghost now—suddenly there, glowering round corners. It's creepy. She's even started showing up in my dreams.' He rested his forearms on the stones of the water's edge, warm from the afternoon sun. 'I thought…I don't know…I thought the Elvis would fix things. Break the ice. Dumb, huh?'

I stood up and I kicked off and I swam over to him with my strongest strokes. I put my palms on his cheeks. I kissed him long. Our lips fizzed stars. I didn't even worry that Summer was watching.

He was right; she was everywhere now.

'It wasn't dumb,' I whispered when we'd finished.

The tips of his fingers traced drops down my chest. 'Hey, Pretty,' he whispered back.

My stomach twirled. I ducked under water, pulled him down with me to where Summer couldn't see. 'Run away with me?' I asked with my hands and my heart.

That night, the sky was thick with stars.

The stars saw me leave my bed in only a blanket. By then we didn't have knickers.

I found Edward. He was still awake.

I lay down on the nest that we'd made him. His head was on the pillowcase, the one I'd sewn with our initials.

I said, 'Sorry these blankets are rough,' because I could feel them now, in just my skin. I could feel everything.

I had to turn and face the wall.

I felt his eyes on my neck. Then his breath on my neck. Then his breath on my hair.

Edward ran his finger down the knobbles of my spine. Like he was looking for dust, or tracing through steam on a window.

'Are you cold?' he whispered when I shivered.

I wondered if he had done this before. I wondered if he could see that I hadn't.

I'd only kissed Summer. She'd wanted to practise.

I whispered, 'No.' I whispered, 'You found the fairy lights.'

'Sure.'

A butterfly kiss. Is that what it's called?

'Did you know we were here?' I whispered, 'Were you looking for us?'

'Only my whole life,' he whispered back. Then he rubbed his ankle against my ankle.

'Ho!' said the stars. But they needn't have worried. That was enough.

'So is this what love is?' I asked them.

'It is more,' said the stars. 'But that is the start. Oh, Winter, you wait.'

Summer

We didn't have any books that, like, specifically advised what to do when your identical twin sister falls in love with a bear with Real Murderous Potential. But as I was looking through the piles for one, I came across *Matilda*, that short, minxy genius, and thought to myself, well, her headmistress, Miss Trunchbull, isn't too far off some kind of unpredictable, bloodthirsty grizzly, and I took myself and that book to the bottom of the bell tower stairs, and suddenly I was eight again in our bedroom in Tokyo and desperately trying to move things with my eyes, and getting a headache with all that staring and straining, but never quite giving up the hope that there was a Matilda tucked in me, and that my little could defeat all the evils and injustices of big.

We had guns. Of course we did—duh, my father was a wanted fugitive. We had guns, and I'm not talking BB guns or antique rifles—I'm talking about the kind that could have split the rib cage of a bear, or popped his head into unstrained raspberry jam. The trouble was that I had seen Pops shoot one of those guns, and I knew that the kickback in them was enough to break the shoulder of a pretty weedy fifteen-year-old girl who hadn't been on the yoghurt regularly.

I had some serious doubts about lassoing that bear in a noose, given that he was now almost twice my height and I'd seen him arm wrestle. And then there were the traps. We had all kinds of traps— Pops had flown them in with us, and some were deer-sized and some were squirrel-sized and some were somewhere in the middle, and truth be told I hadn't thought about them much till now, but I pulled them out and polished them up. And of course the biggest were the bear traps, two of them, and the reason I wasn't so crash hot about using them was that, boy, they looked *mean*, concrete-munching mean, and, let's face it, it wasn't beyond the realm of possibility that I could end up mashing myself, even though Pops had showed us seventy-seven times how to set them safely, but it was usually Winter who paid attention to those boring sorts of details.

And so I chose The Knife—I had to, and don't think I didn't feel sick as I took it out of its leather-pouch home, because it wasn't too far from what a sushi chef uses to gut those fish that are poisonous unless you slice and dice them in a certain way with a blade that is made of, like, diamonds, and, to be honest with you, it made me feel a little queasy, the damage it could do, and had done already to some poor someone, maybe a few someones, and perhaps that is why I was so weird about the forest, if I'm being really honest, which I swear I'm trying to be.

I planned it, drew diagrams in the dirt with my toe of how I'd plunge the blade—like so—into his giant lung. I imagined how it would whistle like a dropped bomb as the air whooshed out. And through and through his chest and out the other side, if the blade would even reach that far, because by now, of course, that bear's trunk was a big old wine barrel and, good grief, how did I even think I could? How does anyone? And how, how could I do that to Winter—literally slice through the one thing she had ever had all to herself?

But every time I faltered, I just had to think of all the things I'd lost, and the only things I had left, which were basically Winter and the memories of our childhood, and how I couldn't lose either of them without dying myself. In my defence, I hope it's crossed your mind that there is a lot of meat on a bear, and I'll have you know I was quite the dab hand with chipotle and our *Little House in the Big Woods* smokehouse. But how I'd ever get Winter on board with that, with chewing on his big old ribs, well, that was a challenge I was still working on when the world stopped spinning. The fortnight

I'd promised Winter was almost up, and Edward hadn't caught anything except her heart—not a squirrel or a tiny forest bird or any woodlands creature you could skewer and roast on a flame till it was crunchy. Boy, was I sick of drinking broth and watching Winter eat nothing but air. Of seeing Edward grow broader each day on her rations. Of fading into a skulking shadow girl, so brittle with envy I could have snapped myself into pieces. I was Oliver-Twist hungry, Dickensian mean.

For almost two weeks I followed them everywhere, chased the ribbons of rainbow that swirled behind them, a trail of love. I watched as they floated each evening in the beaded light of that glowing ocean pool; I shivered on the shore in the hard cold of midnight. Wilting and hungry. Lonely and sad. I was everywhere they were, hidden round corners, flat under bushes, trailing behind them at dawn and at moonrise, trying to be silent and frantically watching. It's only now, from up here, I can see the irony: after all that we'd run from, I had turned into a spy.

I watched Edward watch over Winter as she slept, my heart in my throat as he bent over her, his muzzle so close to the line of her neck. Then he would nose her so gently she'd hardly even wake, just reach out her arms towards him in sleepy love. I would breathe again, feel the pump of hot stress rush down to my toes.

All day my body was taut like a spring, straining for the chance to swoop in to the rescue. But each time I was sure there'd be blood and murder and animal lust, there was nothing. Honeyed, ursine tenderness. Hours, days lost in manic surveillance. Things buzzing round the edges of my vision, small gnats of exhaustion—locusts, maybe. One night I fell asleep in a bush of brambles on the edge of the meadow. I woke up. They were gone. I was shredded and aching.

The next morning I chased them right into the forest. A golden-green cave. Dappled light and no sky. The trunks of the trees dark and sombre, like a field of huge crosses. Quiet on quiet.

Edward and Winter strode out with no path. They flitted so easily into the distance. My sprint was their lope and my breath was a rasp. I ran just long enough to lose the way out.

'Hey, guys!' I called, but they didn't stop.

Now every direction was trees upon trees. My heart sped up. Each shadow was a man hanging from a noose. I spun round and round, searching for a trace of myself—of who I had been a minute ago. I stopped when I realised my eyes were still shut. I struck out in one direction, ran, tried another. There was nothing to show me I wasn't just going in circles. The view was the same whichever way I turned. The spots in my eyes. I would die here—or worse, I would live forever in this infinite cage.

'Mama!' I cried as I sank to my knees. 'Mama,' I sobbed—truly pitiful sobs. I lay down in a ball.

'Not like you to be so glum,' said someone old, and gruff, and kind.

I looked up and there was Walter, blue eyes and white whiskers.

'Come, young banshee,' he said so gently. 'Quit your wailing and follow me.'

He led me out, all the way home. Boy oh boy, did I talk up a storm. As I trotted behind him, I told the whole story: the bear and the love and the starving and me.

'Now listen here,' he said as we came to the river, crossed over the stones. 'You quit all that gawking. Do you hear me? That's nobody's business 'cept him and hers. Chop some wood. Stretch your legs on the beach. Count up your rations. Make a plan. Stop wearing your wishbone where your backbone ought to be.'

'But that bear, he's—'

'No buts, no nothing,' Walter said firmly. 'And have another look out the back of that church—a proper look, not just flitting about. I know you and your slapdash ways. There'll be snacks to be had, for sure.' He reached out to ruffle my hair.

'Are you real?' I asked.

'Are you?' he asked back.

I smiled. 'Good question. Hey—thanks for...you know.'

'See you, kid.' He turned and strode to the ocean, right into the mist of the pretty old sea. He disappeared like the just-waking wisp of a dream.

Winter

Edward built a glass-bottomed boat. In less than two days. Wooden seats. A set of oars. He could build anything out of anything. How did he know? He could do so many things. He just shrugged when I asked.

He lugged the boat halfway up Our Mountain.

I met him there mid-morning, up high where the river split in half. Pete came too. It didn't seem right to leave him behind.

Edward said we'd go rollerskating. 'You'll see,' he told me. 'There's so much you don't know about the other side of the mountain.'

I ran the whole way. I had brought nothing with me. Only fireflies in my rib cage, buzzing. I had expected to be ripped down the middle, like a sheet, from leaving. But here I was, more whole than I had ever been.

'Free,' the stars whispered from where they hid behind the day. 'You are free.'

'Hush,' I said back. 'She will hear.'

The river was cold and the day was bright. Edward carried me across the water on his shoulders. I was lighter now. Like feathers, like dust.

He steadied the boat. I stepped onto the glass that I don't think was glass. 'Will it break?' I asked, then wished I hadn't.

'As if I'd ever risk that,' he said. 'As if I'd ever risk you.'

The wood was warm to lie on. The spray flew up like sparks. We watched it slip by below us, that secret world of the riverbed. Then we lay on our backs. My head fitted his shoulder as if they'd been carved. The sun on my eyelids. My hand on his stomach. I slept.

When I woke, his fingers were circled around my wrist. His pointer and his thumb.

He looked at it, that circle, and in his face was pain. Like he'd hooked a beautiful silver fish and didn't know how he could throw it back.

He looked straight into my eyes.

'What's wrong?' I whispered.

He swallowed. 'I thought...I thought I could predict anything. And then there was you.'

He kissed the patch of skin between the side of my eyebrow and the line of my hair. I had never thought about it, that small patch. But now it was a desert in moonlight, a landscape.

In time he sat up.

'Is it really glass?' I asked. 'The bottom of the boat?'

'No, I think it might be a type of plastic. Your dad had heaps of incredible building supplies out the back—stone cutters and all sorts. Really great stuff. What was he making, anyway? What...What are you guys even doing here?'

The words came up through my throat like a puff of bees. When I finished, I wondered how I'd kept them down so long.

As the river carried us, I told him about our lives before. The church with the tiny tower. The whole truth of our father. I told why and how. The things we were guarding, the things we had hidden.

He listened—with his whole face. Tucked it all safe away so I didn't have to carry it. And it felt so nice. Like leaning back onto the wind.

I told him this.

When Summer and I were eleven, my mother died. We had to leave Tokyo quickly.

We didn't get the chance to find a white coffin. My mother loved white.

Edward didn't say anything. But he looked over at me and whispered, 'I'm sorry, Winter.'

I knew what he was thinking: The Greying. The back bruises. The sick skin. The pits. The bulldozers that bent people up, like plasticine. The huge bags of powdered lime. I knew what he was thinking because of how I'd said it: *Summer and I were eleven. My mother died. We had to leave Tokyo quickly.* He thought that my mother was sick. But that wasn't it. That wasn't how.

My mother had a radio show. It was on each weekday at noon.

Her voice was warm. Like she cared what you liked in your sandwich.

She interviewed someone each lunch hour. A celebrity, an everyday person. A president one day, a postman the next.

They ended up loving her. You could hear, and we did.

They would tell her things—even the rock stars. The shape of their mother's jewellery box. A particular bowl of macaroni as the sun set.

In the supermarket, people stopped her. They would hear her ask us about cheese, and recognise her voice. They would say she made things better. That the hour with her was their only comfort. That the words she spoke were the only truth left.

She was always kind. You knew they'd go home and feel proud as they told.

As I ate my sandwich each weekday at school, I'd imagine the whole world was pausing to listen. I felt proud that she knew the fillings I liked.

'Wait a sec, Pretty.' Edward sat up, his face intent. He leaned forwards. 'Wait wait wait. Your mother...' He whispered, 'You don't mean she was...?'

And I felt that I could. I said, 'Yes, that was her.' I said, 'Yes.'

His eyes filled up and shimmered. Pete leapt up to lick his cheeks clean. Edward patted his head. He started to cry.

Because he had seen my mother die. The whole world had seen her die. I had seen it too, and Summer.

I had thought that I wanted to talk about it. For so long that was all I had wanted. Summer would never.

But now I felt my chest start to ache that hot, sick ache. Lights prickled round the edge of my sight. I started to shake.

'Please?' I said. 'Please forget I told you. Please don't ever bring it up. Please don't say anything to Summer. She doesn't…She can't. *Please.*'

He wiped his eyes with the back of his wrist, but there were tears in his voice. 'I won't mention it. But I can't forget it. I'm so sorry, Winter. I'm so very, very sorry.'

We didn't talk much after that.

'Here,' he said after a while as we turned into a cove. 'Here is good.'

He jumped out to drag us up onto the bank. Pete leapt out to snap at some flies.

'Summer will hate that I told you all that,' I said. I could feel cotton in my mouth. Her foot between my shoulderblades, crushing.

Edward stopped pulling and leaned his forearms on the edge of the boat, right up close to me, his feet on the stony bottom.

'Listen here, Winter. If I only give you one thing in life, let it be this. You need to move out from under that rock or I swear to God, you won't survive. You won't.'

I could feel the truth of his words as they landed, scrunched-up paper arcing across the room straight into a bin, first try.

'But I love Summer,' I said, and that was true, too. 'Without her, I'm…'

'Don't you even fucking say it,' said Edward loudly. 'You are everything, all on your own.'

I felt tears in my eyes. The bridge of my nose tingled. 'Don't swear at me,' I whispered.

Edward sighed, but it was not a mean sigh.

Or maybe that's how I remember it now.

I slipped off the boat. He dragged it onto the shore in rough, sharp pulls. I heard the not-glass scrape the stones. The riverbed pressed against my feet. 'Toughen up, princess,' I heard Summer say into my ear. 'Those wacky guys in India walk across burning coals barefoot all the time, no big deal. You'll be fine—just use your big old brain. And FYI, I'm still mad at you, but I've got so much to tell you, you wouldn't believe. Get back here already. I'm lonely. I miss you.'

The water was freezing. My calves started to burn with the cold.

'Edward?' I whispered. 'I don't know how to rollerskate. Please… Will you take me back home?'

Summer

The after-sunset sky was all plum jam and marmalade. The first sprinkling of stars was out, and I'd been back a while from gathering kindling and was mooching on a pew reading *The Graveyard Book*, thinking about ghosts and dreaming of a giant steak sandwich in that way you do when you've had limp leaves for lunch. I hadn't been to the back of the Emporium yet. 'Coward,' Walter said to me with a wink and a smile, and I wondered for the zillionth time if I had somehow conjured him up to lead me out of the forest. Or if he truly was a ghost now—if that was actually, like, a thing.

At the opposite end of the long church seat, Winter read, too— the book by Obama about love. Boy, did the whole world cry after that caper with him being strapped to the tanks. Us especially. What a guy and what an end.

Our feet were almost touching in the middle, and the air between us was a big old cloud of politeness, both of us doing our best to pretend that there had only ever been peace. Two weeks was up—it had been for a while—but I didn't mention the salmon. The winter settled in.

And now that I had stopped chasing after Winter, she came back to me from time to time, like a baby bird not quite done with the nest. Honestly? It was kind of a relief not to have to follow them everywhere—to trust that if that bear was really up for snacking on my sister, he would have put her on crackers and got it over with by now. And if his love was true, well, I guess it would have happened sometime, and better that she fell in love with a beast than some mansplainer who was deep in love with his own opinions and made her attend all his basketball games, even the lame ones at pre-season training.

They were out in the forest more than ever these days, but they always came back, and I guess I just had to trust in that or I'd go properly crazy. I had to trust in Walter. Calm down. Make a plan.

It was triply lucky that Winter wasn't out running with Edward today, because who knows if she would have survived out there— even tucked inside we barely made it through the jolt when the Earth stopped spinning. Yes, I mean literally.

When the world stopped turning, we were thrown into the air like frisbees. The howl as it ground down was so loud and desperate and long that I thought it had come from the part of me that had missed Winter all these weeks she'd been off with Edward, curling through the trees like steam. It was a shriek like gears stuck and crunching, an arm in a woodchipper, suddenly all pulp and bone. As we lay on the church floor, curled up like commas and sore from the bang, it went on and on, and then we could hear a wind whipping up—slowly at first, but it spiralled into a gale that would have ripped a toupee off a school principal's head as he was walking through the Science-block car park, even one that had been stuck on with ultra-strong superglue because he was so paranoid about slippage. Boy, was it loud.

When eventually the howling stopped and the wind died down a little and we could stand up without fear of being flung against the altar, Winter didn't run off to find that bear, who I guess was having one of his luxurious seasonal naps. She just rubbed her elbow where it had been slammed against the pew and looked at me with knowing in her face, and we didn't need words. We had a vague clue what had just happened, and we were probably the only two living people in the world who did—three, if you included our father, but who knew if he was even in the world anymore?

The whole Why of it was a mash-up of tidal friction, sonic waves, gravity. The tilt of the Earth's magnetic core in the face of that heartbeat of internet waves that had pulsed across the wet blue bits of the dear, sweet planet—waves that Pops had put in the water. And how they actually travelled, well, it belongs with all those science-y things we would have learned if we'd stayed in school, or if Pops had really gone into it all properly when he told us that something like this might happen.

I know now that the water and everything in it rearranged itself, so that the bulge around the middle of the planet sloshed back towards the poles, which did something to the spinning, and I guess that's why Pops had chosen our island so carefully, because we hardly felt a splash of it, even though, elsewhere, the ocean was splitting itself into three different oceans and whole countries were underwater, whole cities already being eaten by salt.

I will say it again in case you missed it: the world had stopped turning, just like they say might happen in corny love songs if the lovers are ripped apart, and little did we know there were earthquakes rumbling all around the rest of the planet, like deep hunger pangs, and a blanket of fog was settling down on the top of the cold slabs of sea, like when you toss a doona up over your bed and it drifts down in perfect rumples that make you want to lie on top of it immediately.

We were so used to everything breaking—glass and engines and branches and computers. But when the world broke down, we couldn't believe it at first; it was like being told we had actually been ghosts all along, and who could take that with a shrug?

The bear didn't understand, couldn't ever possibly have understood, and I'd be lying if I said that this didn't make me feel suddenly, deeply good and, for a few hours there, I almost clean forgot that the bear was a Threat (capital T). When he waddled out from his snoozing, he was all confused and clingy, like a little kid the first time you take them to the movies and the lights go down and they want to climb onto your knee. I can't believe I'm saying this, but he was completely, pathetically gorgeous.

I heard Winter explaining it to him later, what Pops had told us; at least as much as she could, and of course she had remembered more than I had—she always did.

You might think that the most annoying thing about being stuck in the half-light of the after-sunset was not being able to see: having everything in a gloomy half-shadow, and missing the colours that come when light bounces around, or whatever it does—I want to say 'refracting'? But to tell you the truth, it was exciting at first, the candles and the kerosene lamp, and us and the bear all cosy, as if we were having a sleepover in the school gym and the power had gone out, and the teacher had gone outside with a torch to fuss over a fuse box. That feeling you get when everyone says the things they usually only say at sleepovers or on late-night car rides.

We ate the last of the jam I'd been saving, our spoons clinking against each other as they scraped round the jar. We talked about what might be coming next, what might be affected if the sun was stuck just below the horizon, and if right now you're thinking, like, *Ummm, photosynthesis?!,* well, you're a few steps ahead of us, and it wasn't even that whole photosynthesis equation that needed figuring out—it was a thermal kind of question, which is just a fancy word for 'heat'. That's what was slowly draining away from this side of the poor old world, and waiting for us on the other side, six months from now, which, if Pops was right, was how long it would take for us to see sun again. When we did, it would beat down on us for another six months, during which time, well, things wouldn't be great unless you were totally and completely into Death By Barbecue.

At least, that's what could have happened. But maybe you've guessed by now that this is where Pops and the bell tower come in.

Winter

I had gone out early to run it all away.

In the green breath of forest air, I could pretend. That the full set of our secrets was still inside me, caked up the sides of my mind. That yesterday hadn't happened. That I hadn't told. That I wasn't being pulled two ways, in half.

But if I had the chance, would I swallow it back inside me?

Were guilt and regret the same thing? It sounded like something Summer would have loved to debate. But we couldn't. So I ran.

When I was done, I went back to Edward's bed and lay down.

The half-light fringed everything orange, dulled everything mauve.

He opened one eye, closed it and rumpled my hair.

His hands, gentle with half-sleep and morning love. Pete still asleep in the crook of his knee.

'You're soft,' he said. 'Like droopy roses. Whatcha call 'em—petals.'

His palms left star prints all over my skin.

Until he ran his fingers through the gaps in my ribs, the dips like little graves.

He was suddenly awake. He looked up at me. For the first time, I saw fear in his face.

Eat, his eyes said. *Please eat. For me?*

But it had become so easy not to. Like I had fitted the world into a music box, neat and turning. I didn't need food to feel full.

Lying there, I realised: whatever I had done, however bad I was, I still had this slippery magic. It didn't matter that my heart was being stretched to breaking, the past on one side, the future on the other.

I forgot it all when I was running. Each step, each breath, each empty day, I was turning myself into diamonds.

I thought about the feeling I got when Summer ate while I watched. Clean, as if I were praying. I thought about an engine that runs on light. The long white robes of holy men. Repentance.

Summer

I got busy packing my knapsack, all the while imagining karate-kicking through the shreds of mist that floated along the beach on our way to Saving the World. Not that we would need that much once they came to rescue us, surely?

Who exactly are 'they', you're thinking. And I have to admit that I was also hazy on the details, but Pops had said we could trust the people who came to rescue us—and only them. 'They will ask your mother's middle name.'

'June,' I whispered to myself as I walked out the back to the Emporium to finally take that inventory of our supplies. 'June, June, June.'

And can you even imagine my intense and heart-rupturing joy when I discovered, behind some folding chairs and a piece of sacking, a waist-high fort of sweetened condensed milk, which is like heaven in a can, and if you've never tried it, do it immediately and don't ever, both at the same time, it's that good.

'WINTER!' I yelled, and my voice was sort of husky because I hadn't used it much those past couple of days. I'd just been flying around in Colonel Mode through the half-light, and Winter had been—

Where had she been? And where was she now?

'WINTER,' I yelled again, annoyed, because I wanted to crack that sweet milk open—was jittery with it, that need—but of course I couldn't without her. Not that long before I had seen her put lentils in her mouth and chew them and spit them out and give them over to the bear to eat, and I know that sounds gross, but sometimes, let's face it, love is gross.

Perhaps it was the cold, and the half-dark, and the world changing so sort-of-unexpectedly, but from the moment the world stopped turning, their love seemed to glow, as if they had doused each other in brandy and set themselves alight like Christmas puddings, and that was how it seemed to me: that they were ringed in blue flames. And jammed up next to their fire, I was cold.

I came across him, that bear, sleeping on his back by the stained-glass window, his mouth open so far I could have slipped a boiled egg right in, his arms out to the sides and bent up at the elbows, like the limbs of a cactus. He looked so harmless, but then again, so had Pops, asleep in his chair on a Sunday night, with his glasses crooked across his forehead.

Edward's heart was a wide-open target, practically a bullseye.

I stood there for ages. Just looking.

It would be so easy. I could run and get The Knife from under my pillow—wouldn't even need to sharpen it. I could imagine I was slicing a butter knife through the foil skin across the top of a tin of Milo. Lean onto the blade to push it down and through. I could pretend that the blood was treacle, gravy. I would tell Winter that he'd come at me with his claws—right at my face. That it was self-defence. We could leave, Winter snuggled into the nook of my neck, needy in grief, in my arms.

My breath was coming fast. I could do it—I just knew.

But as I turned to go and get The Knife, he gave a snuffle and a little yawn, and when I looked back, he was rubbing his paws across his eyes and for some reason I thought about Wilbur from *Charlotte's Web*, that roly-poly pig, and dear old Fern, the girl who saves him from being chopped up into bacon; how he goes on to live a Full and Meaningful life, befriending all those rascally farm animals, loving that elegant spider.

I shrugged and sighed and turned and grabbed a lamp and wriggled into an altar-cloth poncho and felt very hobbit-chic as I went outside to look for Winter. I shivered as I walked across the meadow to the river bend and, boy, was it all a-flurry out there, like a frozen-yoghurt van had showed up with free samples—birds were circling, going mad with it, the not-quite-night, and the owls' hooting sounded even more hoarse than I did, so goodness knows how long they'd been at it, their croaks searching out the dawn. Above the water's surface, there was a magic carpet of insects, just hanging there and rippling in sync—you could have sliced through them and come away with a wedge the size of half a wedding cake, they were that thick, and all along the riverbanks were the squirrels that Pops had obviously known were there for the trapping, but seeing them all lined up, like those cute mice from *Brambly Hedge* ready for a summer wedding on a mouse-made barge, well, I would rather have stuck my hand in a trap than gone about killing them. So I guess you can imagine my horror when, as I watched them fondly, imagining them decked out in top hats and tails, they all seemed to launch themselves into the water at once, like kids doing soldier drops at the local pool, except here are two things I learned right about then: squirrels can't swim and they're capable of suicide pacts.

'WINTER!' I screamed, dropping the light. 'WINTER, *please*.'

And suddenly she was there, slipping out of the forest, easy as you like, alone, and though she wasn't even sweating, when I picked up the lantern I could tell that she had run far.

'Winter, what the hoop are you doing out running in this? We need to go to the bell tower, like, yesterday and set off the flare.'

'I can't,' said Winter.

'What do you mean? We need to—you know what I'm talking about. Plus it's getting colder by the second and that's bad news for our hair—it'll snap right off if we're not careful, and then what? You know we couldn't pull off pixie cuts. We've discussed this.'

Winter shook her head. 'I can't leave. Edward is sleeping.'

'Well, wake him up,' I said grumpily, 'though I'd like to point out that we haven't even discussed whether he'll actually be coming with us.'

'I mean he's asleep for the winter,' she said.

'That's ridiculous,' I said. 'It's going to be winter for, like, six months now. He can't just snooze around for half a year like some unemployed surfer whose grandma's left him an inheritance. Winter, do you hear what I'm saying? This is important. We have to get going. The things in the bell tower—don't pretend you don't know what I'm saying here.'

Winter looked at me, then—looked straight at me for what felt like the first time in such a long time, and I felt fright run through me like ice-water and sick bite at my throat, because the pillows of her cheeks were gone and her eyes had dipped down into her head and the line of her jaw was furry like a bear's and she was Thin (capital T). And she didn't look like Winter anymore because she didn't look like me anymore and I knew that she knew that—had known it way before I had.

I wonder if you know of the type of pain I'm talking about— types, I guess, because there were so many, but the one I'll start with is the pain of her spidery little arms, which, once I started, I couldn't stop looking at, imagining pinching the biceps between my thumb and forefinger, how snugly they'd fit in that measly napkin ring of a circle. And then her collarbones, or rather, the hollow between them, like a perfect well just right for catching tears, which seemed sadder, even, than the collarbones themselves, like the wooden curves of quaint old archery bows squeezed under her skin. I'm not talking Auschwitz-thin or Horn of Africa–thin, but that deliberate, shrunken thin that says triumph and sadness at the same time, and being somewhere untouchable. I thought of all the time I'd spent glowering at that bear as he grew and realised I'd missed the whole point, which was that her knees bulged like round fruit, and there was space between her thighs for a dragonfly to pass through in that weird, jerky hover they do, and I had let that happen.

I had to remind myself that Winter was there—she was under all that nothingness somewhere. But the more I looked, the more I could only see the cracks and dips of her skeleton pushing greedily through, and the fuzz all over her, like a rash or a secret coating to separate her even more from me.

'You're just scared,' I hissed, wishing I could spit on myself for not ripping The Knife through that bear when I had the chance. 'You're like one of those women who stay in their houses for thirty years eating canned baked beans in a tatty old dressing-gown, staring out the window while hair grows on their faces. You're a coward, Winter. You'll regret it forever if you stay. If you even last that long, because what's going to happen when you run out of food? That bear's going to need to eat something, that's all I'm saying, and by something I mean someone. Obviously.'

'You're talking about yourself,' she said calmly. '*You're* the one who's scared to go—you always have been. But I'm not leaving now. I'm not leaving without him, and that doesn't make me a coward. Besides, I don't know how you can still trust Pops's plan after…after everything. There's no way I could still believe in him.'

''Course I can,' I said hotly. 'Of course you do.'

But Winter just shook her head. 'You do what you like, but please leave me out of it.'

Well! You actually could not even compute my shock. It was like my skin had sloughed right off my body, right onto the floor in front of us. Winter had always agreed with me—always. But now…Not only was she flat-out challenging my Wisdom (capital W), there was something in her voice that I had never heard before, and my mind scrabbled around, trying to place it, and eventually it hit on what that something was, and it was steel.

And maybe that was why I didn't tell her about the condensed milk, even though I'd been busting to, even though she needed it, but who knows if she would have drunk it—if she was shrunken with love sick, or if she had turned away from food to cut herself off from the world, to climb to the top of a tiny castle and sit spinning gold, only letting things in and out just as she liked, even her breath.

Maybe that's why I stalked back to Bartleby, steaming under my poncho, numb and rubbery with pain and disbelief, and waited until she had gone to find that bear. Only then did I sneak off and grab a can and take it over to the piano and open the wooden lid with a bang and climb on in and shut the lid so everything was honeysuckle-sweetness and dark. As I slurped on the holes I'd punched in the milk tin, it was like I was sucking Winter into me, and it wasn't just the ghost wisp of her that had been skittering around with Edward all summer. It was all of her, full and pure and rosy, and it ran through me, and my brain lit up like fairy lights and I didn't empty-ache anymore. Even the sick feeling afterwards didn't stick as much as the golden happiness and the voice in my head that said, *Yes, yes, one more mouthful.* And it felt deeply good in a way that things often do if they're not deeply good for you, and everything slid away.

I don't need you with me to have you, I told Winter in my mind. *You are part of me always. It isn't a choice.*

Winter

Sure, I could have stayed, but the fact is that I didn't.

I left, and not because of the depths of my love; not because I wanted Winter to have her Freedom and Independence and to develop a sense of Self and Identity strong enough that, if she chose, she would have no trouble filling in last-minute as the lead singer in a Queen cover band and belting out the entirety of 'Bohemian Rhapsody', and in hindsight it's a shame that we didn't take our karaoke machine to Bartleby because the acoustics would have been amazing.

I left because I was angry and because Winter had chosen Not Me, and who wants to hang around, starving to death on regurgitated lentils, when you are clearly unwanted? I left because there was a box in the bell tower that contained three things and, to be honest, I thought at least one of them would bring me back to Winter soon enough anyway, on a chopper with a rope ladder that could dangle down for her to climb and definitely could not support a bear, and by then, she would surely have tired of the whole co-habiting thing and be busting to go get some mac and cheese with me and Girl Talk.

I can tell you're going mad for knowing what those three things in the bell tower were, and here's what they weren't: frankincense, gold and myrrh. By now you are saying, *Get to the point, Summer!*, which is what Pops would grumble whenever he was really listening to me, and admittedly that wasn't often, but when he did, I just fizzed up with wanting to tell him everything, and that's one of the reasons I left Winter behind: because, even after everything, I still loved him.

And if you're wondering why I'm stalling so much at this point, it's because it feels weird to spit it out and just TELL: we'd had it whipped into us so often that this was a Secret (capital S), and things depended on it that were so very much more important than our waify little lives, and how I wish 'whipped' was a metaphor. We had travelled round the world for those three things—had been shot at in planes by ground-to-air missiles that only just twirled over us like Catherine wheels; had been grabbed at a bazaar in Alexandria, where Winter was contemplating buying blue beads for our driver because she felt sad that his grandson had cholera, and we'd almost been thrown into a van, so I guess we were sort of kidnapped.

So. Deep breath! I'll just say it, shall I?

Here are the things that I expected to see hidden in the box at the top of the bell tower, 362 steps up, and don't think I didn't count every one.

The first was a flare, and when we let it off, we'd been told, it would fly up and burst into light, like an electric green bird, and a helicopter would swoop in and fetch us—just like that!—and if you're wondering why we hadn't just set it off, like, eleven-odd seasons before, why we'd put up with all the rag-and-bone hardships of living like identical monks, it's because Pops had made it very clear, on pain of death, that this flare was only to be used in three circumstances: if one of us were dying, if the world stopped turning (zing!) or if Somebody had come. We didn't know who would answer that green ball of flame, which felt a little scary and a little exciting, like the feeling you get when you're waiting for the guys at the pizza shop to answer the phone so you can order pizza anonymously to someone's house, but whoever it was who was coming to whisk us away, I just knew they were going to be Handsome, and we were to give them the other two things *immediately*, and one was a book and one was a vial, and I know, I know, that sounds pretty lame after all the build-up, but hear me out.

The book was a notebook, and the entire thing was filled with my father's chunky writing, not that you'd know it, because it was in a code that looked like it had been spewed out by a machine having some really bad feelings, like a midlife crisis in hieroglyphs. And though we'd seen him writing it by all kinds of candlelight, in sunlight—had heard him swear over it, watched him kick over the stone font at the front of the church with frustration when it wasn't going so well—we weren't allowed to know even a scrap of what it meant in case we were caught and dunked in mineral water till we gave up all the secrets in between those black leather covers.

I kid you not, whoever had that notebook could start the world turning again and basically save humanity. It had something to do with the pull of the moon, and magnetism, and restarting the Earth's rotation, though I'd always imagined that once it was translated or whatever, the code was the instructions for building a giant pair of those heart-starter paddles they use on medical dramas—you know, the ones that they rub together and yell 'Clear!', which in hindsight is totally silly. Whoever had that notebook, they had the future and the power and whatever size ransom they wanted to charge—enough to get their teeth studded with diamonds a zillion times over.

The vial was more interesting to me, because at night the liquid inside it was incandescent, like those glow-in-the-dark bracelets people used to wear at dance parties back when more than a hundred people were allowed to get together in the same place. Sometimes when the moon was full, we'd put on three pairs of gloves and go up to the bell tower, Pops and Winter and I, and slide the big block of stone from the wall, and lift out the tin box and click around the little row of numbers until it was the birth date of Harper Lee backwards, and open the box and pull out the notebook, and then fetch the key that was taped to the back of a copper pipe and open the lock of the black perspex box inside the bigger box that could apparently survive the fire of a thousand suns, and from a bed of what felt like dry ice, Pops would take that vial, so green and cold and luminous, and sit it on our gloved palms as if it were a dying glow-worm that could only be kept alive by still warmth and moonlight.

This here, this was why Pops had the laboratory—had flown in all those beakers and Bunsen burners and microscopes/telescopes and all the powdered dudes on the periodic table, and neglected to remember that, at some point soon-ish, we would be needing bras. This was our father's apology to the world: his gift of liquid hope. If he was dead now, this was what he had died for, and if he was still alive, he was living for this, not for us, and that was okay by me, but sometimes, to be frank, I think Winter found it hard to take.

So, now you've got the picture, you're probably as surprised as I was to find that when I pulled out the stone and unlocked the boxes and backwards-Harper-Lee'd and all that jazz, there was no flare, no notebook, no vial at the end. In the black perspex box, there was just a piece of paper that looked like the kind of treasure map an eight-year-old would spend all summer on—I wouldn't have been surprised if I'd sniffed it and found it had been stained with coffee— and it was scribbled with that familiar chunky black handwriting when it was done in a SUPER hurry, and when I held it up, really looked at it, I realised that it was a map of a path that led up to the top of Our Mountain, and I mean, what the hell?

Winter

'Well, are we going to blow this popsicle stand or not?' said Summer. 'You may or may not have noticed from inside your love bubble, but there's nothing left here for us now—not a single thing—and it's only going to get colder. You and I have to leave, and only us, Winter, and don't pretend you don't know why.'

Summer didn't know that there weren't any secrets left for us to guard. That Edward knew everything. That Edward *was* everything now. To me.

I swallowed. 'Edward says that there might be supplies left in the settlement. That there might be help there.'

Summer clicked her tongue. 'Not this again. Read my lips: There. Is. No. Settlement. The only thing on the other side of that mountain is the sea. You can believe some hot dude we've only just met, but I know Pops wouldn't have brought us here if—wouldn't have kept us here—if it was just a hop, skip and a jump to civilisation and, like, an actual future. He wasn't that cruel. Listen to yourself, Winter. It makes no gosh-darn sense. So are you coming or not?'

If I slipped away with Summer, she would never know that I had told. I would escape that shame. I could fold myself back into the cocoon of Summer's love. It was so warm there.

But when I thought about leaving Edward, it was more than handing back the moon.

A butterfly can't crawl back into a chrysalis. And so I said, 'Not.'

And Summer said nothing and her face said everything.

And not that much later, I could feel that she had left.

And for the first time in so long, I was alone.

I thought about cutting off my hair—cutting it short right to my skull; of course I did, because isn't that the ultimate symbol of Rebellion (capital R)? Instead I settled for a lob, which is a long bob, and I switched my part from left to right, and I have to say that I felt quite smart and grown-up when I looked in the mirror, which was actually a saucepan lid because our father didn't think to bring a real mirror, and as I put the finishing touches on my packing, I could just hear the soundtrack to this moment playing around me, it was that cinematic and Meaningful.

Though they were heavy, I packed almost all the cans of sweet milk because, really, we didn't have much else to live off at this stage, by which I mean we had Nothing (capital N) and, truth be told, I was going kind of crazy, could feel my stomach eating itself in a frenzy of unemployed gastric juices. Winter wouldn't have eaten it anyway.

And, though it was long and sort of bulky, I packed the string of fairy lights, because they felt now like a chain of memories, and when I got away, far from here, I wanted to hang them in my new bedroom and lie on my back on my comfy bed, and reflect with all the lights turned off except these little guys, hot with the glow of another time. I suddenly remembered one of those blankets made of silvery stuff that's like aluminium foil that you can wrap around yourself if you're stuck on a mountainside shivering to prevent yourself from getting shock, and I chucked that in too.

And then I went to the bookcase and, oh, that's when I almost sank to my haunches and put my head in my knees and gave up on the whole caper, because how could I bear to leave them, those dear compact worlds of paper and Truth? 'Thank you, thank you,' I whispered as I ran my fingers along the rows and rows of spines, hoping that each book would feel the love in my fingertips. When I had touched each one, and done it again to make sure, I had to choose, and I could only do that by closing my eyes and twirling my pointer finger around my head like a lasso and then flicking it down to see where it landed, and where did it land? Straight in the lap of Ponyboy Curtis.

Oh, Ponyboy. Oh, Ponyboy Curtis, that beautiful golden gangster-child orphan who looked up at the stars and ached for something better. If you've never read *The Outsiders*, I'm so gosh-darn jealous of you right now that I could punch you right in the cartilage of your nose, *seriously*, because it is seventy-seven types of profound and boysy-tragic-wonderful, and I guarantee you that when it ends, when you know his gang and their particular, desperate brand of pain and stupid-bravery, you will be deeply and forever Changed.

I could not really have had a better companion for this adventure than Ponyboy, who, in spite of his unconventional childhood, was so very street-smart and reliable and familiar with difficult circumstances and yet still had the soul of a poet, and I bet if he was with me in real life, he would have totally dug my new haircut.

That's what I was thinking when I marched out of Bartleby, out of the archway and over the moat and over the meadow and down to the sea, which is where the map was telling me to start—right there, on the beach, then around the shore for about a million years until I hit some path, apparently, though I'd believe it when I saw it. I wasn't thinking about Winter—not one bit. And I didn't look back, not up at the river bend or the bell tower or over at the edge of the forest. I just kept walking with Ponyboy in my heart and that big-swelling movie music in my head that said 'this is the start of her new adventure' or perhaps 'this is the end of the world as she knows it', and when I think about it from here, I realise that I hadn't watched enough movies or lived enough life to really know the difference anyway.

My positively triumphant mood lasted approximately forty-five seconds, which is how long it took me to remember that walking on soft sand is possibly one of the most spirit-shredding enterprises a person can undertake, and that all the cans, banging away at the base of my spine, added up to the weight of a tranquillised gorilla wearing an ice vest, and amplifying all that was the fact that the choppy, coming-and-going wind was whipping my new haircut against my eyeballs, and boy, did that *sting*, and it flapped the map around in my hand, wanting so badly to rip it, but as if I was going to let that happen after everything.

Lucky for me, there were some pretty big distractions, and one was the sea, which seemed as if it had been scooped up and dragged out so very far away, exposing miles of sand glowing pearly in the half-light. I suppose that had something to do with the tides or lack of tides, and if you think that sounds beautiful, you would have been right except that what was left behind was like a giant morgue slab for about a million birds lying stiff with their beaks half open, feathers being tickled by the wind, and out further, almost too far to see in the gloom, were the remnants of the ocean floor, as limp and sorry as an aquarium left in the sun in the car park behind a pet store until the water has evaporated, every last drop.

And all those things that used to be life made me even more determined to get to the top of that mountain, where I'd find that flare, which Pops must have buried somewhere sneaky, and bring back help, perhaps a superhero of some sort, who would fix this and pick up the ocean with a single finger and pop it back where it belonged, sprinkling all the dead animals with some sort of shimmery dust to awaken them and—zing!—turns out they'd been sleeping all along, dreaming of one day having opposable thumbs so they could play Xbox.

I would save the world. Because, really, wasn't I the only one on the Earth who could? I would save the world and Winter would come running back to me in full-on slow motion and fling herself into my arms.

Winter

Soon, I will have to admit that I have lied here.
 Not yet. But soon.

Summer

It was a blue whale and, yes, I am well aware that they had been extinct since Antarctica lost the last of its ice, but it's kind of hard to mistake the largest mammal that ever lived when the tide's gone out so far it's touching yesterday and the whale's washed up on the sandy desert of a shoreline, and its body is the length of a post-football-match traffic jam, I kid you not.

Ten minutes down the beach, Bartleby hidden by only one bend, and holy smoke! There he was. I went and sat next to his eye, that big old guy—plopped myself right down next to it and leaned back against his skin because I knew that even if I chugged all those cans of condensed milk like they were the world's most potent protein milkshake, I wouldn't be able to lift so much as a flipper to save him. His barnacles alone were the size of my head, and if you think it's sexist that I just automatically assumed that he was a boy, well, I didn't: he told me himself later on in what was a very enlightening and broad-ranging conversation.

'Jeepers, have we both ever got problems,' I said to him as I pulled the ring on a can of milk. 'You're clearly not going anywhere in a hurry, and, boy, am I mad at my sister.'

'I had a sister once,' he said thoughtfully. 'Got eaten by an orca. Everyone thinks they're so cute but they're vicious little sons of bitches.'

'You're telling me. Don't I know a thing or two about people who come across so meek and mild, and then—BOOM! They blow up your heart into tatters. You want any of this?'

'If you wouldn't mind sharing, kid.'

I cracked open another tin and poured the whole thing onto his tongue and spread it around a bit, because neither of us was quite sure where his taste receptors were, but in the end I think he got the general flavour profile and he seemed to enjoy it. I did some handsprings and cartwheels on the sand to keep warm—basic stuff really, but he was pretty impressed, and it was nice to have an audience after all this time.

'So your sister,' he said. 'She has legs, I presume. She can do all this too?'

'Even better,' I admitted. 'But maybe not anymore because her legs are like toothpicks now, they're so gosh-darn skinny. She's got into running—like, *really* into it.'

'Marathons?' asked the whale. 'The professional circuit?'

'Nah, just scooting around. She's trying to impress a bear. At least, I think that's what it's about. I don't know anymore. I feel like I don't know *her* anymore.' As soon as it came out of my mouth, I knew that was the truth I'd been carrying around in my guts all this while, like a dead star.

'Mmm. That's how I felt about the seabed,' he said, 'when I got my first pair of glasses. I put them on and suddenly nothing was like I'd known it to be. It wasn't good or bad, necessarily. Just different from what I'd expected. Made me a little melancholy. To have lost the sea that I knew.'

I chewed on that for a while. I wondered, had Winter put on the glasses when she fell in love, or had I? Which of us had changed? Or had we been different all along but just blind to it, and the bear was the glasses?

'Sir, was the bear the glasses?' I asked the whale eventually, because he seemed like a pretty smart guy, and I liked his vibe—a poet-philosopher crossed with a clinical psychologist who did TED Talks, something like that.

'The name's Mikie. And I'll need some more facts,' said the whale. 'Why don't you start at the beginning? I think I have time to hear it from there.'

And to tell you the truth, until his peepers shut once and for all, this guy had nothing *but* time, and I would have felt sorry for him if he wasn't so Magnificent (capital M) that he was beyond any pity, and so I sat back down and started from the beginning, with our names. Our mother dying. Winter curled up like a fist inside her. Diving prodigies. Et cetera.

'Some questions, kid,' said the whale when I reached the end, and honestly? It could have been a couple of hours later. Who knew? 'Firstly: did Winter choose the bear, or did the bear choose Winter?'

I frowned. 'Both,' I said. 'Neither. I don't know, actually.'

'And could you have pursued a relationship with the bear? Was there a window of opportunity for you to make these overtures yourself?'

I thought back on how we'd found Edward—how we'd been together in the meadow. How we'd been together every day. I thought about how it was us three and endless summer, and I wondered when it had changed. 'I guess. But you need to understand, it's Winter who does these stupid things—these giant, goofy gestures towards the world.'

The whale blinked a few times and boy, was his big eye gorgeous. 'Can you say for certain this was not romantic love?'

Aw, well, the thing is that I couldn't. I remembered that bear's arms around Winter at midnight under the stained-glass stains of the moon. I remembered how she rode on his back down the river each morning; how she sat up there like a maharajah on top of a wedding elephant, grinning. I remembered sitting up in the bell tower and seeing them down in the meadow, hearing bits of old Elvis songs floating up as she lay on his chest in the sunshine, her fingers through his fur.

'But he was a *bear*—did you miss that part? Don't you think that was kind of a dangerous situation to put yourself in?'

'All love has risks,' said Mikie. 'All love is opening up your

132

clamshell for someone else to poke about in.'

'Dumb,' I said.

'To the outside world. Yes,' said the whale. 'It is so easy for us to judge. But to be in it, to be aware of the risks and wade in anyway— that is life, dear Summer. Your glass-bottomed boat may crack. But to have sailed it and seen into the soul of another realm. Isn't the wonder worth it?'

I didn't like where this was going one bit, and frankly he seemed a bit in love with his own poetic stylings, and I was now regretting sharing any of my sweetened condensed milk with this guy. It's embarrassing to admit it now, but I started to get a real pout on.

'Come now,' said the whale. 'Don't be like that. You may not have been aware, but your love for Winter was a risk, too. A deep dive of courage. At any point you could have ended up here, on the sand, hurting. And yet here you are and you're still alive. With a longer future ahead of you than I have, filled with the chance to yet love and be loved. Over and over. That's a privilege.'

And, as I looked out to the shimmer in the distance that was the promise of a future sea, did I ever ponder that.

Winter

I couldn't find Edward anywhere.

I called and called.

He couldn't have chased after Summer. He didn't know yet she was gone. I was coming to tell him.

I opened the piano lid. Circled the moat. His blankets. Her food store.

As I checked her nook, so bare now, I saw it. My father's knife on her bed. It was unsheathed, naked, shiny. Sharp. It had been cleaned.

I wanted to think that she couldn't—would never. That she loved me too much.

But wasn't that the problem?

I sprinted to the bell tower—ran every step. I was fast. From up high, I would be able to see further. I would be able to spot a body. Perhaps the forest. Perhaps the sea.

As I ran, I said to myself, 'Peter Pan, Peter Pan, Peter Pan.' Three times.

'There's something I haven't told you,' I said to Mikie quietly. 'It's not…It's not something that's easy to talk about. But I guess it might give you a little more context for the whole situation with Winter and me.'

'Is it a sexually transmitted disease?' asked Mikie. 'Because everyone gets one sometime, kid. No shame.'

'Urgh, no!' I said, completely disgusted. 'Where would I even have got that? I'm not old enough for that stuff.' Truth be told, though, by then I probably was.

'Only takes one time without—'

'La la la la la la la,' I sang, my hands over my ears.

'Prude,' said Mikie, a smile in his voice.

'I was *trying* to tell you something serious,' I said crossly, 'but I don't even think I'll bother now.'

'Suit yourself,' said Mikie. 'Your loss. I've been told I'm an excellent listener.'

And dagnabbit, he was right, and that's why I told him anyway, even though it meant going back and correcting some untruths, like unravelling knitting.

'It's about our parents,' I said. 'Our dad.'

'Unsurprising,' said Mikie. 'Show me a girl who doesn't have daddy issues.'

'Really? Even under the sea?'

'Oh yeah,' said Mikie. 'Mermaids—they're just singing with 'em. Literally. Why do you think they're off luring ships? Sea captains are total father figures and mermaids are just gagging for someone to project their issues onto.'

'Interesting,' I said, thinking of Winter and the tall, manly bear, his muscly chest, his swagger that wasn't so different from a sailor's, and what I was about to say next, which seemed kind of heavy compared to the ground we'd just covered.

'Spit it out, kid,' Mikie said with a yawn. 'I'm all ears.'

'How *do* you guys hear? Is it that echolocation jazz?'

'You're just changing the subject now.'

And I was, because I hadn't told this to anyone—never said the words out loud. I had kept it shut away so I wouldn't hurt Winter, which is kind of ironic, given how much she'd just hurt me.

'There is a place,' I said slowly. 'There is a place—there was a place. In America, when it used to be America. I think there were lots of them, but I only heard about this particular one on a podcast once. We listened to a lot of podcasts.'

'I was more of a Netflix man myself,' said Mikie unnecessarily.

'It was a house where kids go when their parents have died, and they can play out all their grief, know what I mean? They can, like, hit things with rubber mallets and roll around on foam blocks, pretending they're being shot out of a volcano. They can scream really loud. No one cares. It's the whole point. I think it's called the Sharing House—something warm and fuzzy like that.'

'You went there?' Mikie asked, more gently now. 'Your mother...?'

'Nope,' I said. 'Anyway, there was a special support group there for children whose parents had...you know.' I waited, hoping I wouldn't have to say.

'Ah, but I don't,' said Mikie. 'Give me the specifics, kid.'

'Whose parents had killed themselves,' I whispered, and then I cleared my throat and gave a small cough and kept going, louder. 'And they went there to understand—understand what it is. Suicide. They went there till they could say, "My dad shot himself in the head with a gun because he didn't want to be alive anymore". That was the aim. They went there to learn that it didn't mean he was a bad person, their dad—or whoever it was. Their sister. Whoever. And that despite what anyone said, it wasn't their fault—I mean, the kid's fault.'

I didn't say anything for a while. Mikie didn't say anything either.

'One little girl,' I whispered eventually, 'kids at her school said her dad had gone to hell because he'd killed himself. But the people at this house—they told her that wasn't true. She knows that now. Because of the special house. She had such a sweet voice, that girl. And when we heard it, Winter cried so much—wanted to find her and hug her. "How could he leave her behind?" she kept asking. "Didn't he love her even a bit?" And I didn't know what to say,' I whispered. 'My throat just closed. I said nothing and I think about it so often, that moment when I could have made it better.' Eventually I asked, 'What should I have said, Mikie?'

And as Mikie thought and blinked, thought and blinked, I got that ache that you get when you can't fix the ache in people you love—when you can't scalpel the hurt out of them and bandage it up so it can heal.

'Sometimes,' said Mikie slowly, 'for some people, the end of the world is bigger than love. It's too much to live through, their suffering. And that's so hard for us to understand from the outside.'

'But I'm suffering, too,' I said angrily. 'No one remembers that.'

'Kid,' said Mikie slowly, 'I don't know what you're saying and you're scaring me a little. Is this about your mother dying?'

I shook my head.

'Or are you having those thoughts yourself? Because it's okay if you are—everyone gets them sometimes. Doesn't mean you have to do anything about them, though. You can just stay right here with me till they pass, like a bunch of clouds on their way to another sky. You can stay right here with me.'

I wanted so much to tell him, to be able to say it out loud:

how the rope turned on itself in the breeze, first one way, then the other, like some trinket hung up on a porch to catch the twist of the wind.

How the noose knot was neat, precise, scientific.

Our dog jumping up on his hind legs to paw at my father's shoes, barking like it was a game.

His glasses, which had slipped to the ground but hadn't cracked, so small and familiar in such a big and horrifying moment.

How the death thoughts had slipped into his mind and captured him, like ninjas.

How I wanted to take Winter to the Sharing House so she could throw herself against the foam, over and over, and not be hurt.

You're probably expecting that it was me, all nosy, who was the sleuth. But it was Winter who started to ask, and wonder, and then doubt till our father had explained it all. But not before he smashed Winter's face in.

And, sure, maybe it wasn't her whole face, maybe it was just her nose, but with all the blood that poured out of her, I'm talking the kind of gush that you get from a chocolate fondue fountain, I wasn't really expecting her to have much of a face left, and for a few weeks she didn't—she was just two eyes blinking out of a giant plum, and you can imagine how well I coped with that.

'Do they smile?' Winter had asked Pops one evening when we were in the place that could have been Turkey or Greece.

'Whales?' Pops asked, not even looking up from his notebook. We had been *Moby-Dick*-crazy for weeks, and though we'd moved on now, Pops was always a bit behind.

'No, axolotls,' said Winter. 'Do they smile when they're happy?'

'That's an ignorant question,' Pops said in a voice that I'm sure was much colder and brusquer than he meant it to be.

'But how would I know? I've never seen one,' Winter said, and

I could feel my father freeze and whatever he'd been reading, he wasn't anymore, just staring at the paper so intensely that I expected the page to burn up.

'There weren't ever any axolotls in the rivers we visited,' Winter said, and I could hear the realisation in her voice, as if a sun had just popped up in her brain. 'We never found any. Anywhere.'

And she was right: we hadn't actually seen any hauled in nets, or pickled in jars on the shelves of his study, all pink and transparent, like the raccoon foetuses we'd stared at for ages in the Natural History Museum. No diagrams, articles, books—nothing at all— and as we looked at each other, Winter and I, we were wondering why the hoop it had never occurred to us to ask about this before, though I have to admit that my dad wasn't exactly the most approachable guy. Seeing him glowering, his brow all scrunched, for some reason Voldemort popped into my mind. I sent Winter my most urgent twin telepathy: *No no no! Cease and desist! This isn't going to end well!*

But Winter and my dad, it was sort of a thing—a clash of minds or something—and looking back, I can see that her stubborn streak was basically just an extension of his, and though she'd never have dreamed of sticking pins into Edward, when it came to my father she really knew how to poke a bear.

'You were never actually studying axolotls, were you?' Winter asked slowly. She thought for a minute, her eyes bright with so many types of fire. 'It's not just a coincidence. None of it is a coincidence— the people following us. Our new names. Those people who took Mama. You're doing something else. Is it something bad?'

'No!' said my father, and I think this is the right place to use the word 'vehemently', but I'm not 100 per cent on that, so don't quote me.

'Then what is it?'

'This is none of your fucking business,' said Pops.

'Why won't you say?' asked Winter. 'Are you ashamed?'

And if he wasn't then, well, he sure was two seconds later—you could see on his face that he regretted jumping up from his seat and striking her, the full force of his fist on her nose, the sound it made when the cartilage broke, like the pop of a bottle top opening. I already knew it would leave a scar.

Winter

From up here, you could see the whole island. I'd avoided the bell tower so long that I'd almost forgotten. Now the view from each arch was a map of our love. To the south was a bend in a path where Edward had knelt to tie my shoelace; to the north, a curve in the sand dunes where he had swung me up to lie on his chest. Even the sky felt marked, as if we had carved our initials in it.

And there he was at the top of the stairs. Pete by his side. My smile was so big it shone out through my chest.

In his hands was my father's notebook. Black, just as I'd told him.

On the ground was the box and the other box. Pulled out from the wall. The open lock. Harper Lee's birthday backwards. The secret block of stone, just like I'd described.

'What are you doing?' I whispered.

He barely glanced up from the notebook. His eyes were hungry. 'Interesting stuff, this,' he said as he chomped the core and the seeds in one. 'It truly is.'

'But...But you can't read,' I said. 'We've been forgetting to practise. Besides, it's in code. Isn't it?'

I walked over and reached out my hand.

But he held the notebook to his chest. 'You've got to be kidding. The last eight months I've been waiting for this.'

'And then?' asked Mikie, as I paused to sip some more condensed milk, though truth be told I was stalling a little. The next part of the story wasn't pretty. Winter and I, we never spoke about it. If I'm being really honest, I never let her.

'Well, we went back to Tokyo, some stuff happened, yadda yadda yadda, and, long story short, we ended up on this island.'

Mikie raised an eyebrow at me and I sighed. 'Just go with it for now,' I pleaded. 'Not long after we got here…my father shot a guy.'

I explained how we were in the moat, Winter and I. This dude wandered out of the forest and BAM! Pops was suddenly there with a rifle. Shot him right in the head. And because Mikie didn't seem like a squeamish guy, I added, 'Blew it clean off his neck.' I swallowed and skimmed past the part where I'd grabbed Winter's hair, shoved her under the water so she didn't have to see. How she'd flailed against me but I'd held her down.

'And the kickback of the gun,' I continued, 'it did something to Pops's collarbone. Chipped a piece out of it, something like that.'

That night, after he and I had dragged the body into the forest, he slumped on the altar, sipping whiskey for the pain while Winter sat beside me on a pew in the first row, not reading the book in her lap, shivering.

'Who was that guy?' I asked him.

'Nobody,' Pops said. 'A nobody.'

'How do you know?' Winter asked, her voice a bit shaky. 'You didn't even ask him.'

'Nobody you need to know,' said Pops, slurring a little.

'But he didn't get the chance to say anything,' Winter insisted. 'You just—you—'

'SHUT UP!' roared Pops, so loudly that even I shrank back a little. 'SHUT. THE FUCK. UP.'

Winter cowered, as if he had hit her again. Our father saw her flinch. He groaned. He held his head in his hands and rocked.

And then, I kid you not, he actually started sobbing. It felt as if we'd been standing on a trapdoor that had opened up; we were *Alice in Wonderland* falling down into another realm. We looked at each other, Winter and I, not quite sure how scared we should be. But ultimately, I can't ever give up the chance to be a hero, so I grabbed the bottom of my shirt and I ripped—ripped as hard as I possibly could. I tore off a strip and I swallowed and I stood up and held it out to Pops to use as a hanky, and I said, 'You know what? I reckon you owe us an explanation. What are we doing here, Pops? Start at the gosh-darn start.'

He looked at me and then slowly he nodded. And through his tears, he explained it all. About the internet in the coffee cups—his dream for it, his vision. How he was a hero and all that jazz. But then came the parts we weren't so across. Because even though we were smart (have I mentioned the International Maths Olympiad?) and we'd been trained for some very specific scenarios, we were kind of oblivious in that way kids are. More into redecorating our room with a tiki beach vibe than the whole geopolitical situation that swirled around us.

Pops told us how things went swiftly downhill after Operation Freedom was launched. Once there was internet everywhere all the time, people quickly became Obsessed (capital O) on a whole new level. Local councils started padding poles, trees, parking meters, because people could not tear their eyes away from those little backlit rectangles. But all the fractures, the facial bruising, that was actually the least of anyone's worries.

Hate groups popped up like mushrooms after autumnal rains. They came from many places—the deep folds of the internet, the cold insides of mountain caves, the slums that didn't get put on a map, crowded camps, hot with desperation, air-conditioned basements. After a couple of years in isolation, they quickly formed chains across the globe, those groups. Some of them fused together in clumps. They started to do things—horrible things. They started to figure out how to make people watch those things against their will. Then hate groups formed against those hate groups, which were equally hateful in different ways.

'But surely someone tried to stop them?' Mikie asked. 'I'm hazy on the specifics of human conflict, but it's my understanding that there's usually someone fighting back.'

I nodded. 'The Resistance. I'm getting to that. But first, do you guys know about climate change?' I asked. 'Global warming? All that stuff? Because that's why it really got hairy.'

'*Mate*,' said Mikie with emphasis. 'If there's anyone who knows about environmental catastrophe, it's me.'

I felt stupid, then, because of course he did. Duh! That's what killed the blue whales in the first place. Well, except this hunk. And I felt guilty, because you could probably draw a pretty straight line between our dad putting wi-fi in the water and Mikie losing 100 per cent of his family, his pals. At least, it seemed like a pretty straight line to me, but once the internet truly got up and running again, nothing was ever that simple. Facts and truth and lies became all sticky and tangled. 'Like a real *web*,' I told Mikie. 'You get it? Like the world wide web?'

Mikie just looked at me steadily. I got the message and sped the whole story up.

Winter

I threw myself onto the ground, then. Onto the box. My heartbeat slammed against it as I ducked my head, steeling myself against what came next.

The way Pops explained it was that, with the internet up and running again, people were bombarded with new info, all the things they'd missed in the last year, so that it felt like everything in the world was escalating quickly. Whole oceans turned to acid. Pockets of malaria blooming where it shouldn't have been. Then a huge seam of coal was found off the coast of Alaska, which started that bizarre stand-off—one country disease-bombing another and trading the vaccination for coal. New Zealand completely evacuated, nobody left to fight the flames.

'And then…' I told Mikie. 'Cyclone Cooper.'

'Mmm,' Mikie said sadly. 'Dear old New York City. RIP.'

People were going mad with helplessness by then. Sort of frenzied and half out of their minds with anger about how the planet was already cooked or why it absolutely, definitely wasn't, depending on who you believed. There was blame spraying out in every direction, and at the same time, cooking videos became ridiculously popular, as did re-runs of a TV show from Norway that was basically twelve hours straight of a crackling fire.

But in among all that was a call that was growing louder and louder for the biggest companies to be held accountable for what they were doing to the planet—or not doing, to be more precise. 'And that,' said Pops, 'included Big Tech.' Because by then, they were the biggest.

'Not the governments?' asked Winter, who had a touching belief in the enduring power of democratic institutions on account of a Grade Four project about the preferential voting system that she had presented as a rap.

'We-ell…' said Pops. 'You girls might be too young to have

registered it properly, but it turned out that a ring of supposedly trustworthy governments was behind that whole business with deepfakes, and after that?' He shrugged.

Turns out those governments had paid that dude in the baseball cap, Pops's old boss, to get a hurry on with deepfake technology. Deepfakes were those creepy videos that mashed people's faces and voices to make it look like they were saying all kinds of wacky stuff that they never actually said. They'd been around for a while, and at the start, you could teach a computer to recognise that they weren't real. But once some serious cash was invested in the whole thing, you honestly couldn't tell the difference. Everything looked fake, and nothing did. You could make it look like a scientist was saying that climate change had been reversed. You could have a president giving a warning that a nuclear warhead had been fired and we all had forty-four seconds to live, and you *literally* could not tell if it was actually happening.

'And that's what was behind the whole video with the Queen and the ham sandwich?' asked Mikie, and truly? I was impressed he knew about that.

'You get YouTube down there?' I asked.

'Saw it through a cruise-ship window,' said Mikie.

How could anyone really trust anyone after that? And then…that thing with the driverless cars, the yoghurt shops. All those children around the world. Oh, it was so awful. That's when the Resistance officially formed. And TBH, it really wasn't that hard to get people signing up for a life lived completely offline.

That was also the day my father quit his job. But he didn't give it up to pursue his lifelong dreams of communing with the souls of axolotls, like he told us.

My father was breeding a special kind of bacteria. It took years. Eventually he bred something that could eat the seabed cables that were wrapped around the planet, spreading that hot, fast internet and fuelling the whole shebang. It was supposed to be the toppest of secrets.

'But they found out,' Pops told us that day in the church. 'A couple of years in.'

'Who found out?' asked Winter.

'That dude in the baseball cap?' I asked. 'And all his groupie tech bros?'

Pops nodded. 'I suppose I always knew they would. They followed me—all the way to Belarus. They wanted to buy it so they could destroy it. But of course I wouldn't sell it. They started to make threats.' He paused, picked at the label on the whiskey bottle. Then he looked up, and I could tell from the pain on his face as he gazed at Winter that those threats had something to do with her.

Through the Resistance, Pops found people to share his vision, to help him spread that bacteria. When the moment came, they released it simultaneously on the edges of oceans around the world. It spread faster than fire. Ate the cables in hours. It shut down the internet. Just as he'd planned.

But there were other things he didn't plan. That he suspected but claimed he didn't have time to test for.

'There *wasn't* any time,' he said desperately, wiping the back of his hand against his nose. 'And I'm trying to fix it. I've found the cure.'

'What do you mean?' Winter whispered. 'A cure for what?'

Oh, my hat, you can't even imagine the scene that unfolded when Winter found out about The Greying—that it was Pops and whatever he had put in the water that had caused it, that awful dripping away of life and slipping away of beautiful minds, greying of skin and certain death. She trembled with a sorrow so deep, it went right to the layer of the Earth that was molten. Tears dribbled down her face. She didn't even bother to flick them away. Eventually she whispered to herself, 'Minami.' And she was right.

Minami had died in one of those death hangars. We had seen her being led away on a street corner in Akihabara, her eyes glossy and vacant, a strange half-smile on her perfect lips, her walk still the glide we used to mimic. Through the cut-out window in the back of her shirt, we had seen the dark web of bruises, intricate and beautiful, like the inky brushstrokes of Japanese calligraphy. Boy, had we cried that night in bed for all the things we'd never said to Minami. Somehow it was worse that we'd loved her so much from afar.

'She wouldn't have suffered,' I said helplessly. 'They just sort of... fall asleep. Isn't that right, Pops?'

'Well...' he said cagily. 'There's some initial pain. Intense pain. Bruising. A fevered state. Confusion. But yes, once they pass to unconsciousness, they—'

'Is that why we came here?' Winter interrupted. 'You ran away because you made people sick?'

Pops winced. Then he nodded. 'Partly. And there will be government agencies after me because of all the laws I broke—the security risk of the things that I've done. There are others, too, who want what I know.' He sighed. 'But that's for another time.'

Winter glared at him. 'Tell us now.'

And so he explained about using The Greying as a weapon of sorts—how it was being tested in remote areas by groups who were up to No Good. How everyone would be after a cure. How they'd be hunting him down to find it.

'Is that everything?' I'd demanded, my tiny mind blown with the hugeness of it.

'But it wasn't,' I told Mikie, stroking him absentmindedly as I looked out at the mess my father had made of the ocean floor.

Pops explained to me and Winter the effects of his work on the water, the seas, the Earth's tilt, the shift of its axis, the turning of the world. I tuned out a little, I've got to admit, but Winter seemed to follow. Truly, she was always the cleverer one. 'If my modelling is correct,' he said sadly, 'the Earth will stop turning sometime soon. And the consequences…I'm still figuring them out. But needless to say, it won't be good.'

'Will that be the end of the world?' Winter asked.

'Oh, the end of the world is already here,' Pops said gloomily. 'Has been for a while. It's just not that evenly distributed yet.'

'So is there any hope?' I asked.

'Depends what you mean by hope,' he said.

'Don't you listen to that,' I had whispered to Winter as he threw back his neck to drain the glass bottle.

Winter

'Well, you'll just have to choose,' Edward said calmly as Pete scrabbled in his arms, trying to lick his face.

I held the black box close to my heart and stood up.

I thought about my mother.

Pete's head on her lap the first time she wore reading glasses and felt sad about getting old. Her brown eyes that looked green when she cried.

'Who are you?' I whispered. 'Where are you from?'

He swallowed. Pete squirmed. Edward tightened his grip.

'Give me the box,' said Edward, 'and I'll give you the dog.'

I said to Mikie, 'I bet right now that you're thinking that Pops was a monster, and good riddance to bad rubbish, and that we'd have been better off without him. The world, too.'

'Heavens, no,' said Mikie. 'I get it: people are complicated. Besides, he can't have been a complete waste of space. He gave the world a kid like you.'

I glowed pink with pride then, as if someone had turned on a torch inside me. This dude really understood. Like I'd told Winter a zillion times, people aren't just their best bits and worst bits—not just a length of a prison sentence, the weight of a medal on a ribbon. 'Haven't you read enough by now to know that human nature is all about the nuance?' I asked her once when we were blindfolded on a plane, tucked somehow into an overhead locker, and I have to admit, I felt pretty sophisticated right about then.

As I leaned back against Mikie, exhausted by the sweep of my own saga, I remembered that flight in the overhead locker. How Pops had sung Elvis the whole way so we wouldn't be scared—till his throat sounded raspy and sore. How he'd done 'Moon River' in a fake opera voice while someone shot at the plane, how he'd used the voice that always made Winter giggle. The shake in his legs as he carried us out, one on each shoulder down the spindly stairs of that plane into the heat of another long night far from home.

'He wasn't all bad,' I whispered to Mikie, and maybe to Pops, wherever he was now.

Winter

I thought about my father.

The chance to hand over the contents of this box and get my mother back safe.

How he'd brought us here and built this church. How that's when we knew he'd gone mad with grief, his bleeding hands on the rough stone. How he left us before he quite finished the roof.

I swallowed. I said, 'No.'

I didn't watch Pete drop from the bell tower.

I closed my eyes and imagined his yelps were singing. Imagined him flying, up, up, towards the stars, like Laika, the first dog who ever went to space. Perhaps they would meet out there.

Ten minutes later, Edward snapped my wrist and he got the box anyway.

I was glad Summer wasn't there to see it.

Mikie seemed kind of tired, and I wondered if I'd worn him out because, let's be frank, my narrative style is somewhat barrage-like if you're not used to fast-talkers, and I wasn't sure how much hip-hop or spoken-word poetry this guy would have been exposed to, which would at least have provided him with some context.

And then it hit me that perhaps—perhaps it wasn't me that had worn him out. Perhaps he was dying.

I jumped up. 'Oh, gosh—shouldn't I be wetting you with water like they do on the news? Spraying you with a hose or something—buckets, at least? I'm so sorry. I just sat here jabbering and let you get all dry. If I were Winter, I would have thought of that. When we used to go out for Chinese food she would spend the whole time spinning that round little table thing—what do you call them?'

'The lazy Susan?'

'Yeah, she'd be spinning that lazy Susan from person to person, making sure everyone had their soy sauce and their sweet chilli and their jasmine tea. We'd get to the end and she'd hardly have touched her meal, and she wouldn't even let us get a doggy bag for it because she didn't want to make any extra work for the waiter.' I shook my head. 'She's too much.'

'Sounds like a honey. I think I would like her,' said the whale.

'Everyone does,' I replied, somewhat annoyed that I couldn't even have a whale to myself without sharing, but I guess that wasn't old Mikie's fault.

'You don't need to hose me down, kid. We both know it's too late for that. But…If you wouldn't mind…'

'Yes, Mikie?'

'If it isn't too much trouble, will you stay with me?' said the whale. 'Until the end? Won't be too much longer.'

I swallowed. 'It would be an honour,' I said. I sat back down and pulled my backpack over and rustled through it, seeing if there was anything else he might be interested in. I came across *The Outsiders*, tucked down the side, and blow me down if that isn't a book to get into you before you kick the bucket, even if you're an oversized marine creature.

'Do you know anything about gangs—teen gangs?' I asked. 'That's what this book's about. Not the druggy ones. I mean, like, the bratty ones who run around town and think they're so tough.'

'What do you think dolphins are?' said Mikie.

'Show-offs,' I agreed.

So I read it, all the way through, because even though I was Tired (capital T), there wasn't a night and a day to put me to sleep, just the winds coming and going, whipping my hair into my mouth, which didn't even seem that annoying, given the context, and the gentle half-sunset, which felt thoroughly appropriate for a twilight-of-life situation. As I started each new chapter, I would put my head to Mikie's jowl to feel his pulse, the beat of his heart ('Larger than a Mini Cooper,' he'd told me proudly. 'And you, kid, you could actually swim in my arteries, they're that big.') and though it wasn't exactly racing to start with, by the time we got to the whole 'stay gold' moment, it was only beating once a minute, max.

'Mikie?' I whispered.

'Mmm?' he said sleepily.

'Just checking,' I said.

I sat there, feeling how strong he was against my back, wishing that I could have known him out in the ocean, the sun splashing over his belly as he arched up to the sky.

'Mikie?' I whispered again.

'Hmm?' He opened his eye.

'Do you think this haircut suits me?'

'Real elegant, kid. Like one of those old movie stars.'

'You know about movie stars?' I asked, impressed.

'Sure,' he said. 'Can't get enough of that Ryan Gosling.'

'Mikie? If you…If you were Winter, would you have run away from me too?'

For a while he didn't say anything, and I guess it was a leading question, but I wanted to know the truth, and my instinct was that this dude could tell it to me straight and easy, like an arrow made of peace; that he'd run out of time for the lies and half-truths and types of sweet nothings that you pull out of fortune cookies.

'I do not know Winter on a personal level,' he said slowly. 'But I know this. Winter wasn't running away from you. She was running towards herself. And when she finds what it is she is looking for, she will run back.'

Boy, did I ever cry then, really cry, and I still don't know why exactly, but I don't think Mikie minded, because my tears were salty and I cupped them all in my palms, and when I'd finished, I climbed up, really carefully, just with my shins, and rubbed them on the bit that I think was his forehead, and he seemed to like that.

'Mikie?' I said one last time as I lay with my back on his big old back. 'I don't know how to love anyone who isn't Winter. It's so natural for her. But it's harder for me.'

'Summer,' said Mikie. 'You are doing it now.'

Winter

I held them close to my heart, the pieces of hand and arm joined just by skin now.

I was sick with the pain. I said to Edward, 'But you cried. When I told you about my mother. You cried real tears.'

He said, 'Too easy—that was one I practised a million times in role-play. I did theatre...you know, before. Plus our training was pretty thorough. Had to learn five languages. You oughta put that arm in a sling.'

'Edward?' But as I said it, I realised it wasn't his name and was sick again—over the side this time. There he was, Pete, so far and still below.

'I'm only saying this to be helpful, okay, but if you get desperate,' said not-Edward, 'you might want to think about eating him.'

I thought back to what my mother had said to me the last time we spoke. 'Edward?' I said again. 'Did you never love me, not even a little bit? Was it all made up? On the boat—that, too?'

He didn't answer. He turned away.

And so he was gone, just like that. Mad, am I right, that people—souls—really do fizzle out of existence in a hot second, like candle flames. I was glad that dear old Mikie got saved the indignity of being blown up with explosives, which is what they used to do with whale carcases when they didn't want them stinking up the beaches. But, boy, did I miss that guy, like I had a whale-sized hole in my heart. And, yes, I know it sounds corny, but here's the truth: love hurts, and it's just like they say in all those pop songs.

I set off again, my feet sinking into the cool of the sand under the weight of my pack, like a turtle with a shell made of marble. As I plodded, I peered through the half-dark at that crumpled map, the chunky writing. And suddenly I wondered why I was even bothering, because weren't we all going to die some day anyway? And wouldn't it be better to drift off, thirsty but content, like dear old Mikie, than to march headlong into who even knows what?

Winter

I watched Edward leave from up in the bell tower. He took the opposite beach path to Summer's, started up the mountain. I was so thirsty.

I stood up and the pain of my arm flashed all around me in bursts of stars. I thought about Ponyboy from *The Outsiders*, who looked up at the stars a lot. How Summer loved Ponyboy.

Down each stair with a clunk and lightning through my wrist and Ponyboy Curtis.

'Swoon,' Summer would say. 'Ponyboy, what a hunk. Bags kissing him first when we get to heaven, and don't even think about pushing in because you know you don't actually like guys with ponytails in real life.'

'Ponyboy doesn't have a ponytail in my heaven,' I had said. 'I don't think he had one in the book, either.'

'Since when is heaven yours? We'll be in the same one, anyway, though I might not see you all that much at first if Ponyboy has anything to do with it, and especially not if he's gadding about in a toga.'

'Ponyboy is not a Roman,' I said. 'He wouldn't have a toga.'

'Hey—nobody's forcing him to wear it,' said Summer, 'least of all me.'

When I got to the bottom of the steps, I went to Edward's bed. There was shock in my veins. Even after everything, I needed his smell. I hadn't learned yet to hate it. Like a dog, I guess.

On the pillow I'd stitched for him, he had left a note.

The boat was real.

And next to it, small and glowing, cased in glass, an apology.

Here is the lie that I warned you about.

I ate that dog. Forced it down my throat. The meat was stringy.
It caught in my teeth, like coconut shreds.
But it wasn't Summer who made me.
I did it myself. I did it to myself.

Summer

As I finally reached the end of the beach, I felt something swoop inside me—a joy bird, Winter would have said. The wind was only a wisp round here, and as I tucked my lob behind my ears, I realised I didn't have heavy boots anymore. Boy oh boy, is that a good feeling, like getting down off the stage after you've done your compulsory audition for the school musical that you never wanted to be in anyway, and not having to sit there waiting your turn with a sore stomach, knowing that your singing really isn't good.

Even in the dim light, I could see that the sand was softer here, like sifted icing sugar, and up ahead, there was a small rise covered in tiny pink flowers shaped like little trumpets. They were resting in a clover so bright that, even in the dim light, it glowed green and, just where the map said it would be, a path led up over the rocks to the headland. Then there seemed to be a big flat field to cross, and beyond that, I guessed, was the base of the mountain. From there, well, it was up, up, up.

I shucked my pack and lay back on that lush carpet of grass. I thought about the hotel in India that used to be an old fortress, where we'd stayed once at the end of a summer that went on forever; how we'd gone up to the roof to lie on our backs, just like this, and watch the moon rise. Except there wasn't a moon now, by the looks of things, and I guess it was there somewhere, just below the horizon, forever waiting to appear.

On the roof of that hotel in India, we felt so close to the sky. The rubies and diamonds of traffic spun below, and the clatter and the horns and the bleats and the smell of spiced sweat and fried-egg rolls cooked on petrol drums—it all floated up. Warmth wrapped round our bare legs, so brown after a hot week in the hotel pool learning to do somersaults underwater. We were ten, had just turned ten, and for our birthday we got a camera with film (Winter's request) and a giant '10' cake with tiny purple flowers on white icing (my request), and we'd had leftovers of that cake for dinner up there on the roof. Our hands in each other's hands were sticky with icing, my right in her left.

'If a plane flew into this building,' I said, 'right this exact second, and our bodies floated all the way down to the ground like the Falling Man, I would die happy. That was *really* good cake.'

We knew all about the Falling Man, that poor, beautiful guy from the Twin Towers who'd jumped out the window rather than be burned alive, and tumbled down through the air, turning over and over, like an autumn leaf. By the pool that week we'd read *Extremely Loud and Incredibly Close*, so we were all obsessed with 9/11, and there are pictures of the Falling Man in the back of the book but they've been reversed so that he floats up, up, up as you flick through to the end. And even though Pops read the blurb and sniffed and said, 'American schmaltz', we both agreed that we had been Forever Changed by the main character, Oskar Schell, that complicated little inventor whose dad was trying to phone him from the top of a tower as it burned around him. And though it was sad, sad, sad, that book, is there anything better than feeling Forever Changed?

'Remember how Oskar wanted to make that device that flashed above an ambulance when the person inside was dying? GOODBYE! I LOVE YOU! GOODBYE! I LOVE YOU! Of all his inventions, I think that's the one I liked the most. That, or the—Ow!'

I yanked my hand away because Winter's nails were digging into my palm, and below us a truck beeped and a man yelled and when I looked across, Winter was crying.

'What's wrong?' I asked. 'I thought you loved that ambulance sign.'

'I don't want to die,' she sobbed. 'I don't want any of us to die.'

'Everyone dies some day,' I said unhelpfully. 'Besides,' I added, remembering something my mother had said in an interview about the people who'd died in the Twin Towers that Winter and I had listened to seventy-seven times. 'The ending isn't the story. Remember?'

'I don't want to die,' Winter said again through strings of snot, 'but I don't want to live like this anymore, either.'

'Winter, we're in a gosh-darn five-star hotel,' I said, but of course I knew what she meant.

Remember we were only ten, and it's easy when you're ten to imagine that there's another way—that surely someone can fix it, whatever 'it' is. When you're ten, you think that everyone should have a home and their own bed, their own bedroom, even, with posters on the wall, and some sort of pet, and an after-school snack, and a school, as if all those things are possible for everyone everywhere.

'I want to go out on the street. I want one of those egg rolls we saw from the car. And I want my old name back,' said Winter. 'I miss being—'

'HUSH,' I said urgently.

Winter

Time passed, and still the questions dripped off me, froze in the air, hit the ground.

I bent down and splashed them onto my face, the hard chips of alphabet. They ticked against each other like flint.

Did Edward ever love me? Even a bit?

Was it duty? Was it easy?

Had he planned it, his touch? His fingers through my hair? Had he practised that part? Who was in my soul if it wasn't him?

Did he ache like I did now? Would I always? Would he ever?

'I could find him,' I said to Summer. 'I could ask him. Maybe he's taking that notebook to do something good. They said that—remember? That guy from Big Tech with the baseball cap. He said he was sorry. After the driverless cars…He said he would fix it. He truly cried.'

'That guy was just a really good actor. And besides, even if you did find Edward—if you could,' said Summer, 'how would you know he was telling the truth?'

'I would know,' I said. 'I'd be able to tell.'

'Like you knew he was an undercover agent?' asked Summer. 'You will never know, Winter. You just won't. That's the risk you run. And FYI, if you want my two cents, he's one hundred per cent spy, and a good one, too. I didn't even pick it myself, and that's saying something.'

But when I looked hard, it wasn't Summer after all. It was me reflected in a window. It was me.

I sat on a pew. Everything was a gap.

My whole self ached for Edward as I tried to pull apart the lies from the truths. I tried to find the end of the roll of the sticky tape that was our love. Or whatever it was.

I curled myself around my knees and closed my eyes. All I wanted was my mother.

Her warm calm. Her cool wise.

'Hey there, chicken,' she would say.

I would tell her about Pete.

The glass-bottomed boat.

Giving up our secrets.

I would ask her.

Just in case she was listening, I said it out loud.

'Mama?' I asked. 'Why do people do all the things that they do?'

I listened for the answer. But the voice wasn't hers.

It was a man's voice, and loud.

It said, 'Speak no more.'

I turned and there he was.

'Do you know Edward?' I whispered. 'Can you take me to him?'

He raised his arm. He spoke into his wrist. 'Peter Pan. Peter Pan. Peter Pan.' From his belt he pulled—

Summer

The rocks were red and big and smooth and really pretty easy to climb, given that it was gloomy and dusky, and I got so totally into picking a path up and around them that I was singing to myself by the time I clambered to the top—a really stirring version of 'Shake It Off' because, boy, did Pops have a thing for Taylor Swift when he was younger, before people cottoned on to the fact that she was one of those humans bred in petri dishes for world domination. When I scrambled over the ridge of the headland, I found myself on a cliff, looking out over the sea. And as I turned to look at the field I'd have to cross, every thought was scraped clean from my mind, like scraps from a plate.

Have you ever burned a pizza—I mean, *really* burned it—like, left it in the oven till it was black and no part was even the tiniest bit eatable? That was what I was looking at—a huge expanse of scorched topping, stretching out to the base of the mountain, chalky and dark.

Here and there were the white stumps of trees on the blackened ground, their roots exposed, like pale hands cut off at the wrists. And the ground—it was crunchy with the ends of things. Stone? Bone? I couldn't tell in the half-light, but it felt like stepping on popcorn. That carpet of death went on for miles, thicker in some places, hotter in others. Above me the sky was all orange clouds, the ones that bloom like cauliflower, backlit in violet—a sky I swear we'd seen in a gallery, Winter and I, in a red-walled room in Paris. Through the middle of that big old plain cut a wide stream, a gash of silver. I ran all the way over to it and plunged my head in. Was that water ever frosty. As I squeezed out my hair, I thought of how this side of the island was eerie like an old convict prison, or an empty house after a removalist has been, or a dry fish bowl: somehow heavy with the absence of everything that's been before. No wonder Walter hadn't let us come here all those moons ago. Or was this something more recent?

I kept trudging, crunching across that weird ground cover and thinking of so many things, none of them good. I thought about the fire in the Amazon to smoke out all the refugees who were hiding there—how it burned for four years before the whole forest disappeared. I thought of the camps in Mexico after the US built the wall across their border. I thought of the mass graves for corpses from The Greying that were dug in a day; the legs sticking out, bent into Ls and Ds and Vs, so geometric.

'What happened here?' I wanted to ask Winter, or Walter, or Pops. 'Was this a fire or, like, something more sinister? And why is it only this part of the island? How's our side so healthy?' But nobody answered. There was nothing here, not even the kinder parts of my mind.

I felt as if I had been walking forever when I turned around to clock how far I'd come. But, hoo boy, the trail of footprints was short as a skipping rope and the sea still seemed ridiculously close.

I needed to rest, but I didn't want to sit down on that black dust; somehow it seemed so dirty, like the smog from the nuclear power plants before they were all blown up. I took off my pack and dug around for that foil emergency blanket, and I spread it out and pretended I was having a Famous Five–style picnic—that the sweetened condensed milk was a treacle tart, that the water I scooped from the stream as it trickled by was actually ginger pop or lemonade, and on reflection, it probably wasn't realistic for those five to have had so much time for adventures, given all the trips to the dentist they must have had to make to get their sugar cavities fixed.

I sat with my back to the mountain, because I wasn't quite ready to face just how huge it really was up close—topped with snow, like a dozy brontosaurus dusted in icing sugar. How I was going to make it up there without a scrap of polar fleece—without shoes or protein bars or a fancy breathing machine—was anyone's guess. I sighed and instead I looked back out, down over the cliff, at the sand and beyond that the sea, that big opalescent field glowing faintly in the distance, and I wondered about George from the Famous Five—whether she was just a run-of-the-mill tomboy, or if she was really a boy trapped inside a girl's body, desperate to crack out, miserable with the unfairness of it all. *Good old books,* I thought with true thanks in my heart. *You're still with me. Without you I'm never really a—*

And then there she was.

So far in the distance that anyone else would have thought she was a rogue buoy, the head of a curious sea lion. But I knew. Of course I did.

It was Winter. And she was running—running into the water, as if she were hunting down the horizon. It was up to her waist and she was still running. She was running and she was alone—completely alone—and my heart grew wings.

She had left that bear behind and come looking because of our Love (capital L). Winter was trying to find me. I smiled. I was sure of it.

I like to think that the plane was heading this way anyway—that it wasn't attracted by the shine of my silver emergency blanket, crinkling in the half-dark like a fallen star. But suddenly it was there, swooping over the mountain and down towards me, sharp like a flying syringe. I felt it in my teeth, the thrum of it, as I threw myself onto the ground facedown. The sweetened milk sloshed in my stomach. It circled and circled, that plane, first nearer then further away in turns, like a mosquito whine on a hot, still night. I could feel the heat of its lights through my eyelids, but they didn't pass near enough to cut over my body, and I guess that was one thing to be grateful for. All I could think of was Winter, down there in the sea. Had they seen her? Did they want her? Could anyone want her as much as I did?

Eventually I couldn't stand it, and I raised my head, keeping my eyes squinted up as much as I could, like Pops had taught us, so they wouldn't reflect the glare. And, holy smoke, you wouldn't believe what I saw.

The plane was spraying something—a sky-blue mist that hung thick in curtains. When the light hit a patch, it glowed rainbows, as if it were made of unicorn's tears. It would really be a hit at a school disco, whatever it was.

Then the lights dipped and circled and headed out over the sea, and I stood up so fast, I hit my head on yesterday. I sprinted back down through that crunchy potting mix of death, and I reckon I could even have kept up with that bear, my fists were pumping so hard.

I had to run right through a cloud of that blue stuff, and you want to know something weird? It felt warm and cold at the same time, like when you put your fingers through the trails of a sparkler. At first I tried to hold my breath in case it was Nazi death gas, like we'd read about in Anne Frank's diary. But when it swirled around my face, it didn't feel harsh or stingy or toxic; it was balmy and gentle, like a drying-up puddle after a sun shower.

PHEW, all caps, because when I got back to the edge of the cliff and the big red rocks, the plane was a fleck on the horizon, and Winter was still out in the waves—a version of her so tiny, I could have threaded her through the eye of a needle. But then, so quickly, she wasn't. Her head surfaced a couple of times, but soon I could only make out an arm, a hand, a ripple. And then nothing. I practically popped out my eyeballs looking, but she was gone.

Because Winter couldn't float.

Of course she couldn't, because you need body fat to float, and it's something to do with buoyancy and I bet Mikie would know, that gentle, gracious blubber king, but he wasn't here to ask.

Winter was just skin and bone now. She couldn't float, and out there, far from my reach, she was drowning.

Winter

Speak no more, speak no more.
    As I ran, it matched my footfalls.
    As I ran, I thought, *Of course.*
    Out to sea, I ran on water.
    Speak no more.
    I thought, *Of course.*

BOOM! You actually cannot imagine how fast I threw myself back down that wall of rocks, how I shot into the sea, half-stroking and half-running in the way that you do when the water is waist-deep and flashing around you. Boy oh boy, you cannot fathom how many dead sea creatures I crunched to get out there, and how bad I felt about that, as if I were having a dance party on top of a mass grave.

By the time the seabed dropped away and I had to swim, I had lost sight of her. Frantic doesn't even begin to describe all that flailing around, dashing in one direction and then the other, diving under, grasping with my hands, my desperate fingers. The memory of diving head-first into the dress-up trunk, the lid slamming shut above me, the certainty that I would die. Each second that passed rang heavy like a gong, meant something worse and then worse, until it was too much to hold in my head.

'MIKIE,' I screamed when I came up for breath. 'HELP ME!'

But there was no Mikie, no Pops. It was us alone, and as I dived under again, that just didn't seem fair.

It dawned on me while I treaded water and paused for breath that this was my fault. If I had stayed at Bartleby like Winter wanted, she wouldn't be stretched out, drowned, on the ocean floor. She would be lying in the moat, floating on her back, her head nestled into the nook of that bear's armpit, the water shimmery like silk, her hair fanned out. I came to a realisation then, and you might think that I was getting carried away in the drama of the moment, but I promise you it's true: I would have lived happily alongside them forever, orbiting their love like a stringless kite, if it meant that Winter was safe for always.

I sank back down, blowing out every last wisp of air so that I would drop further, and I waved my hands around and around, and pretty soon I was dizzy with the effort of it all, and I wanted to just fall down like you do when you're a kid spinning in circles with your face to the sky.

Right about then was when my big toe hit the jelly of her eyeball, my heel struck the bridge of her nose and I felt it give a little. I took a gasp so huge that I gulped in a whole lot of sea water, and I had to shoot back to the surface to get the air to go back down, which was incredibly tedious, as you can imagine. 'Idiot!' I said to myself, but secretly I was kind of in awe of my mad search and rescue skillz, because, really, what were the chances I'd actually find her? Usually it was Winter who had the patience to look carefully for things while I was doing Couch Gymnastics.

I duck-dived, and now that I knew where she was, old Winter wasn't that hard to spot. I kicked down and snatched her by the hair, which sounds kind of brutal, but do you know that a head of human hair bunched together has the strength to lift two elephants? I yanked with everything I had, but it was harder than I'd reckoned— she was so heavy that I wondered if she'd come across a buried stash of Nutella while we'd been apart, and I think I grew doubly strong with my anger at that injustice. I gave up on the hair and grabbed her under the armpits and kicked, kicked, kicked till I was certain I'd dislocate my ankles with the effort of it.

All the while I was thinking back to when we did our lifesaving certificate training one weekend at a pocket-sized public pool in Tokyo, which had so much chlorine in it I swear it permanently burned the hair off our nostrils. I was trying to remember the breathing, mouth on mouth, how many times to pump the chest, but the only thing that came back was how funny it had felt to jump in with all our clothes on—jeans and a hoodie and our shoes, too— and try to swim two laps, which was part of the requirement for getting the certificate. At least I'm not wearing sneakers right now,

I thought, as we burst through the surface of the water. And you want to hear the weirdest thing? As I gasped for air, a big, wet, suck of a gasp, Winter gasped too, as if she'd been holding her breath the whole time, and while I was relieved not to have to remember the finer points of resuscitation, a small part of me was peeved that I didn't get to bring her back to life, like, literally.

I had my arms around Winter like you're supposed to, floating her on her back while I egg-beater-kicked us towards the shore, and I could feel her lungs working, her rib cage pushing in and out like bellows, and though we were both breathing pretty hard, honestly, Winter seemed fine. I was so gosh-darn relieved that it took all my self-control not to duck my head down to kiss her smack on the lips, which I know that she hates, but sometimes I had to—my feelings for her were just too big to keep in my own mouth all the time. By the time my foot hit the sand and I could stand up, she was standing up too, and we sort of flopped ourselves to the shallows and then stood folded over for ages, our hands to our knees, panting.

It could have just been a post-exercise rush of endorphins, but I felt a booming wave of love wash over me. 'You're safe,' I said with wonder in my heart, and I looked over at Winter to smile.

But, oh my hat, oh my hat, she most definitely hadn't been mainlining Nutella. And what part of it was me forgetting while we'd been apart and what part of it was new, and worse, and ambulance-ready, I don't know. Winter was so thin, I thought I might throw up. She was so thin, I wanted to shake her till she rattled. I wondered what it is in us that cracks open when we see them, these tiny people—why it is that we feel that sick sadness, that strange darkness; what strings they are twanging deep in our hearts.

All I wanted was to hold her down and force sweet milk into her mouth like a mother bird.

But I didn't. Can I tell you, was that ever *hard*. I said to myself, for the first time ever I said, 'Step back, Summer. If this is what she chooses, let her be, like they say in that song, which was a top-of-the-pops hit for a reason, so just follow that advice. Let it be.'

'Hey there, chicken,' I said, all deliberately light-hearted and not-care-y, squeezing the water out of my hair. 'What's with the ocean, am I right? So weird. We need to get up that mountain and light that flare for the chopper ASAP because this whole caper is starting to get a bit too *intense*. FYI, I think that smell is dead octopus, and you know how I feel about those guys—they're smarter than dogs. Scientists have done tests. Talk about a tragedy. Hey—what happened to your arm?'

But she didn't answer.

Winter didn't talk. Couldn't, wouldn't, didn't—it's all the same, isn't it?

She looked at me for a bit and then turned and waded back to the shore, picking her way over the crusty old sea life with her toes pointed, chest high, as if she were striding across a balance beam, one arm folded into herself like a wing. I followed behind, still breathing hard with what I swear to you was lung-ache, feeling a little dark at her lack of appreciation for my heroic deed.

By the time I made it back to shore, she had settled herself on the sand and was rifling one-handed through some kind of bag, which I later realised was the ratty old pillowcase that she'd love-embroidered with You-Know-Who's initials. She pulled a notebook and a pencil out of that pillowcase, wiped off the cover and opened it, and I thought it was going to be a situation where she wrote instead of speaking, flashing me notes with smiley faces at the end of them. But it wasn't that at all.

She just wrote to herself, her good hand flying across the waterproof page, as if she were dictating the voice of God, she was that intense about it. Every time I tried to look over, she hunched her scrawny prawn of a body over the page, and, boy, did that ever make me burn right up. She knew it and she kept writing anyway.

And then I realised, in that way you do when your hands are busy: of course, you fool, she is writing about *him*. It was in her eyes—the way they wouldn't quite settle on me. Something about her face reminded me of a cow we'd once seen stuck in fencing wire, just standing, still working cud around its mouth. A word popped into my mind, and the word was mourning.

I'll bet it was love poetry, whispery, fairy-floss love poetry, with a beautiful metre, an exotic rhyme scheme, because if anyone had the soul of a poet, it was Winter. And if it wasn't that, it was a letter telling him to meet her on the top of the Empire State Building at midnight, though of course it's not around anymore, but how would a bear know that, anyway?

And all that joy, and all that light, and all that love, and all that hope—everything I had felt when I fished her out of the sea, it was gone. She didn't even have a thank you to spare. I was back here again in this tight, spiky world.

Winter

He followed me out to sea. I dropped to the bottom. He found me there. Kicked with his heel, caught the jelly of my eye.

As he dragged me up to the surface, I wished that he had let me be.

When I opened my eyes, I saw my own face looking down. For a beautiful moment, I thought I had died. Or had I rescued myself?

'What's with the ocean, am I right?' said Summer. 'So weird. We need to get up that mountain and light that flare ASAP because, boy, this whole caper is starting to get a little too intense. FYI, I think that smell is dead octopus, and you know how I feel about those guys—they're smarter than dogs. Scientists have done tests. Talk about a tragedy. Hey—what happened to your arm?'

I couldn't tell her. My wrist was broken. The flare was already gone.

Guilt sat on my chest. I could smell its rot.

I would see it break, her glowing heart, with all its wasted love for me.

'This stuff is the weirdest,' I said to Winter as we trotted back across that squeaky dirt to the spot where I'd had my picnic. She didn't seem shocked at all by this big old charcoal prairie, which was strange, but then again I had always been the effusive one. 'But you should have seen what shot out of that plane—like octopus ink, if the octopus had done it with a giant fairy. Don't make that face— you're the one with a boyfriend. Where is he now, anyway?'

She didn't say anything, just sped up and left me behind, that dirty pillowcase bumping against her tiny back. 'Why do I even bother?' I muttered.

But once we hit the road it was better, because when you're bushwalking or mountain-climbing or any of those wholesome activities that they did in the Famous Five—watching for smugglers through binoculars, that sort of thing—you just have to be in the moment, you know what I'm saying? Everything else is just a faraway radio.

Soon enough I was trying to be zen again, trying to keep up, whistling our old school song. 'Do you think Pops knew about this—what it's like on this side of the mountain?' I asked Winter when she stopped to hold her swollen blue wrist in the freezing stream, gritting her teeth through the ice pain. 'Wait—what am I saying? He made this map, so of course he did. But when would he have even had the chance? I thought he was always up there in his lab, doing his thing. Makes you wonder, doesn't it, what else he was up to—like, was he watching those weird sexy robot cartoons? Remember the ones they had in Japan?

'Well, I guess it doesn't matter that much now. We've just got to make it to the top of this big old hill and set off that flare and

BOOM! Back to civilisation. And I don't care who I have to kiss, I'm getting a packet of cheese-flavoured corn chips from someone, and don't start with all your chat about artificial flavouring. And FYI, I'm still obsessed with that gingerbread milkshake we decided not to get last time we were in Sydney—boy, was that ever a mistake, and not one I'm going to make twice, let me tell you. That's what I'm going to ask for in the helicopter when it comes to scoop us up. And if they can't make one in the helicopter, well, are they *ever* going to get a piece of my mind.'

Winter started to weep right then, and while it could have been to do with the mention of artificial corn-chip colouring, I think it was actually about that bear—about leaving him behind for good when we eventually got rescued. I wondered what he was doing back there now. Sleeping, maybe, that heavy sleep that we used to sleep after diving training—the one where we had to do side-planks, pretending we were ironing boards.

Winter sat right down and pulled out that notebook and started scribbling furiously again, her face leaking straight onto the page.

'Cheer up,' I said in a rare moment of compassion. 'All love has risks. All love is opening up your clamshell for someone else to poke about in.'

But that just made her cry harder. *There truly is no reaching some people*, I thought as I gave up and stood up and dusted the weird soot from my legs and set off again, and eventually she followed, loping along, still sniffling.

And I guess I should tell you that I sort of screwed up here, because I actually knew the only thing that could really cheer Winter up—that could draw words out of her in spite of herself, like splinters, could maybe help her forget whatever was going on with that swollen arm. With each hour that passed, I wondered if I should bring it up—knew that I probably should. 'Hey, chicken,' I could have said, all breezy. 'You know what I've been thinking about?'

It was the story of how our parents had met. Boy, Winter used to shine when she heard it, all girly and hopeful and dreamy. Like we began with an explosion of glitter, she and I. I knew it all, every heartbeat—had heard it told so many times. 'Forty-three minutes and twenty-six seconds'—that was all I would have to say to whisk us away from this blackened crust, at least for a little while. That's how long it took them to fall in love.

But I didn't. Or maybe I couldn't.

So instead, I just got all Robert Frost–crazy, reciting every single one of his poems that I could remember even a crumb of, and though Winter often worried that there were other poets who weren't Male and White and had subsequently escaped our attention, I think she found old Frost comforting in spite of her trickle of tears, which was pretty constant. I hoped she was going to remark on my A-plus oratory skills in her journal. I'd always loved that bit in *Anne of Green Gables* where Anne gets dressed up in her string of pearls and recites 'The Highwayman' at the White Sands Hotel, and perhaps, when all this was over, I could do that at an open mic night—the pearls, the whole bit—if people were still doing things without a measurable outcome by then, things like art and kindness. They'd been on their way out by the time we'd boarded that seaplane, both scrunched into the passenger seat, Pops swearing, stabbing desperately at the controls.

Hours of walking, walking, walking. After trusty old 'The Road Not Taken', I did that one I think is called 'Birches' where he talks about a farm boy not being able to play baseball because he lived too far from town, which had always caused Winter's eyes to pool up, but this time drew sobs from her little wire frame of a body.

'Cheer up,' I said. 'I bet he practised kissing on his sheep out there on the farm, and he got so good he could tongue better than any guy in town. I bet he had, like, a zillion girlfriends, all mad for his smooching, and he married a film actress who could wear a scarf around her hair without looking silly and had champagne for breakfast, and he got around in those aviator shades that I like.' The more I talked, the less I had to think about the ache in my legs/ back/heart, and the glue in my throat and the sting my blisters made when they passed through the air.

When I ran out of all the Frost I knew, I just whistled 'Moon River', which had been Pops's favourite song that wasn't Elvis, and I was secretly hoping that Winter would start singing—she was such a pretty singer. Everyone had always said so. A song seemed like such a little thing for her to give to me.

But she didn't. Or maybe she couldn't. So much had gone down since we'd heard it last.

'Who even are we now?' I said to Winter's silence. Lucky for me I wasn't expecting an answer. I wondered if even her voice was thinner.

I went back to 'Moon River', and when I got to the part where the violins kick in and the lyrics talk about two drifters setting off to see the world, blow me down if I didn't get all teary myself. Because that's all anyone wants, isn't it? To be one of a pair, going out into a shiny new world. That had been Pops, once, him and our mother, before we were born, so young and beardy and full of hope; I had seen a picture. And hadn't that been me and Winter, criss-crossing all those countries in the back of that tiny plane, everything so small and simple from up there that we felt like we could pick it up in our fingers? None of it had turned out how you hope the world will be when you hear that song, all warm arms around you in the moonlight. And as I looked at my sister's sweet face, at the past as it rolled around us like a young cloud, I thought, *What have we done to deserve this?*

When we stopped for a rest, Winter sat with her head on her tucked-up knees, and I could see that she was shaking, could hear the click of her teeth like an insect's hum.

When Winter was running, she seemed immortal, dazzling, all fairy child and blazing light. But now that she had stopped, the power was draining out of her so quickly I could almost see it leak, and I was starting to Worry (capital W) that she might not make it, because could pain—the gnaw of it—actually kill you? And when had she eaten last? How long had we been climbing? Did I know how long a person could even live without food—was it a week? But there weren't any weeks now that there weren't any days, on account of the missing sun, and even though I was so very sweaty, I could sense a new chill, perhaps the ancient cool of the mountain now that we were higher up or maybe the cold of the planet in stillness.

Winter

'Are you there?' I asked the stars. I couldn't see them—hardly any. The world was so dark.

'We are here,' they assured me. 'We are here and we are waiting. We will always be here. We always have been.'

'I've done something bad,' I confessed to the stars. 'Really bad. And I can't tell Summer, but I can't not tell her.'

'Then you must tell,' said the stars. 'Always tell. You're just delaying the inevitable if you keep it all inside, Winter.'

'But she loves me so much,' I said.

'And that's why you can tell—tell her anything.'

'But she thinks I am perfect,' I said.

'Then it's about time she let you be human, no? So you stuffed up—who cares? Everyone does it sometime. This is just your time. Telling always helps.'

'Not always,' I said. 'Remember?'

And they didn't say yes and they didn't say no, but I knew that they did.

Have this notebook, the white masks told me. *Write about where you think it might all have started. Write your truth. Write it down.*

When we finally reached the base of the mountain, I had to hit the hay immediately and have a nap so deep it hit the Earth's core. And when I woke up, I felt a whole lot better and I was relieved to see that Winter was where I'd left her, quietly scribbling away in that notebook—that she hadn't run back to the forest, or whatever. 'Come on,' I said to her as I stood with a yawn. 'Let's get cracking.'

But on closer look, it wasn't going to be so easy, because once there had clearly been a path up from the base of the mountain, just like on Pops's map. At some point, though, perhaps some yetis had had a brouhaha, because there'd been a big rockfall and now there was just a huge pile of stones, grey and black and sharp, like a steep ramp. The path started up again on a ledge above that— about the height of a three-storey house—but to get there, we'd have to do a whole lot of clambering, because either side of the rockfall was just a sheer wall of granite. Those stones didn't look too stable, quite frankly, but there was no other option: the mountain stretched so high above us, it was like looking up at the Chrysler Building, which we had done a lot back when just anyone could go to New York, and we'd arrived there for the International Maths Olympiad, all quaking and full of wonder and drilling each other on Fibonacci sequences.

I tell you what, it's lucky that we had such strong ankles from all that tiptoe work on the diving boards, because you really had to watch your feet in the half-dark or you could tumble right over, tear up your ligaments, crack your patella, and then where would we be? I had to feel out each rock hold with my hands, and then move my feet all stealthily, transferring my weight at just the right point so it didn't cause a landslide. It was actually kind of satisfying, like stacking up Jenga blocks.

'You should probably overtake me and go up first,' I called down to Winter over my shoulder once I was a few metres up. 'I don't want you getting squashed by an avalanche if my foot slips. These rocks look *mean*.'

But she was still just standing at the bottom, holding her pillowcase, a big question mark on her face.

'Put that in my backpack if you like—I'll wait here and you can pass it over when you catch up.'

She didn't move. My foot slipped a little from underneath me, and the rubble caught one of my blisters, right in its watery centre. 'OW!' I yelled as I turned back to the wall and scrabbled to get a hold again. 'Winter, hurry the *fuck* up. This whole thing has a time limit, you know.'

Behind me I could hear the slightest scrape of stones, which meant that at least she was making a start. And as I paused to wait for her, my feet stinging, it struck me that this whole mountaineering thing was going to be harder than I thought, and absolutely nothing like the time we'd practically jogged up the steps to the top of Montmartre. Up there, it was all rooftops and chimney pots and blocks of cream light, and you couldn't find a single ugly thing to snag your eye on—it was totally, dreamily, heartbreakingly perfect. Boy, did we ever love Paris. Didn't everyone before it got bombed flat out of existence?

There was nothing there now—just scorch marks in perfect, elegant rings. I had seen pictures from a drone. I'm not sure entirely how Pops came to have them, those shots.

'Hey,' I said as I tried to shimmy back towards Winter, 'do you remember when we climbed up the—'

I turned to see Winter, still at the bottom, vomiting nothing over and over again, like a cat trying to get out a furball.

'What's wrong?' I asked. 'Food poisoning?'—which I thought was pretty funny because she hadn't eaten for about a zillion years.

Winter didn't look up, not even to acknowledge my dark comedic genius. She just ghost-barfed again with a terrifying combination of effort and agony. You've probably guessed this—and, yes, I probably should have thought about it—but it was her wrist; she couldn't raise it up to shoulder-height without being sick with the pain, and her face was completely white, and the shaking was bad now, like she was holding a jackhammer, and I want to say 'convulsing' but I'm not entirely sure that's right in a medical sense. How Winter was going to get up that mountain was a Mystery (capital M), almost as big as what happened to King Charles and Camilla when their plane disappeared.

I threw off my pack—could come back for it later—and half-climbed, half-fell down to where she was doubled over. It sounds gross, I know, but if there's one thing I loved doing, it was holding back Winter's hair in these situations. 'It's okay, chicken,' I said as I bent over beside her, trailing my fingers along the back of her ribs, trying not to shudder at the hollows they found there. 'Hop on my big old back and I'll give you a ride till you're feeling better.'

She nodded, the tiniest nod, and for some reason my throat closed over with trying not to cry. All I had wanted for so long was to hold her. As I knelt down so she could lay herself across my back, I wasn't sure if she was actually on there or if she'd just slung her pillowcase over my shoulder, she was that tiny, and I felt Sad Sad Sad. She could only hang on to me with one hand, and even that didn't have much strength, so I had to reach back and grab hold of her legs.

Oh.

Truly, they were just bones, and even touching them felt wrong, like she was made of chalk dust and would crumble. But if I wasn't holding on, she'd just slip straight off. How was I going to balance—to climb? As I paused to think it over, I smelled the waft of Winter rotting.

Should I have been force-feeding her all this time, holding her down and pressing her jaws shut like you do when you give a dog a worming tablet? Should I have gone on a hunger strike of my own—refused to eat till she did too? Should I have made her eat to prove her love? Withdrawn my love until she ate? And maybe I should just have asked straight out: why?

But the trouble was, there were so many things we didn't like to talk about, so many knots that were too tricky to untie, and so I had chosen the coward's way, trying to convince myself at every step that Silence = Love.

I tried to steady myself, my hands around her legs, her good arm tucked under my chin, which I'd clamped down over her wrist. I lifted one foot to set off. But my centre of gravity was all off, and the rocks slid under my feet, and the orange-purple of the clouds loomed above us, and that leaden sky was so oppressive that sweat was running down into my eye sockets. There was no way I was going to risk toppling backwards onto Winter. It would be like squashing a duckling in a sandwich press.

'This isn't going to work,' I said down into my chest. 'I need a second to figure this out. If I lift my chin, can you slide back off?'

She didn't answer, of course, but I felt her little muscles tense, ready for the landing. And even though I tried so hard to do it all gently, when her toes hit the ground, the jolt of it—the pain—made her sick again. Through the gloom I could see tears on her lashes and I felt that particular anger that is part despair. I thought back to that bear—how he had ripped the door clean off the drone plane and tossed it to the ground. He could have carried her now so easily, and knowing that made me want to rip things off the sides of the world and throw them around. Everything was always squeezing shut around us.

I gloomed and stormed for a while, wondering where all the heroes were who popped up in novels when you needed them most.

'Why isn't life ever as good as it is in books?' I asked Winter, who was sitting writing in her notebook again. 'Are we doing it wrong?'

It wasn't until I was lying with my legs up the wall, which in yoga is called Viparita Karani (the Fountain of Youth pose), that I figured it out, the climbing thing. I knew that pose from when we did Gifted and Talented Yoga. It took about three hot seconds for the G&T kids to memorise seventy-seven Indian pose names and, boy, was Zephyr, the teacher, impressed. And while we're discussing extracurricular activities, it was lucky that we'd done all those Flexible Thinking workshops at our school in Japan, because that's how I came up with what Pops would have called an Elegant Solution to that big pile of rocks, and, yep, I'll admit, I was smug.

'You just kick back, One-armed Susan,' I said to Winter as she sat writing in her Book of Love. 'I've got this.' I pulled everything out of my backpack except *The Outsiders* and the one crucial item I'd need, left them in a neat pile, and put it back on my back. I set off again, feeling the lightness that comes with big ol' fashioned hope.

But soon every single stone found a corner of my blisters to poke in to, like I was stepping up onto little blades. Every three seconds I had to pause—I was panting like that bear used to pant when he had spent too long by the stained-glass windows in the heat of the afternoon.

But I made it.

And the moment I hoiked myself up onto that path, I actually gave myself a cheer. 'You can see everything from up here!' I told Winter as I shucked off my pack. 'I reckon when we get up a bit higher, we'll be able to see old Bartleby.' And she looked up, like she was actually interested.

I got to work then, finding a good anchor point, and it wasn't far along the path before I found what I was looking for: a boulder, immoveably heavy, plump like a panda's stomach when he's been hitting the bamboo hard. I took the string of fairy lights out of my pack and tied one end around that big, friendly rock, using the knots that Walter had showed us, proud that I still remembered. I paused for a second, thinking about that guy. It seemed so beautifully impossible that he had ever been with us; we had been alone so long.

When the knots were done, I pulled on that rope—I mean *really* pulled, to see if it would hold us, and I guess if there was one upside to my sister being light as an actual feather, I had just found it. It seemed pretty sturdy, and so I tied the other end round my waist and stood with my back to the edge of the path, which felt scary, but not in that familiar way that our lives usually were. I leaned back out over the shelf of rocks and I let some rope go. And I jumped— BOING!—over the edge and down, shrieking a little as I swung back in and had to push my feet off the stones to swing and drop again. Over and over I abseiled down that slope, till the rope ran out, which was only half a metre before the bottom and not a hard drop at all. You probably think that the whole thing sounds risky, but it's okay—we did Gifted and Talented Abseiling when we lived in Tokyo, too. Our instructor was called Eric and he wore a purple bumbag—even inside—and was he ever a nerd for safety. The climbing wall where we went each Sunday was forty floors up a skyscraper, so we were used to heights. Pops could hardly bear to sit in the cafe there and wait for us, because he really wasn't, so eventually he let us go alone, across town, and boy, were those fast trains packed with a trillion girls in white knee socks who I was dying to be friends with. It had its own karaoke booth, that climbing gym, and weren't they the most golden afternoons, the two of us harmonising through the soundtrack to every Disney movie ever in between drinking peach bubble tea, which you could order just by pushing a button on a screen.

'Didn't that remind you of Tokyo?' I asked Winter when I reached the bottom, and she looked up in surprise, because I didn't talk much about Tokyo usually. 'The abseiling, I mean. Hop back on. We've got this nice old handrail now.'

With the light rope to pull us up on, hand over hand, I didn't need to fret so much about my poor feet or toppling backwards. Once Winter was on my back, I put my pack on over the top of her, sort of wedging her in, like one of those carriers that strap babies to dads' chests in the park. She felt more secure there, like a bony koala, and once I got up some momentum, boy, were we swinging along. As we got a little higher, the air felt cooler, and though the mountain was so tall it was an actual joke, the idea of reaching the summit didn't feel quite as ridiculous as before.

I really had to grunt to heave us up to that boulder and get us over the lip of the rubble, onto the path proper. I thought my knee would pop right out of its skin with all the weight that was on it, like a pea splitting out of a pod. But we made it, and I stood there at the top, wheezing, feeling Winter flicker against my back with the pulse of my breath. I swear I saw stars with all of that effort—that they were actually saying to me, 'Nice job!' And when eventually my vision cleared, the path ahead was curving round the mountain to my right, smooth and dark and wide and even as the road of icing on a race-car cake. It was beautiful to me in that way that breaks your heart—you know the one. A choir in a church, the glow of a candle lighting a face, the soundless swirl of falling leaves.

The endorphins from all that climbing were flooding my brain so fast that I was actually laughing. 'Imagine if endorphins were actually mini dolphins!' I said with delight, and promptly started crying. Boy, brain chemistry is weird.

When I'd composed myself, breathed deep, I said, 'I should probably fetch the fairy lights. Do you think you could walk?'

I felt her shake her head. Hot joy ripped through me like fire. 'It's okay, kid,' I said. 'Rest in me.'

Winter

Where I Think It Might All Have Started:

Egypt—Alexandria.

My father was already here. Another flight through the dark. We brought nothing from Tokyo except Pete and books, which came with us everywhere. We thought that our mother was working on something super secret. We were excited to be allowed to come along.

My parents were often at the apartment. It felt strange at first, to have them home, and then cosy. So we didn't bring up why we weren't back in school when weeks stretched to months. They only left to take turns going somewhere we weren't allowed to follow. My father's lab, we assumed. A recording studio where my mother charmed guests.

After a few weeks, our father hired a driver, Ammon, who was allowed to take us out on our own. We would bring back treasures from the city. The big citadel on the edge of the sea.

We found a favourite spot for hibiscus ice cream.

I liked the way Arabic felt on my tongue.

'We could spell Mediterranean practically the minute we were born,' Summer told Ammon as he pulled up at an outdoor market on the way back to the apartment, where Pete was always panting on the white, shiny floor. 'Mississippi, too.'

Ammon had a son. And his son had a son. He had cholera, that boy. 'No good, no good,' Ammon had said, shaking his head. 'Okay, I stop here. You buy something nice your mother? Pretty things.'

'We're on it,' said Summer, bursting out of the car. Even the time taken to swing out the door was wasted for her.

'Thanks, Ammon,' I said. 'We'll only be a little while.'

'A turquoise scarf,' Summer said above the clatter: the donkeys and the bartering, pots clacking, wheels of all sorts through the dust. 'One of those pashmina things—you know what I mean? That's what she'd like. And don't go getting all emo about the people with nobody buying stuff at the stalls. This is capitalism at work, and it's fine.'

'I want to buy something for Ammon,' I said.

'Pops is paying him, like, a squillion dollars to drive us round,' said Summer. 'He's not doing this out of the goodness of his heart, Winter. He doesn't need some touristy piece of—'

'Because of his grandson,' I said.

I found a necklace of blue beads at a store at the end of the row. They clinked in my hands, like teeth. The day was so hot. They were like cool chips of ice in my hands.

'How much?' I asked the lady in English, then in Arabic.

She smiled and reached out to stroke my cheek. Her hand was so hard and so soft.

'WINIFRED.' It was a man's voice, loud and urgent.

We had been trained. We had practised this exact scenario a thousand times.

And perhaps I was distracted by that lady's hand.

And perhaps I was happy just to hear my name—my real name—after all those years. Because I did exactly what we'd been told not to. Just this one time.

I looked up. I turned my head.

Above the din of the market, Summer shrieked, 'RUN!'

But I froze. I hadn't learned, back then, what it was to run.

Someone grabbed my ankle. My stomach hit the ground first. The necklace broke, beads skittering out like my thoughts.

My wrists behind my back, the door of a van.

And then Summer's toes against a man's shins, down at the height of my eyes. The crack of a kneecap. How she grabbed my hair, right at the skull. How I thought it would break. How I thought we would die.

Summer half-carrying me, half-dragging, under stall tables, a body-roll over a storm drain grate, back to Ammon. How bad I felt for the dust we left on his car seats as he drove us in wild loops to an airstrip on a sand dune.

It wasn't hard for them to trace us after that through a chain of money and hidden eyes.

They took our mother from the apartment.

By the time my father returned from wherever he'd been, she was gone.

We weren't allowed to read the note.

Sometimes at night I'd imagine fingers around her neck, pushed in so far that purple bloomed on her skin, an opening iris across her throat.

On one side, above us, was the smooth, dove-grey rock of the mountain, and on the other side, the drop beneath us was ankle-snapping. But the path was easy to walk, and it kept curving around to the right, which was towards the side of Our Mountain that we knew so well and away from that purposeful swirl of blue mist and the squeaky charcoal carpet.

Even in the half-light, the meadows round Bartleby glowed green, the colour of emeralds on museum pillows, lit from below. We could hear the rush of the river working its way down the mountain, wending through the trees, and FYI, I have always wanted to use the word 'wending' in an actual sentence. The trail was so wide and smooth I could practically have skipped, but I trod very carefully on account of Winter's arm. I imagined I was gliding with a book on my head, that the path was a pillow to cushion my steps.

'Remember the story about the street being covered in hay?' I asked Winter, hoping to trick her into talking again, because it was just the kind of heart-swelling story that Winter loved. And, sure, I failed, but I went on anyway. 'How the guy in—where was it? Milan? He was dying, and so loud noises hurt his poor old brain. The mayor sent out a decree: "Cover the streets with hay!" So that the horses' hooves wouldn't make that sharp clopping, you get it? All the footfalls would be cushioned, like on carpet. Isn't that the nicest—hey!'

We had rounded another little bend, and suddenly there it was, way below: Bartleby. Tiny and perfect, like a miniature wooden carving from an old-fashioned railway set. It looked so peaceful and idyllic that it was hard to imagine all the awful things we'd seen there. It was like a picture of the outside of a concentration camp taken in swirling snow, and when you don't know any better, you see all that European wintery goodness and think, *That's pretty*. I stopped walking just to stare at it. I know it's impossible, but I swear I could smell its particular smell: cool stone, sun on grass, the mossy walls of the shady moat. I felt the part of my mind that says 'HOME' light up in flashing neon, and that sort of surprised me. We had lived in other houses longer, and Bartleby was such a complicated knot of refuge and prison and heaven and hell. But I guess now it was all we had.

And from up here, I felt nothing but fondness and peace, like an astronaut must feel for Earth when he sees it from space, and a saying popped into my mind. It was Winter's favourite, for reasons that shall not be discussed here.

I recited it: 'We live on a blue planet that circles around a ball of fire next to a moon that moves the sea, and you don't believe in miracles?'

I felt Winter reach around and brush her lips against my cheek, soft as they ever were. And I thought about that feeling you get when you love someone so much you want to die first so you're not in the world without them. 'Dear old Bartleby,' I said. 'Shall we stop for a snack and remember the good times?'

But Winter made no move to slide off my back. I felt her tiny body tense, her grip tighten. She must have heard it before I did, the long, low whine of the war-shaped plane that swooped in from the horizon towards us. It flew in a line so straight, it was unnatural, like a robot dog or a fake plant.

As the plane swooped past dear Bartleby, it spat two black droplets. And that was the start of the confusion, not knowing whether to look at those dark seeds as they shot towards the church, or to follow the arc of that plane up over our heads, over the mountain, the force of its flight whipping our hair around, the noise so loud I swear we went deaf. I remember the next bit in silence, unspooling before us like an ancient, twitchy film.

The church didn't crumple down in a majestic waterfall, like the Twin Towers in all those old news clips. It shattered, like a skull hit by a bullet, blowing apart in chunks. Boy, I wish I didn't know how both those things looked in real life.

As the pieces fell, Winter vomited something hot and putrid, like rancid squid ink. I felt it against the back of my neck just as a wall of heat blasted past us, so thick it felt like running through a banner, the way they used to do at sports games when they had real audiences watching, not just holograms projected onto the seats. Around us, stones rained down—small at first, but then larger chunks thumped into the earth like unexploded cannonballs. I should have thrown myself to the ground just then, right onto my stomach, like we'd practised in Tokyo. But there was something so enchanting about the storm of rocks, like being inside of a shaken-up snow globe. Looking back, I get that I was probably in some kind of haze, but I couldn't stop gazing, and so I wasn't quite prepared for the aftershock. The Earth gave a huge shudder, sharp like the buck of a horse. The force threw us across the path towards the edge of the mountain, the edge of the path, to the slope that wasn't much more than a flat wall of rock below. I felt my head whip back, snap forwards, and an ache slime down my spine, like the innards of a cracked egg oozing.

Then my feet left the ground. And in that second, I did something I never thought I would do.

It still haunts me, even up here.

I let go of my sister.

I threw my arms over my head to protect my face.

She was ripped from my back so easily, along with my backpack, like the Velcro strap of a kid's shoe, pulled apart.

Winter

We left Alexandria quickly and blindfolded.

We held hands through the dark, Summer and me. Stumbled up steps; the cushioned seats of a plane. Cars and vans and different rumbles.

The cloth of the blindfolds mopped up our tears.

We arrived in a house high up on a hill. We thought we'd gone blind, the light was so bright when our eyes were set free.

The walls were thick, the windows glassless. The ground was dry and the trees were gnarled. No one for miles. The soft click of bugs.

'It's Greece,' Summer guessed.

'It's Turkey.' I was sure.

There was a pool that was never cleaned.

It got so hot we didn't mind the green fur.

As we swam, my father went mad.

He couldn't sit still, stalked around through the day. Sat down, stood up. Wrote in his notebook. Disappeared and came back. His feet turned black from the old slate floor. He'd hidden things in a cellar cave.

'Don't go down there,' he snarled, and then wept at the tone of his voice.

As we tried to read, he moaned. He held his hands round the neck of my mother's dog.

I held my breath each time, waiting to see if he'd snap Pete's head back.

'Don't watch,' Summer whispered. But how could I not?

And he drank.

Till his eyes were red and spidery, thick like glass.

His breath smelled like rank fruit.

While we slept, he made wounds on his body that blazed red, then wept with old custard.

We stayed six months.

'Fuck this,' he said one night as we were reading *The Little Prince* under the kitchen table. 'We're going home.'

He threw his bottle into the fire. It popped so loudly, Pete sprang up and whimpered. The pellets of glass white-hot on the rug.

'You shouldn't have done that,' Summer said slowly.

I whispered to her, 'Will Mama be at home?'

My father heard. 'Fuck you,' he slurred.

Summer

I turned around to grab on to Winter, but there was only air. And as I fell backwards through space, stones were raining down around me and my eyes prickled with lights and I could have sworn I was an astronaut out raving in a meteor shower. The slope of the mountain above us started to tumble, like a sheet of Arctic ice in a documentary on global warming.

You know how I'd just said the blue planet/ball of fire line and got that feeling you get when you love someone so much you want to die first? They actually have a word for that feeling in Arabic—one word—and our driver in Egypt, Ammon, had taught it to us. The word is *Ya'aburnee*, and the direct translation is 'you bury me'.

Hoo boy, was my life ever flashing before my eyes. It wasn't a quick flash, like blinking. It was scenes from an old home movie: Winter, four and brown in bathers on a driveway, six and eating a doughnut off a string with her hands behind her back, eight and dressed as a unicorn with a party hat for a horn. A snippet of memory and then a clicking noise and the next and a clicking noise and the next, on and on, until eventually I realised that the clicking was my breath, in and out, further apart each time, and it suddenly dawned on me that I was dying.

By some miracle, I was pretty much upright—must have flipped the full way around as I fell—but the stones were all around me, pressing down and in, and here's a word I've always wanted to use contextually: entombed. I could still feel my toes, so my neck wasn't broken, and though my lips were jammed up against a rock so that I was basically tonguing it hard, by some stroke of Xtreme luck or misfortune (I wasn't quite sure yet), I had an air pocket around my nose. But it didn't take an International Maths Olympiad Champion to figure out that with each breath, I was coming closer to choking on my own carbon dioxide emissions, which, FYI, is what kills people in these situations, not the lack of oxygen, which is the common misconception and one that I can forgive you for. And those clicks, were they my ribs, snapped off and poking into my heart? Because that's what it felt like—as if knitting needles had been jammed deep through my aorta. Jeepers, was I *thirsty*.

'There's hope,' I told myself, thinking of miners caught down shafts and skiers under avalanches and babies under earthquake rubble, all yanked, blinking, back into the light. But the difference was that people were looking for those guys—knew they were there, were searching for them with torches and rope and resolve. I only had Winter, and who's to say she wasn't buried beside me, already dead? But then again, surely I would have felt that—the weight of her absence—wouldn't I?

And, let's face it, even if she were still alive, Winter was half ghost now, and though they've got some neat tricks, a ghost can't move a mountain.

'You've always wanted to know what it felt like to die,' I told myself chirpily, 'and here's your chance, and it's not even a mediocre one, like stroke or heart disease or listening too hard to your headphones while you're crossing a road. At least it's original.'

But obviously some part of me wasn't buying it, that cheeriness, because a voice that wasn't mine ripped through my head like a bullet, and that voice said, 'Speak no more.'

'That's probably God,' I said to myself. 'And if he's around, well, I guess the time is nigh.'

I thought about what I needed to ask forgiveness for—how long it would take, all the repenting. Did I just need to confess the serious crimes: letting Winter starve, the times I'd dreamed about stabbing that bear? Or was it every little lie, every pebble of untruth? Boy oh boy, I hoped God wasn't in the middle of binge-watching a really good TV series, because this was going to take a while. I decided to really concentrate on my breathing—keeping it steady but small—because, let's face it, by staying alive I'd be doing God a favour as well, giving him a nice deep pocket of alone time, which he probably didn't get a lot of. It might make up for some of my misdemeanours. A few of them, anyway.

Was I scared to die? Such a good question, and one that I was pondering myself. I thought about Mikie: how dignified he had been at the end of his life, and calm. I thought of Pops, and then tried not to. And truly, I wasn't scared of the moment when my soul left my body, which I'd always imagined would be as momentary, as fleeting, as a flower popping open into bloom. As I hung there cased in rocks, I was scared that I'd lived in a way that would banish me to an eternity alone. A forever without Winter, without Pops. Without our mother. I hadn't always been truthful or faithful or kind. Was it too late?

As time ticked on, I thought I could hear people talking, and eventually I swear I could see them, and—blow me down!—they were the Glass family. Have you ever come across them? They're a gang of child geniuses that J. D. Salinger made up, that grumpy old author who basically shut himself in a cabin as soon as he got famous for *Catcher in the Rye* and spent the rest of his life writing a web of stories about the Glasses, so tender and perfect. If you've never found them, go out looking—it will make your life seventy-seven times better to know those seven charming siblings; how they were on a radio show called *It's a Wise Child* when they were young, and how stuffed-up they've been ever since in ways that will tear your heart apart. And, boy, in spite of the dysfunction, did Winter and I ever wish we'd been born Glasses—into a big, chaotic family, bubbling over with eloquent drama and brainy love. In car rides out to remote rivers, we'd ask each other the sorts of things we imagined they would have had to answer on the radio: *What are the four stages of mummification? What is the difference between altocumulus and cirrocumulus? How many bones in the skeleton of a blue whale?*

Our mother had all the short stories about them in different collections and, I kid you not, every single page was dog-eared, as if she couldn't read two paragraphs without being face-smacked by a profound truth that made her stop and go in search of tea. Perhaps that's why we loved them so much, those Glasses: perhaps they made us feel closer to our mother. Perhaps they had inspired her to be on the radio, which was her job before there was us, and apparently she was pretty dang good.

'I think I would have married Zooey,' I would say to Winter. 'The handsome actor brother. What a babe. I think you would have ended up with Waker.'

'The monk?'

'Sure. You like the quiet.'

'I don't think—'

'Protest all you like. I know you best,' I'd assure her.

In my pre-death dream haze, Winter and the Glass family were standing in front of a huge piece of canvas in a New York loft, dipping their hands in black and white paint and making prints, the hands overlapping so their fingers made little grids. All seven siblings were there, laughing and arguing, and Winter was among them, so easy in their company that I knew she had been there a while, because she can be shy at first around people she doesn't know.

And I was not there. I was nowhere, and I searched for my handprints on that canvas—for evidence that I had been—and there was nothing.

I was already thrashing when I woke up, jerking around in some claustrophobic fever, and though I could only move a few millimetres in any direction, I was twisting so violently that I could feel things were beginning to shift—a pebble here, some gravel there, stones crunching against each other. For some reason, our father's voice popped into my mind, gruff as always. 'If you keep flipping around like that, Summer, you'll bring the whole lot down on top of you and that will be the end. Enough with the hysterics.'

And I heard him, and I understood him, and I just kept going, because the thought of Winter out there, making abstract expressionist art with the Glass family—without me—was enough to make me want to break free or die, it was that powerful.

You know the sound of a scuttle in the roof at night when you're just falling asleep and you hear those little foot-scrapes and your eyes pop open and something deep within you says 'Animal!'? Well, that's what I heard, just when I was starting to tire, when my heart was loud in my neck.

'Winter!' I tried to yell, but it was just the vibration of my teeth on the rocks and I thought my throat would burst with the effort, so I signalled with my mind: *Winter! I'm here! Winter, I need you!* And we had done enough experiments over the years that we had grudgingly accepted our lack of Twin ESP, but perhaps we just hadn't been conducting our research under the right conditions, because this time her mind whispered back.

Winter

We left that green swimming pool in the place that might have been Turkey. Days of flying. We went home to Tokyo. Everything we owned on the floor, like in a movie. Nowhere to step.

Our beds rumpled, thick hairs on the sheets.

A big wooden wardrobe tipped on its side. Magnets gone from the fridge. My snow globe cracked on the kitchen tiles, leaked dry.

Couch cushions slashed open, yellow stains through the stuffing.

The remains of our rabbits laid out in a cage. Their bodies so flat without all that blood.

My mother was nowhere.

'It's nice to be home,' Summer said with false cheer. 'Are we back now for good?'

'Start packing,' said my father. 'Only the necessities. Don't leave this building. I'll be back in three days.'

'Can't we come?' Summer asked.

But he said no.

'Well, can we at least take the karaoke machine wherever we're going?'

He left without saying goodbye.

'Fine,' Summer said. 'Then I'm not taking anything.'

While she sulked on the window seat, I packed my mother's books. I found a necklace with a grain of rice inside that said my name. I stared at it, sore with remembering. I tucked Summer's fairy lights into our striped cotton bag.

I slipped out while she was glowering. I tiptoed to my mother's study. I knew which floorboards creaked. We had listened at the door so many times.

The floor was a carpet of papers. Whoever had been here had

pulled out old logs from the fireplace, stomped the charcoal around. A drawer on the ground, its front pulled off. A paperweight bluebird flipped on its back.

A broken frame that had held a photo of me eating a doughnut off a long string. It was empty now, the glass in shards across the floor. The largest piece was the shape of a kite.

But her computer was still here. So many nights I had fallen asleep to the sound of her typing across the hall. As I sat in the leather chair at her desk, I felt my mother all around me, as if I were sunk down deep in her lap.

'Pops says no to taking the karaoke,' I told her. 'But can I bring this bluebird? I'll give it back when you get home, I promise.'

I felt her fingers through my hair, felt them catch at the knots. 'I haven't been brushing,' I whispered. 'I'm sorry.'

'Keep the bluebird, my sweet,' she whispered. 'It's yours.'

'Think of me sometimes,' she said, 'when I'm gone.'

Beside me, her screen whirred to life. And there she was, as if I had conjured her up. Jolty and pixels, a bright-orange jumpsuit, but definitely her.

'Mama,' I whispered. I reached out to not-touch her face on the screen. 'How did you know we were back?'

'Hey, chicken,' she whispered. 'How's tricks?'

Just when I was starting to get light-headed—I mean seriously dopey—and wheezing all tightly, like the pumping sound of a fly-spray can, I heard it: stones being ripped away. And not one or two, I mean whole sections being pulled apart, tumbling over each other to the ground. I knew immediately who was doing it, the only one strong enough: that mother-flipping bear.

He was back, Edward, and he was about to be my knight in shining armour, and I would be indebted to him for this rescue—would absolutely have to put up with his presence forever and always—and I wondered if it wasn't too late to make myself asphyxiate to avoid that horrifying fate. Then I almost spewed up from my own lack of gratitude, and all those feelings came back: jealousy and loneliness and sad, sweet rage. It felt as if I were pushing my thumb against a bruise.

Winter

The orange of her suit was so merry, so bright.

She said, 'Winter, I don't have much time but I need you to listen, because I might not have a chance to say these things again.

'Winter, when you are walking behind someone and they are going too slowly, it won't hurt their feelings if you want to overtake them.'

She said, 'When you know someone is home but they haven't answered the door, it's not rude to knock again—louder, the next time.'

She said, 'If you're at a market, you don't need to spend all your money at the stalls that nobody visits because you feel bad for them. That isn't your fault.'

I rested my cheek against the computer. It felt warm. She felt close.

It didn't seem right that Summer was missing it.

'Winter?' my mother said sharply.

I opened my eyes.

She said, 'Don't hide behind kindness. Behind anyone. One day you'll disappear.'

'Mama,' I whispered. 'Come back. Come home.'

I could hear her swallow. 'Winter,' she wheezed, her voice suddenly hoarse. 'The ending is not the story. Promise me you will remember that. The ending is not—'

And then she was gone. The screen went blank.

In the emptiness of her study, I leaned back in my mother's chair. I picked up her paperweight bluebird. I threw it hard against the wall.

Its beak broke off. The hole in its face gaped like a ghoul.

I remembered a man with a white mask from a bad dream. 'It

felt real, didn't it,' my mother had said as she'd sat on my bed. 'But there's a way you can tell if it's all just a nightmare. You say to yourself three times: Peter Pan, Peter Pan, Peter Pan. And then you wake up. Easy as that.'

Huge chunks of rock were being tossed to the ground, landing with thumps I could feel in my bones, and then ribbons of pale light started to shine through and I could hear his breathing, not that different from the sound made by the guy who had followed us through a park in Boston after dark when we'd taken a cheeky shortcut after watching people skate at the ice rink that played Buddy Holly songs on a tinkly old loudspeaker.

And then suddenly I could feel air against my skull and I realised there was something sticky dripping through my hair, trickling down my face, but do you think I minded? Hells no. Hoo boy, what a roller-coaster this whole trip had turned out to be. Suddenly I was completely and utterly High on Life, and as the rocks slid away around me, I flicked out my limbs and pushed, like a caveman breaking through a block of ice in an old cartoon. I didn't even care about that bear—would put up with him, whatever—because in 3.5 seconds I would see Winter's scrawny little face again, and that was Enough.

Here is the best part, and you're probably not going to believe it, because I didn't either. When my head popped up, meerkat style, Edward wasn't there—wasn't anywhere.

'Winter! Boy, is it good to see you. Hey, where's the bear?' I asked as I wrestled my shoulders free, and then my hands.

Winter just looked at me, confused. She held my backpack out to me and said nothing as I took it, which should have annoyed me, that continuing silence, but it didn't. Because as I watched she grabbed a rock the size of a netball with her not-busted hand and threw it to the side, and it dawned on me that this time the bear was Winter. The bear was inside her.

I squeezed that backpack tight against my chest with all the love I had for the world. Boy, were we *survivors*. Pops would have been proud—Walter too. I hoped wherever they were, they were watching with hot, buttered popcorn, cheering us on.

I don't know how to explain it, but maybe once she'd barfed up that gunk, Winter felt better—maybe she'd been feeling nauseated that whole time, and once it was out, she was back on form. Or maybe it was something to do with Bartleby being gone—with being free. Perhaps butterflies *really* hate cocoons. How would we even know? She had a real spring in her step; she had found that ridiculous pillowcase among the rubble, the swelling in her wrist seemed to have gone down, and even though she still wasn't speaking, Winter's face shone a little, and I like to think it was something to do with me being around and alive because of her.

Even though my body was bruised—hoo boy! Was it ever—I was keen to get moving quickly, and as I pondered the best way to go forward, I made a splint for her arm from a flattened condensed-milk can and ripped-up bits of my shirt, and I combed my fingers through her hair, trying to work the matted bits out of it so that when we eventually hit civilisation, we'd at least have some scraps of dignity left. The section of wall above us had fallen down in a neat slope— like a wheelchair ramp that led straight up to the next section of path, curving ever higher towards that snowy old summit. As I was hoisting my pack back onto my back, Winter was already scampering up that rubble, eager and coltish.

'Wait—water,' I called, my mouth claggy with thirst, and immediately she skipped back to me, went round to the back of my pack and found that big old sheet of silver that was scrunched at the bottom. She trotted over to fill it up at the stream. I watched her the whole way, willing myself not to fixate on that gruesome gap between her thighbones. 'Just choose not to see it,' I told myself.

'Stop wearing your wishbone where your backbone ought to be.'

Once the water was in, my pack was so heavy, I even considered ditching those fairy lights, but of course I decided against it—we'd come so far together, that rope of love and me. Those first steps, first minutes, I was sore in a deep and profound way, as if I had aged centuries. The air smelled of factory smoke, of tar. Though I was queasy with hunger, I was saving the milk for when we climbed higher—surely we'd need it more up there, where the air would be thinner, colder? But as we set off, I made a special effort to trot alongside Winter, just chatting away as if everything was how it had been in the spring. I brought the chat around to books, which had always been where we felt safe.

'You know, I've been thinking a lot about Ramona Quimby,' I said to Winter, and I knew that would get her attention because the Ramona books were her favourite growing up and, boy, did we spend a whole lot of summers, back when we had a yard, acting out those stories. No prizes for guessing that I played feisty, impulsive, misunderstood Ramona, and so Winter alternated the other parts: Ramona's big sister, perfect old Beezus, curmudgeonly Howie, her best friend who refused to get excited by anything, and his sticky, bratty little sister, Willa Jean. We loved Ramona the way we loved fairy bread and cartoons—because her world felt like a secret cubby that adults couldn't climb into, not even with their minds.

'I've been wondering what she did when she grew up, Ramona—like, what did she study at college, or whatever? And I reckon it was probably textile design, because remember how she was mad for drawing cats? And how excited she was when she got her own room? So I'm thinking textiles and interiors—haberdashery, or whatever you call it.'

And, boy oh boy oh boy, I kid you not, Winter actually smiled—that smile you smile when you're trying not to smile—and my heart soared like a drone flying over the White House washing line.

'And Howie,' I went on, 'this is controversial, but I'll bet he ended up being a spy for the Russian space program, based in Florida, secretly beaming shit back to Eastern Europe. Nobody would ever suspect Howie, those blond curls and his unimpressed affect, am I right? As soon as I get to heaven, I am hunting down that author to ask her, that sweet old Beverly Cleary. And Beezus, well, that's easy—a paediatric oncologist who had a stress-related breakdown at thirty-five and became a Pilates teacher. It was written in the stars from Day One, I'm telling you.'

She laughed. That pretty little twig, she laughed out loud, and it was husky from coatings of silence—husky like her laugh had been the time we'd caught laryngitis on the plane back from the International Maths Olympiad, but it was laughter all the same. How I beamed. And I tell you what, I may have been slightly high from being wrestled out of the Jaws of Death, because the sunset felt like a sunrise, all hope and glory, and I swear I could hear the golden hum of bees. I looked across at Winter and suddenly it dawned on me: for the first time in forever, we were so very happy.

All was so definitely, completely Not Lost, and though the path was narrow, and at some points you had to hug the wall as you scooched around bits where it swelled and bulged, and though the fall over the side was pretty monumental, suddenly life was peaches, because she was coming back to me, little by little, and so was my hope. And so was my heart.

'You know what I've got in my backpack?' I asked a while later. 'Actually—I'm not going to say. I'm going to save it for the summit, and mark my words, Winter, you are going to go batshit crazy for this, I just know it. We can read it in the plane when we—aww, man! I just gave it away. It's a book, but I'm not telling you which one. No way. Wild horses couldn't drag it from me.'

I should have remembered that Winter is the patient one—that I'm the one who is always gagging to know how things turn out—

because she just smiled even more, and looked up at the sky, down the mountainside, out at the sea, and I could feel it rising in me, that Need To Tell, and even at the best of times I'll admit that my impulse control is, like, zero. As I followed her gaze, I licked my lips and I opened my mouth and I said, 'It's *The*—'

But I didn't get any further than that, because there was a flash, a green flash—a flash so bright you could see the bones in your hand. A whistle like the screech of torn metal. Something rose up, like an electric green bird, and hovered right where the moon should have been.

Winter

As I went to shut down the computer, I remembered the audio file that had sat on the desktop forever. Could I somehow bring it with us? It was a recording of the moment they fell in love, my mother and father. You can hear it—the whole interview. Forty-three minutes, twenty-six seconds. We must have listened to it a hundred times, Summer and I. A thousand. Over and over and smiling.

'With me today is the man of the moment—the world's favourite scientist, affectionately known as the Coffee Cup Bandit,' she begins. 'Here to explain the vision behind his bold invention, it's—'

'Pops!' we would say together.

When he says good morning, he sounds the same as always. Gruff and clever.

My mother sounds so young, but her voice still twinkles big. You can hear that her soul is bright. You don't even have to listen hard.

'Truthfully?' she says when he's explained the whole coffee-cup wi-fi thing. 'The science seems complicated to me,' she says. 'Though I must admit to being distracted. Dear listener, this man is *handsome*.'

They never get around to discussing his bold vision. They talk about his childhood, which was spent on a moor. How he skipped two grades of school because he was so clever. How he earned seven different degrees. They talk about the absence of tin-can stilts these days. How my mother loves the stages of the moon. They talk about a breed of dog that belonged to a carpenter in a TV show they both watched when they were young. How they both loved that dog; how they always dreamed of owning one like it. They talk about deep-fried shallots as a garnish. They talk about their favourite seasons before there was us.

'Tell me again,' I would say to my mother some nights as she tucked me in bed. 'The feeling you had when you met.'

She would kiss me on the forehead, smooth the sheet. 'I felt as if I had always known him.'

'And it made you feel safe,' I would prompt.

She would smile. She knew that this was my favourite part. She nodded as she stroked my hair. 'It made me feel safe. Like leaning back onto the wind.'

Summer thought the best bit was the ending. 'And now for the question I ask all my guests, because, let's face it, it's a classic,' says my mother. 'What are your hopes and dreams?'

'*Great* question,' Summer would say. 'Nailed it.'

He pauses. He says, 'My hopes? My hope is to make the world a better place—for all humanity.'

In my mind, I can see my mother lean in with excitement. Summer does that, too. 'If you don't mind me saying, how is that different from the answer given by every beauty pageant contestant ever?' she asks.

My father laughs—he actually laughs. A deep, husky laugh. And when he is finished, he gets serious again. 'I'm talking about making a difference in a real way. In a practical way.'

'But what you're talking about here...' My mother pauses. 'It seems risky—doesn't it? Freedom, yes. But at what cost?'

Pops goes kind of quiet then—or maybe just thoughtful. 'So much of life is sacrifice,' he says. 'Think of everything that has been given up in the name of freedom. Even love is a sacrifice. When we fight for our freedom, we are fighting for love.'

You can hear my mother stop in wonder. Like a bucket's worth of rose petals have been dropped from far above her head.

So my father continues. 'And my dreams? I only have one. It's to take you to dinner.'

This time my mother laughs. I hear the scrunch of folded

215

newspaper hats. I hear the crunch of honey crumpets. The tinkle of Christmas ornaments. So much of my life was that laugh, my childhood. But it is gone and she is gone.

'Dear listener, I'm really—I'm blushing,' she says. 'It's not often you can make dreams come true.'

Summer

'But if Edward has the flare, what the hell is this map for? What's even up on the mountain? Winter, do you know? *Look at me.*'

But she wouldn't. And so I shoved my face in her face, my eyes up to her red-rimmed eyes. I grabbed her broken wrist in my fist and I squeezed. I hissed, 'What else did you give him?'

Winter gasped with the pain. But she did not speak.

Instead, with her free hand, she reached inside her shirt slowly, trembling, and pulled out something tiny—a tiny bag on the end of a long piece of string, and I wondered how I had missed that, old Eagle Eyes that I was, and then I looked over at the flare, suspended in the sky like it was hanging from a wire, and I almost laughed with all the things that I'd missed.

She handed me that tiny pouch, and I knew what it was, but I opened it anyway, tipped it up, and it was just as I remembered, that little freezing vial, filled with droplets of incandescent light, like liquid fireflies. 'And the notebook?' I whispered, when I had finished gazing.

Winter shook her head, and the only word I can think of to describe her face is destroyed. The worst part was, I had seen it before, that expression, twice before, and I should have expected it, because don't they say that bad things always happen in threes?

And, yes, yes, yes, I knew everything she'd gone through—had lived them with her, the mistakes she had made—but I was still Mad (capital M).

So the loud, raw thrum of the chopper that came over the horizon at just that moment, towards the green blob of suspended light— well, I'm not going to lie: it felt good, the way it battered my ears, shook right into the gaps between my organs. And when Winter watched it drop down to the beach, her misery felt just right.

Winter

Whoever we had been hiding from knew we'd come back. That we would return to Tokyo eventually. That's when they gave my father twenty-four hours to choose.

My mother in exchange for his secrets.

A soul you loved in the place of nine billion souls, most of whom you'd never know.

Big Tech knew he had been making something to attack the cables under the sea. He'd suggested it back when he worked in their labs—that someone might try it. That they should be ready. At a long, glossy table he talked through his modelling. Possible outcomes: a fast-catching sickness, the world half in shade. Someone had laughed, then. His boss rolled his eyes. A ridiculous notion. Impossibly hard. An improbable feat. They moved to the next point.

Years later, in Guam, on the banks of a river, my father was spotted. Then followed. Then bugged. In the cool stone lobby of a hotel in Rajasthan, his old boss made an offer.

My father claimed he'd given up. There was nothing to sell. That he'd never been able to get it right. That he couldn't live with himself if it all went wrong. 'I'm sorry,' he said. 'You'll have to excuse me. It's my daughter's tenth birthday. The answer is no.'

As the Resistance grew, Big Tech grew uneasy. People withdrew all their money from banks. They met to throw their phones in large pits. Then they met to lay themselves down in larger pits so they wouldn't drain what was left of the world.

Suddenly it wasn't so ridiculous. If it existed, Big Tech needed to get it before it got out. And if it got out, they needed Pops alive to come up with a plan in case there were consequences.

So they took my mother instead. Nothing meant more to my

father. He would cave. They were sure.

'What would you have done?' Summer had asked me. 'Same as him? I would've—I just know it. It was right, what he chose.'

'But…but she wasn't just a soul,' I said. 'Words made coloured fireworks in her mind.'

And people loved her—which was the bonus. Publicly, on the radio, she never took sides. 'But her whole vibe was truth,' Summer would say. 'She was, like, the least fake thing on the planet.' When it became impossible to tell truth from lies, real people speaking from their digital clones, her voice became the symbol of the things you could still believe in.

I thought about the video, the first to be seen simultaneously on every screen around the world. How hot it looked where they'd taken her. The stains on her orange jumpsuit. How her eyes were closed, as if she were dreaming.

But if you look very closely, you'll see her lips move.

There is no sound, but I know what they're saying—the same thing three times.

Peter Pan, Peter Pan, Peter Pan.

My father knew it too.

He saw it for the first time in the back of a car—the screen on the back of the taxi driver's seat.

And that, for him, was the end of the world.

So I shackled Winter to me. With rage through my veins, I threw that string of fairy lights around her in loops, round her waist, round her shoulders, and knotted it viciously, so that she couldn't lift her arms, even to scratch her nose, and especially not to write in that stupid fucking notebook, and the cable was digging in enough to cause a burn.

'You think you're so pretty,' I spat as I bound her, 'all tiny now. But you're not—you're *disgusting*. I can't hardly stand to look at you, rotting away like a zombie corpse. And holy fuck, you *smell*.' As if that wasn't a pot calling a kettle black or whatever, but mad doesn't even begin to describe what I was feeling—Does. Not. Even. Begin.

Holding the two ends like reins, I whipped them up and down so that they smacked against the back of her prison-bar ribs. And I was almost disappointed that she didn't fight against me, didn't scratch and hiss but instead just dropped her head and closed her eyes and stood, the fairy globes winking in the half-light, like the shimmer of tears on a sad midnight car trip away from home, and boy, had we done enough of those.

'WALK,' I yelled in a voice I would never dream of using on a horse. But I didn't care that I had basically turned into Stalin. It was Winter who had killed us anyway, because there were only four cans of milk in my backpack and even if she could survive forever and ever on the sugar of her own breath, I couldn't. My only hope now was that there was something else waiting for us on the top of Our Mountain—something in the spot that my father had marked on the map that could save us. Some buried supplies, perhaps—some Doritos, some peanuts. A two-way radio. Some new books by J. K. Rowling—and not those adult crime-y ones. Another flare. A tiny fold-out plane, just right for two. A gun, loaded, two bullets in its chamber.

As I looked up above us, it was all sheer cliff striped with time, and a few ridges with fir trees perched as if they were stuck there, too scared to jump off, and had we ever seen that scenario play out during our time as International Diving Prodigies. And snow, which was going to be interesting, given the whole lack of shoes.

At first, Winter strode out, pulled against me, and I had to trot a little to keep up. Where she got her energy from, I don't know, though I wondered if, at some deep level, she wasn't ablaze with a fury of her own. And maybe it was aimed at herself, that anger, and that's what was driving her toothpick legs, and for half an hour or so I felt sorry for her again. Perhaps she was starving herself with the shame of all the things she'd done, and it was my job to save her, my chance to be Noble (capital N) and oh so mature.

So the first time we stopped, I held a can of milk up to her, holes punched in the top, tried to tip it down her throat, but she coughed and gagged and turned her head, back and forth, back and forth, and eventually her lip caught against the ragged edge of one of those holes, and oh my hat, there was blood, wriggling down her face like a worm. I gave up then, and it all came tumbling back, my anger. *Let her starve*, I thought to myself. *Fucking traitor.* And you might have noticed that I don't swear all that often, so hopefully you get how riled up I was by the whole thing. I want to say livid but it's not strong enough—nothing in the thesaurus is.

We kept on and on, the cliff on one side and a zillion-foot drop on the other, and only the occasional burbling sound of the river wafting over as we rounded bends, ever upwards. The path was there in front of us, zigzagging back and forth just as Pops had marked it on the map, smooth and dark and easy again. And in spite of everything, I felt a sudden rush of love for that guy as we strode on in our weird horse-and-cart arrangement, and I pondered for the first time how lonely it must have been to be him, stuck in a cage of his own making and blazing with fury.

I must have been contemplating all this pretty hard, been really deep in love with my own metaphor, because I hardly noticed that the fairy-light reins were slack in my hands, and then dragging on the floor, and then Winter was only the slightest bit ahead of me. And then there I was by her side, our steps matching exactly, as if we were North Korean soldiers, back when there was a North Korea, and, boy, wasn't that a beautiful story, that elegant people's revolution that caught everyone by surprise back in the day.

I should have asked Winter if she was okay, should have unravelled her. It wasn't like her to slow down, not these days—but I didn't. I just walked ahead of her with my hands behind my back, trailing the reins, until eventually I could feel that I was pulling her along. And I'm sort of embarrassed to write the next bit but I'm trying, really trying, with the whole truth thing, so here goes: I tugged on them, those reins—tugged sharply, and BANG! I heard her trip and smack against the ground, and I was thinking to myself, *Good*, when the reins jerked out of my hand, catching me by surprise. I stumbled, toppled right over, and by the time I stood up and brushed myself off, Winter was nowhere to be seen.

Winter

On the day my mother died my father came through the front door and looked at me without seeing me. He knelt and held out his arms. But when he closed them around my shoulders, his grip didn't feel tight enough.

Then he disappeared into his lab. I left food outside the door that he mostly didn't eat.

Within seventy-two hours of her death, he had done it. With revenge in his heart, he set fire to the future, put his secrets in the sea.

Nothing happened—not for weeks.

I slept a lot. Curled around the packed boxes of my mother's books, Pete coiled into the crook of my knees. When I was asleep, I didn't have to remember.

But Summer had nightmares. She couldn't bear to stay inside. At least in Turkey we'd had the pool.

Eventually, we snuck out. We wore hats. We mooched around parks. We went to the teahouse at Shinjuku Gyoen. Walked in the park, threw stones in the pond. We'd been there last for my mother's birthday to see the blossoms. That gave us the idea to visit the places in the city that she'd always loved.

At Itoya, that's where we saw it first. How our mother had loved that big old stationery shop. The rainbow rows of thick patterned paper. The neat rows of inks. The place to try nibs. She would sigh when we left and say, 'Twelve floors of heaven.'

On the seventh floor, a man fell to the ground. He clutched at his back and started to moan. I ran over to help, stepped back when I saw. His skin was the colour of a pigeon, a kerb. I could feel he was burning.

After that it spread quickly, The Greying. Masks and fear and quarantine. Windows cut into shirts. People led away to die in huge sheds. The whole world sick-panicked, the internet gone. But we didn't connect how it fitted together. It all seemed so strange, that upside-down time, newly missing my mother.

We watched from our window. Minami. The end.

That was the night that we left in the dark. A drive to an airstrip. A fat wad of notes.

My father was flying. He banked the plane steeply away from the lights.

'Goodbye,' I whispered, my head on the window. 'Goodbye. I love you.'

You are pretty much just going to assume that I'm lifting the next bit out of *The Power of One* (and if you haven't read it, how are you even alive at this juncture?!) but I swear on my new lob that it's true: Winter found a crystal cave. I'm talking a cavern with a roof so high that we shouldn't have been able to see it, except we could because it sparkled like a disco ball. The cave smelled like a church that's been filled with the sea, limey and salty and musty and dark, and if you think dark doesn't have a smell, you're crazy in the coconut. As she lay on the ground where I'd tripped her, Winter must have seen the glow of the opening and commando-crawled in and, boy, was it lucky that she was trailing those fairy lights, or I'd never have found her.

'It's Doc's cave,' Winter said, gazing around at the glittering walls, the columns that shone with sequins of light.

And, oh my hat, I know that just a few seconds before I'd wished that she was being chomped alive by flesh-eating ants, but you can't actually imagine how good it was to hear her voice. I'm sorry, you just can't.

Doc was that beautiful old German professor/pianist/genius in *The Power of One* who teaches a little guy called Peekay how to Look at the World—teaches him about nature and music and compassion and humanity, and if you think that sounds soppy, it's actually a pretty brutal read on account of all the competitive boxing/South African race relations.

And, as weird as it sounds, I felt Doc there with us, in the crystal cave, his strong but gentle presence, and suddenly I knew, I just knew, that we were going to make it—that in spite of everything, it was going to be okay now. He'd make it so. Whatever was up the top of the mountain was going to save us, and soon enough we'd be under someone's wing, and after all this time, wasn't that all that I wanted?

In the story, Doc is so patient, so forgiving, so filled with unwavering love in the most horrible of circumstances—he's practically Jesus. And under the imaginary gaze of his crinkly blue eyes, I felt my heart bloom.

I forgave Winter. Just like that, I forgave her everything. I maybe even forgave myself a little.

'It's so nice to hear you speak,' I said as I unravelled her from the rope of lights. 'Boy, Winter, I missed you. I missed you this whole time and I'm not going to go on and on about it, but I just want you to know that. Now let's never talk about this again. Want to go exploring?'

And she did, and we did, side by side, and it took ages because it was huge, that cave, and one part was a garden of stalagmites that looked like stone cacti, and there was a lake in the middle that reflected the roof, and as we waded in, it felt like we were sloshing our way through a puddle of stars.

'It feels like Christmas here,' Winter said, and I knew what she meant: hushed magic, safe and true. As if nothing bad could ever happen. 'Can we stay forever?' she asked. 'Please?'

And part of me wanted to say yes, of course, and so I said, 'Yes, of course,' and we laughed for so many reasons, because it actually wasn't that different to Bartleby, and how could we ever have thought that staying there was a good idea?

Winter

As the world turned grey, our father brought us to Bartleby to fix it. He thought there was a third way to live, a balance that could be found. A world not all online or off it. He muttered to himself about how we could get there. He paced at night. He scribbled things down.

But he didn't live to see it through.

We had been a year on the island when we found him in the forest. Long enough to carve out soft little lives in this prison of his guilt.

Pete had run ahead, threading through the trees. By the time he caught up, he was dancing around my father's feet as they dangled down. Jumped up to paw his shoes. He thought it was a game, that dog. He grabbed the laces, yanked down hard.

As my father's body swayed, I screamed.

When I stopped, he was still swaying, the dog still jumping. The rope creaked like the chain of a swing in the park.

My chest beat like wings.

His tongue.

I thought Summer was running away to be sick. But she came back. She had The Knife.

We cut my father down.

He crumpled.

There was a crack that was one kneecap breaking, and then another that was the other.

The top of the rope was still tied to the tree.

We started to dig a hole for my father. But it was cold, and the earth was so hard. After two days we'd hardly dug deep enough to cover our ankles.

'Screw this,' said Summer. 'Let's cast him out to sea, like a brave old sailor.'

'Won't he be eaten by sharks?' I whispered.

'He'll probably end up in the belly of a wise old whale. Spend eternity cruising the sea in style. Boy, do those guys live a long time.'

'I don't think whales eat people,' I said. 'I think they eat krill. I think they suck it in through their baleen.'

'Well, what do you think the krill are eating?'

I knew the answer—microorganisms—but I didn't want to say. Summer was trying so hard to be brave.

'Will he sink?' I asked.

Summer thought for a minute. 'We can put rocks in his pockets—special ones. We can write messages on them.'

'What kind of messages?'

'*Goodbye, I Love You.* That sort of thing. Does that sound okay?'

And now that we had covered his face, that we knew we could carry him between us—Summer with her fingers jammed into his armpits, me wrapped round his broken knees—it sounded okay.

'Summer?' I whispered when she came back with a pen. 'We are orphans.'

'And who doesn't love a story about orphans?' she replied. '*The Secret Garden, Oliver Twist, The Outsiders*…they all end well. Trust me on this one.'

I sat with the pen for ages, the lid off. The words wouldn't come. Eventually I looked up. Summer was watching me closely.

'Winter?' she said gently. 'He…he wasn't all bad. Pops, I mean. He was just a person doing his best. Promise you'll try to remember that. There were good times, too. When all this is over, I bet they'll come back.'

'Why do you think we never used it earlier? The flare, I mean,' I asked as we were walking to the far end of the cave through darkness as thick as a milkshake. 'Why didn't we just get ourselves rescued after Pops was taken away? Isn't that what a normal person would have done? Are we not normal people?'

And beside me Winter tensed, just as she did whenever we talked about our father, and she didn't have to say anything after that. Pops was an arsehole, no two ways about it (aren't all geniuses?) and we had lived in fear of his moods so long that even when he was gone, we were frightened to disobey him. And to top that all off, after he left, life felt delicious—so free and easy and uncomplicated—that we were happy. In the weeks and months that followed, I felt a new kind of empathy for Maeve, our old class guinea pig, who used to escape all the time and just run, eyes half-closed in bliss, to the furthest corner of wherever she was, and eventually nobody wanted to take her home on the weekend because it took hours to catch her, particularly if you'd walked her down to the local park, and nobody's parents had the time.

'Yeah,' I said eventually. 'You're right. Stupid question.'

'I'm the stupid one,' said Winter. 'Look where we are because of me. I always have been,' she added.

'As if,' I said as we reached the back of the cave, where a hole high up in the ceiling haloed down light.

I looked up and made one of those breathy 'wow' noises and believe me, you would have too—this wall was something. Once Pops came back from a business trip with a chunk of stone, like half a big egg, and inside was amethyst, all glittering crystal shards of violet, and, boy, did we swoon. And even though we weren't eight anymore, that's how I felt looking up at this wall, which, now my eyes had adjusted some, I could see was the same kind of deep violet. Pops was confusing that way: he wasn't all good and he wasn't all evil, and just as you got to thinking one of those was true, he'd go and do something like bring home a gosh-darn piece of gemstone heaven just for you, and upset your apple cart of certainties.

'Remember that big chunk of amethyst?' I reached out to grasp Winter's hand and she flinched. But she didn't move it away. I felt so hungry for her. 'Lie down, Winter,' I said. 'Please? Lie down here with me.'

We lay side by side looking up at all the Beauty of that star-studded roof, and we didn't say a single thing, not for ages, and eventually our breathing synced so perfectly that I couldn't tell which exhalation was mine. And even though Winter was all bones now, as if her skeleton was on the outside, I still scooched up next to her and laid my big old head on the nook of her collarbone, and I tried not to think about crushing her, tried to pretend it was all just how it had been before.

'Can you tell me how it feels to be in love?' I asked, eventually. 'Was it like you thought—like Amy and Teddy in *Little Women*—sort of steely pure? Or more like Jo and Teddy—brotherly and smouldering? Or was it more Harry Potter and Cho Chang—sort of just epic crushing? Or Gatsby love—throwing silk shirts around the room, all silly?'

'Do you really want to know?' said Winter. 'You won't think it's dumb?'

I clicked my tongue. 'I asked, didn't I?'

'It was like…' She looked up at the ceiling, her face as tender and love-filled as if she were looking up at a fresco of labrador puppies. 'Like my whole body was nervous but without the fear. Everything felt electric. But I was safe.'

Without thinking, Winter was running her not-broken fingers

over my hair. It was so long since anyone had touched me, and I got what she meant by electric.

'There was a fuzzy outline all around me. A sort of force field. Of happiness. And I could do anything—be anyone. Because who I really was—the parts I never showed—they were safe in someone's pocket, and someone thought they were worth keeping there.'

I'd be lying if I didn't say that was hard to hear, because hadn't I been keeping Winter safe in my pocket the whole time? And what were these parts she never showed, exactly? But I let that go, because this was the most she'd talked since she'd come back to me, and I didn't want to discourage this Opening Up when I had so many other important questions.

'What about the kissing? Was it better than kissing me? Did you like it?'

Winter laughed again. 'Well, at first I didn't like it that much. I kept stopping to breathe in really fast because I wasn't used to touching and it made me, sort of...'

'Gasp?' I asked, loving this Girl Talk moment, which was like something from a magazine—something we'd missed out on all these years, and definitely an area I would have been exceptionally good at if circumstances had allowed.

'Yes, I guess, and that made me embarrassed.'

'I bet you blushed. You always blush.'

'So much blushing. But eventually I got used to it. And he liked it, the...the way I breathed.'

'The gasping,' I said eagerly.

'Yes. Because the thing was...The things about me I hated, some of those—lots of those—were the bits he liked best,' said Winter.

'Your appendix scar?' I asked.

I could feel Winter duck her head in happy-shyness. 'He kissed it so many times, I thought he was going to—Sorry, is that too much information?'

It was, but only because my heart was hungry in the way that I guess every teenage girl's heart is at some time, and it felt good to acknowledge that sweet, hollow pain.

I said, 'Nope, not at all. Tell me anything. Tell me everything.'

'Well, he…' Winter paused. She sighed, as if she were suddenly remembering something that had been so freeing to forget. 'You were right,' she said. 'You were right all along. He wasn't who I thought he was.'

'Maybe he was exactly who you thought he was but he was someone else as well. People are complex, am I right?' I said, trying to channel my inner Mikie. 'Besides, you're so easy to love that the guy never really stood a chance. Trust me. It only took three hot seconds for Mikie to start swooning once I told him about you. He thought you were a honey.'

'Who's Mikie?' she asked, because she's great at deflecting when she's just been given a compliment. People saying nice things about her is excruciating to Winter.

I paused. It was a good question. Who *was* Mikie? 'Nobody, I guess.'

'But Summer,' Winter continued, 'now Edward's got the notebook. And what…what will he do when he gets into that helicopter? To the people who think they're coming to help us?'

'Simple,' I said. 'Two options. Number one: he'll be so lovesick for you that he'll see the error of his ways and hand them the notebook and join the Resistance, and BOOM! The world starts turning. Without the internet to make things all murky, people get their shit together and rise up. The planet is saved!'

'Or he gets on board and he kills them,' she whispered. 'I think he's been trained.'

'And I'm guessing the people he's working for will want to keep what's in that notebook on the down low. They won't be using it anytime soon.'

'What do you mean?' she asked. 'Why wouldn't they want to? Won't everyone die if they don't?'

'The usual,' I said breezily, feeling kind of smug that I'd thought this part through. 'Money. Power. Greed. Think how much they could sell it for. Plus, if the world's not turning, it's probably a good excuse to fast-track that whole scheme where people pay truckloads to relocate to Mars. Boy, what a cash cow. Like that guy with the baseball cap needs any more cash, am I right?'

Winter didn't say anything to that, and after a while I felt her tears drip onto my forehead, still a tiny bit warm from running down her cheeks. I shifted myself a little away from her so I could prop my head up on my elbow and look right into her eyes.

'Kid, most people most places—they're just doing the best they can. That includes Edward. That includes you and me. We didn't know any better. You'd never blame Anne Frank for being stuck in the annexe, would you?'

I thought this was a masterful argument but, truly, Winter was always the smarter one.

'Anne's family didn't get stuck there because of something she did,' she pointed out quietly. 'It wasn't her fault.'

'That we know of,' I said. 'The diary's probably a little biased in her favour.'

'So you took a risk and it didn't work out,' I continued. 'But Winter, for a little while, boy, you were in love, and that is why we are alive, am I right?'

'I guess...' Winter laughed through her snot, which is one of the ways I loved her most. 'Summer?' she asked. 'Do you forgive me? For Edward, I mean? For telling.'

I paused. I did—I had. And yet...

'If I say yes,' I said slowly, 'will you drink some of that milk? A little bit—a bird's beak.' I could feel the fur of her body stand up. 'If you loved me,' I whispered, 'you would eat.'

'If you loved me,' she whispered back, 'you wouldn't ask.'

I swallowed. 'I'm sorry,' I said, trying not to show how much that broke my heart. 'I *do* forgive you. And…' There was something else I needed to say—something that had been boiling up in me since I had left Bartleby, or maybe since I was born. 'And Winter? I'm sorry you felt you needed to escape me and I'm sorry I couldn't help loving you so hard. After everything, I couldn't handle losing you too, and if that makes me a monster, well, sign me up with a lifelong contract to appear on *Sesame Street*.'

Winter shook her head. 'You weren't a monster, Summer. You were brave and strong and fierce, like a lion. Like a bear.'

My heart felt full to bursting and I smiled at Winter, a smile so deep I felt it in the soles of my feet. And Winter, she smiled back.

We slept facing each other, our knees tucked up in each other's knees, noses close enough to catch the warmth of our breath because that cave wasn't exactly tropical, though Winter was surprisingly toasty. Winter fell asleep first, she always did, and I spent a whole lot of time looking at her tiny, hollowed-out face while it was up so close to mine, trying to figure out which bits were still the same— the same as before, the same as me. I reached out to touch her hair, just as she'd done to me, and as I stroked it she murmured a little, a happy murmur, and so I twirled gentle spirals around her scalp with my fingers, and that would have been enough right there, enough to make anything bearable.

Except that when I eventually pulled my hand away, a clump of her hair came with it—I'm talking a bunch like a bunch of raw spaghetti when you tap it out of the packet, trying to figure out how much will make a bowl. And after that, I was so disturbed that it took me ages to fall asleep, as I'm sure you can appreciate.

Winter

'Do you love me?' Edward had asked as we'd sat side by side under the tree in the forest with the rope still tied round the branch, its end sliced through.

This was back when he was working on that little guitar. Everything around us glistened with the ends of a sunshower. We had come here to shelter, where the leaves were the thickest.

'I love you,' I said. Like they do in a movie—the type Summer swoons over. It made me smile, to sound like a script.

He turned his head and leaned right over, kissed me deep, touched my forehead with his. And then he'd said, 'Go and get me that knife.'

I froze.

I knew the one. We had had it since Tokyo. Sharp and bright. Long—as long as a torso is deep.

I swallowed and I whispered, 'But what for?'

He looked into my face. His eyes were sad. 'Winter, don't you trust me?'

I went and took that knife from where Summer had hidden it.

Edward smiled when he saw me walking so slowly, the blade pointed down as I slipped through the trees.

He stood up. Held out his hand. I gave it to him. 'Turn around,' he said, 'and then don't turn around.'

I started to shake, but I turned.

He said, 'What are you thinking, Winter, right now?'

I kept my voice steady. 'I am thinking of my mother.'

I woke because Winter was unhooking her legs from mine. 'What are you doing?' I whispered, all groggy, because however long we'd been asleep hadn't been long enough.

'Running,' she whispered back.

'Winter, your wrist is broken,' I said, trying to keep my voice even. 'You probably shouldn't move it around.'

She just looked at me, or was it past me? I sat up and pulled my scrap of a T-shirt over my head, and it was cold but I didn't care, not really. I tied the two raggedy ends in a knot and handed it to Winter. 'Here—a sling,' I said. 'At least put it on while you're running.'

'I—'

'Yes, you can,' I said, turning my bare back to her so I could rub my eyes and think.

I wish that I had come to terms with her Xtreme running addiction so squarely that it didn't bother me, seeing her lope off, knowing there was nothing in her stomach—literally nothing—and I thought about what Mikie had said about her running back to me one day, tried to hold that inside me, but, boy, it wasn't easy.

I'm a little ashamed here, but my motives in letting Winter go weren't exactly pure, or even a tiny bit. Truth be told, this whole time, I'd been dying—DYING—to figure out what was in the notebook she kept writing in so feverishly, and now was the perfect time to sneak a peek. And while my money was on soppy love poetry about the bear, probably in haiku because it was a form we were pretty familiar with, what I was really hoping for was a juicy account of what had happened while we'd been apart. I felt that gap of time deep within me, like a toothache. What had she done, and what had been done to her, and had she missed me, even a bit? She had written so much, so intently, that it had to be in there, blow by blow, her thoughts and feelings, all untangled and tidied, and even the thought of it made my mouth water.

I was running, I mean running *really* fast, and if you find that surprising, well, so did I, but there I was, positively sprinting around that cave, jumping over rocks and puddles and slopes of scree like I was Anna-May Barnes, who was the hurdling champion at our school and also ridiculously popular and also blonde, and why those things so often go together, beats me.

I was yelling Winter's name. And though I imagined it would bounce around the cave like in a cartoon and smack me right back in the face, it didn't: my voice just disappeared, and I want to say it was sucked into a vortex, but I'm pretty sure that's wrong in a number of ways—semantic, scientific, whatever.

I was panicked.

That notebook, boy oh boy, it had freaked me out on seventy-seven different levels. And not because of what was in it, but because of what wasn't, which was anything of anything that made sense, and I would even have been okay with some hardcore erotic sonnets compared to what I found.

Which was this:

Summer Winter Summer Winter Summer Winter Summer Winter Summer Winter Summer Winter Summer Winter Summer Winter Summer Winter Summer Winter Summer Winter Summer Summer Winter Summer Winter Summer Winter Summer Winter Summer Winter Summer Winter Summer Winter Summer Summer Winter Summer Winter Summer Winter Summer Winter Summer Winter Summer Winter Summer Winter Summer Winter Summer Winter Summer Winter Summer Winter Summer Summer Winter Summer Winter Summer Winter Summer

Winter Summer Winter Summer Winter Summer Winter
Summer Winter Summer Winter Summer Winter Summer
Winter Summer Winter Summer Winter Summer Winter
Summer Winter Summer Winter Summer Winter Summer
Winter Summer Winter Summer Winter Summer Winter
Summer Winter Summer Winter Summer Winter Summer
Winter Summer Winter Summer Winter Summer Winter
Summer Winter Summer Winter Summer Winter Summer
Winter Summer Winter Summer Winter Summer Winter
Summer Winter Summer Winter Summer Winter Summer
Winter Summer Winter Summer Winter Summer Winter
Summer Winter Summer Winter Summer Winter Summer
Winter Summer Winter Summer Winter Summer Winter
Summer Winter Summer Winter Summer Winter

But that was all. *Pages* of it, over and over. And the writing, it wasn't Winter's writing—well, it was, because I'd seen her do half of it right in front of me, but the style wasn't hers at all, so scraggly and uneven, like she'd done it blindfolded after a cheeky swig of sherry.

I knew about this—something like this. Your starved body sort of eating your starved brain. I should have known by the smell. I should have known when her hair came out in my hands that this was Serious (capital S). Winter was starving to death.

And I knew that—I had known back when the world was still spinning.

And I didn't do anything—not a thing.

And that was why I was running so hard, backpack slamming against me, screaming her name into the void, hoping it wasn't too late.

Winter

'Tell me about her,' Edward said, 'Anything you like.' Behind me, I could hear that he was moving.

'My mother…'

A part of me was waiting for Summer's knuckles against my face. For the heat of her slap or the slice of her nails. But there was nothing—just rustling.

Where was The Knife?

'When my mother washed the dishes,' I continued, feeling bolder, 'she was always talking.'

'Just when she did the dishes?' Edward interrupted.

'No—all through the day. When she was home, I mean. Because often she wasn't.'

'Where was she?' asked Edward.

'Away. Different places. She interviewed people.'

What was he doing? I heard rubbing. I went to turn.

'The dishes?' said Edward quickly.

I paused. I closed my eyes, remembering. 'When she filled the sink, she would be talking as she put in the washing-up liquid, so it was always a big slosh. She never noticed. And when this huge mountain of bubbles rose up, she was so surprised, every time. I loved to watch for it, that big slosh of green that came out while she chatted, all absent-minded. She had so many ideas—she wanted to know everything about everything and chat it all through. Like… like Summer, I guess. She would put the bubbles on my face, like a beard or a hat. Or a mushroom cap. When she was home, it felt like home.'

I turned around to look at Edward. He also felt like home, but in such a different way.

He had cut down the rope—what was left of it. Held it out with both hands. 'Want me to take this some place?' he asked quietly.

Winter was lying by that star-speckled lake, facedown, her knees tucked up under her, with one hand, the not-broken one, stretched forwards, fingers dangling into the water, the other still tucked in that sling. I recognised that pose from Gifted and Talented Yoga. It's called child's pose and its Indian name is Balasana, and it's supposed to be a good one for contemplation.

'Winter!' I yelled. 'Get up! We have to go, like, NOW.'

'Go where?' said Winter dreamily.

'You know where, dickhead,' I said, and I do that—I get grumpy when I'm scared so it doesn't show, and it's an unattractive trait, I know.

'Home?'

But we didn't have a home. I stomped my foot down hard then, right on the edge of the lake, hoping that a good splash of water would wake her up a little. But the droplets just sat on her, gently shimmering, and it reminded me of the Christmas Eve when I'd wrapped her up in our fairy lights, like a parcel, and switched them on, and how she hadn't told me that the tiny globes were getting hotter and hotter because she could see how much I loved her there, shining and gorgeous and trapped.

'Winter, I need you to come with me to the top of the mountain, and I can carry you if you need me to—just let me know, but we're leaving right now.'

Slowly, she stood up, and it really did look like she'd been showered with liquid diamonds.

'I've been there,' she said, 'before.'

'Course you have, sugar,' I said, a little more gently, because aren't you supposed to just go along with people's fantasies when they're kind of going demented? 'Sure you have. You can show me around when we reach the top.'

I threw my backpack down for what felt like the zillionth time, and I pulled out the silver blanket, folding it up into a sling so that I could have my shirt back. And I know it seems stupid now—so stupid!—but a tiny part of me wondered if Pops might be up there, at the top of the mountain, waiting after all, in which case the last thing he needed was to be confronted by his daughter topless rock-climbing. After nearly two years, that wasn't the impression I wanted to make.

In spite of the snow, it was hot work, summiting that mountain, and, boy, did I ever wish I had deodorant, because today more than any other day, I totally stank. 'Great,' I said to Winter. 'Our rescuers will get a whiff of us and take off again, no questions asked. This is terrorism right here, how bad I smell.'

When the towpath ran out, petered down to nothing, it was just your basic rockclimbing, that last little bit, scrambling up and over and across, the stone cold and sharp on my palms. Winter refused to let me carry her, and in truth I didn't blame her, so it took forever. Every time I thought that we surely must be about to pop over the lip, there was another slight rise, and another, until I could have cried with frustration. But I didn't have any tears left. I'd entered this weird phase of cool, grounded calm where I knew I had to watch over Winter, get her safely to the top—to wherever came next. Truly, I might have made a pretty great astronaut, because once I am totally focused, boy, I am on, on, on and it's Mission Accomplished.

My lungs were puffing and creaking like an old accordion, and I wondered if the accordion wasn't actually first invented as an instrument of torture that somehow mistakenly found its way into the hands of a merry, gormless troubadour, and we've all been

242

suffering ever since. And, I kid you not, that's what I was thinking about when I reached the summit, which is so un-triumphant and unromantic, and gazed out to the other side.

But maybe it took the shock away from the fact that up there, touching the skin of the sky, I could see more than clearly that this was not an island but just a sticking-out bit of the mainland. And below, twinkling through the gloom, there were lights, and I'm not talking fireflies here—I'm talking the lights of actual buildings, and there were plenty of those, it seemed, scattered below like Lego blocks on a play mat.

It felt like discovering an extra set of limbs on the back of your body that nobody had bothered to tell you were there: creepy and wrong and possibly useful and confusing in so many ways.

I guess you could call it a settlement. And I guess that made our father a liar. I guess.

Winter came up beside me and slipped her twig of an arm into mine and she whispered, 'Summer, I am sorry.'

Winter

We took that frayed piece of rope to a riverbend, cast it into some rapids, watched it streak swiftly away as we held hands.

Then we lay in the meadow, side by side, with Pete snoozing between us, his paws in the air.

Edward stroked my hair so lightly, as if it might melt if he touched it too long. The sky blazed above us, impossibly wide.

'"We live on a blue planet that circles around a ball of fire next to a moon that moves the sea, and you don't believe in miracles?"' I recited. 'That was one of my mother's favourite sayings. She knew so many poems. She could memorise things so easily because of her synaesthesia. Do you know what that is?'

'Crossed senses?' he said. 'Like, when sounds have a taste, days have a colour, that sort of thing?'

'How did you know?' I asked. 'Most people don't.'

'Seriously,' he said, kissing the back of my hand. 'Do you honestly think I'm just most people?'

I let go, stood up, did a handstand, flicked up my feet and rested them on the trunk of a tree. *This isn't a dream*, I said to myself.

'Letters made colours in her mind—little pops of coloured lights, like fireworks.'

'That's crazy,' said Edward. 'The sounds? Or when she saw them written down?'

'Both. So everyone's name made a different rainbow inside her head. Isn't that pretty?' My arms burned, but the muscles down my back felt firm, felt strong. I could stay here forever, I thought, with him. 'And that's how she remembered things—the order of the colours that they painted in her mind.'

'What would my name look like?'

'Well, let's see. Vowels are white and yellow—pale. "R" is purple—'

'Urgh, I hate purple.'

'—and I think "d" was blue. But a really light blue, like, softer than the sky.'

'Oh, great,' said Edward, 'like the colour scheme of a nursery school. That's just dandy. I bet my surname's mauve and peach. And yours?'

'Well, "w" is navy blue, and then the vowels are pale, and "n" is grey and "f" is black and then "r" and "d" are purple and light blue, like I just said.'

'Whoa, whoa, whoa—what do you mean, "f" and "d"? Where's the "t" in all this, Winter?'

I swallowed. 'It's not.'

Summer

I shrugged Winter's arm off gently, pretended like I didn't care that basically my entire life seemed to have been a lie, and she sat straight down, curled herself into a little ball, so small that I might have mistaken her for a teensy boulder. I threw down my backpack and went walking around the top of that mountain, feeling how thin the air was up there, how my head ached right between the eyes from the altitude, like I'd just shovelled in some serious amounts of ice cream. The snowdrifts were so big that walking was basically just lifting your feet high and sinking them down again till you were almost halfway up your thighs in powder. But I hoped that would make it easier to dig up whatever it was that was marked with the X on old Pops's map. You see? I still believed in him. Sometimes it's crazy, how blindly we love.

It was so peaceful there, on top of Our Mountain. You could hear a tear drop. It was beautiful.

I turned my back on the settlement. In the other direction, the rubble of Bartleby was no bigger than a chocolate chip. I sat down in the slush so I could look properly and, though it was wet, the cool of the ground felt lovely. I lay back. Swiped my arms around. 'Look, Winter—snow angels! Remember the Christmas we were in Belarus? Remember how Pops said—ow!'

My left arm struck something hard and I banged my funny bone, which has never and just will never be a source of comedy. I felt like I was going to up-chuck with that weird, tingly pain, and I also felt disproportionately angry. I would dig up that stone and throw it over the side of the mountain, out into oblivion, and it would spin so many times that it would probably leave the Earth's orbit, and wouldn't that serve it right. And, sure, maybe I was angry at other things too. How our father had deceived us, even though we'd trusted him—trusted him all around the world. How my sister had turned herself into a skeleton. There was nothing, now, that was still pure.

I dug around that stone, ripped the snow up in chunks, smashed it into snowballs, threw them at the sky, and when the tips of my fingers went numb, I thought, *What do I care?* I kept on anyway, and pretty soon I figured out that the stone I was uncovering wasn't a stone. Well, that's not entirely right. It was the top of a stone and I'm not just talking any stone, I'm talking a gravestone, that unmistakable slab that says Death and Not Forgetting.

'Someone died up here,' I called over to Winter.

But she just sat with her head drooped down, breathing.

'Are you okay there, kid?' I said, but I was sort of distracted. I'd cleared off enough snow to see the top of the inscription, chiselled out all chunky and tender and perfect.

And that's when I started flinging the snow out behind me like a desperate dog, because I knew those letters. Though I hadn't said it for three years, I knew that name.

And though her name was here, she wasn't.

That someone hadn't died up here.

She died on a desert dune. The sand looked hot. I had wondered if it burned her knees through the jumpsuit, though I guess it was the least of her worries at that point.

And this is the part where I need to tell you that I lied.

Not one time: lots of times. Over and over I told the same stories—a serial liar. A weak little fraud.

Because our mother didn't die with Winter curled inside her.

She died when we were eleven.

They took her out to the desert and ripped open her prison jumpsuit and wrote something on her bare breasts. It said, SPEAK NO MORE. They left it hanging open.

247

They made her read something, and her voice was still so warm and clear and pretty, just like it was on the radio, even though I could tell she didn't believe what she was saying.

Then they made her say her name and she did, so proudly, such a strong, regal name. And then she turned and vomited onto the sand, because she knew what was coming next. Everyone knew what was coming next.

Everyone in the world saw it, and that's not just me exaggerating in my Summer-speak. It was the first killing they spliced into the news, into movie theatres, on every screen across the world. It flashed into computer labs full of strung-out uni students high on No-Doz, and classrooms full of kinder kids with iPads playing treasure island alphabet games, and nursing home rec rooms, the old-timers propped up in their chairs, not really knowing if what they were seeing was real or dementia haze, and onto the TVs in gyms with those buff corporate guys pounding squeaky treadmills on their lunchbreaks. In Times Square and department stores. On every mobile phone.

Nobody could work out how to stop it—not for days. By then people could see her face, her head, every time they closed their eyes.

Over and over, every hour, my mother came back. Her name. The vomit. Her chest.

Her head.

We were in Tokyo when we saw it. My father had taken us back to Japan while he organised the seaplane to bring us here, got all the supplies together. Our mother had been gone for months by then but somehow we still had hope. She would be back some day soon, red glasses dangling round her neck. We were supposed to be in hiding in our apartment while we packed up her books and he packed up his lab.

✧

But they found him. Through a chain of threats and whispers, they gave him twenty-four hours.

His secrets for her life.

'Let's celebrate! Should we go and get peach bubble tea?' Winter had said that day when we'd sealed the last box—the one with *To Kill a Mockingbird* stacked on the top, waiting to greet us wherever we'd be when we opened it next. We went back to the skyscraper climbing gym and, boy, was Eric happy to see us. His bumbag was blue—blue like a peacock's chest. We did karaoke and drank our favourite bubble tea, just like old times. Except it wasn't.

Suddenly there she was, our mother, on the screen of that karaoke booth. And on every screen, wherever we ran, wherever we turned. Boy oh boy, there are a lot of screens in Tokyo—on the sides of buildings, in lifts, in trains. We couldn't escape. It was burned into the backs of our eyes, and I want to say retinas but I'm pretty sure that's only half right.

Her death was a message to the Resistance. To everyone around the world who had been trying to fight back—who had listened to her words about freedom, beauty, hope. Were they all for nothing?

And now there it was, her name, on that smooth piece of stone on top of this very tall mountain, and the date she was alive and the date that she'd died, which wasn't the day we were born, and I'd run from that date for so long that, as I knelt to clear the last of the snow from the bottom of her gravestone and trace my finger around the letters of her name, I felt relieved that I could stop running now.

Winter stood up and came over and looked at those words for a long time. Then she sat down and leaned her head against the stone and closed her eyes. She whispered, like she had a million times across our lives, 'Read it. Out loud. Read it, Summer. Read it to me.'

I couldn't. I swallowed and tried again. I couldn't. I swallowed and tried again.

'You made me live without her,' Winter said sleepily. 'You tried to make me forget until all I did was remember. I just wanted to love her with you, so it wouldn't feel so lonely.'

I started to cry, then, and I know I've said that before but I mean *really* cry.

On and on in ripples and waves, until I felt I could have filled the moat at dear old Bartleby, if it still existed anywhere but our hearts. There were so many things I was crying for and I'm not going to itemise them here like a shopping list but I bet if I gave you a pen and paper, you'd be able to have a good crack at that yourself. Everything you've ever heard about my mother—and people talked about her a lot—it was all true. She was brave and bubbly, clever and noble, wise and funny and good. If anyone deserved not to...Well, you get the drift.

When I had wiped away enough tears to be able to see and dealt with the strings of snot and the sore-throat hiccups, I looked across at Winter. She was lying in the snow with her back to me, curled around our mother's gravestone as if it were the last true thing left in the world. And through her singlet, the outline of her spine was a foot-long string of pearls.

'Winter,' I said. But she didn't move and I couldn't see her face to know if her eyes were open or closed.

'Winter, I'm sorry,' I said. 'I wasn't as strong as you. I never have been.'

That was the truth—all of it, bundled up so neatly. And at that second, as it came out of my mouth, I realised I had always known it and that Winter had, too.

But she didn't say anything.

'Winter,' I said, louder now. 'I admit it—I lied. And I made you live that lie, and I get that. I just didn't want you to have to remember what you did—at the market. I'm sorry. I couldn't *be* more sorry. Please forgive me. Say you forgive me?'

I went and lay down and curled myself around her tiny back and tucked my knees in the crook of her knees and put my chin on her shoulder, and it was lucky I was so close, right up in her grill, because even then I could hardly hear as she breathed out, 'Yes. I forgive you.'

And then, high on relief, I put my arm around her chest and squeezed her to me, and you actually, literally cannot imagine how she screamed—the shrillness of; the brutal pitch. How her body arched, all writhing animal, flipping fish. She sprang up, her hands on her back, moaning.

'What did I do? What is it?' I asked, trying to grab hold of her, but she was thrashing against me and her eyes were rolling around, all whites, and in the half-darkness, boy, was that spooky. I said, 'Stop it—you're scaring me. Calm down and just tell me what's wrong.'

But she didn't say anything.

When she had slowed to a shiver, I looked at her wasted little body, and that's when it suddenly dawned on me, and maybe you've guessed this all along, but clearly I didn't, and oh, oh, oh, it would have been so obvious in the daylight from the colour of her skin. Minami's eyes flashed through my mind, so brown and gentle, like a bright young deer's.

'Winter,' I said slowly, calmly, as I stepped towards her, though inside me was so very Not Calm. 'Turn around and pull up your singlet. Winter, show me your back.'

Winter

Winifred

If I hadn't turned my head that day in the market, in Egypt, they wouldn't have taken my mother.

In my dreams I have unturned it a thousand times. A hundred thousand.

I have whispered to the sky, *Come back. Take me instead. I will be so well behaved in heaven.* I was always good—it was just this one time.

But then I think about Edward, and my father, and I wonder, *What is good? What is bad?*

Summer

It's ironic, how beautiful that web of bruises was, blooming across Winter's back. So delicate—I'm talking spider-web fine—and dark against her skin, like a chocolate pattern marbled in white icing. I wished Winter could see it up close and we could study it forever.

And as I pulled Winter's shirt back down, I thought about how the things that make us vulnerable also make us beautiful, and how the parts of ourselves that we hide away are the ones that we should probably hold up to the sun.

I felt it as a stillness in me, Winter's Greying. And for once I didn't say anything, just folded her into my arms as if she were a paper girl.

Winter

On the night before Edward betrayed me, we stood side by side on the banks of the river in the moonbeams. The light flowed like liquid silver. He ran his fingers so softly over the back of my wrist.

I said, 'There is nothing more beautiful than this here now.'

He turned and he flipped my hand over to look at my palm.

He looked up, right into my eyes, and he said to me, 'Your mother, your father—that wasn't your fault. None of it. Do you hear me, Winifred? They would have found them soon enough anyway. They knew she was there. They knew he was here. They know everything about you. You didn't stand a chance.'

'You can just call me Winnie,' I said. 'Then it's Winter and Winifred together, you see? Not one or the other.'

'Stop changing the subject,' he said. 'I want you to say: *This was not my fault*. None of it—past or present or future. Whatever happens, promise me you'll remember that you haven't done anything wrong. You're the sweetest thing that ever lived. Say it: *This was not my fault.*'

The future was him. I see that now, the things he took: my mind, my heart, the truth.

The past was my mother being captured, and my father hanging himself, mad with grief and the ghouls of his own mistakes.

And the present was my love for Edward.

I say it again and it means something different.

The present was my love for him.

I am standing on top of a mountain.

I shout out to the world, 'THIS WAS NOT MY FAULT.'

Summer

As I set off through the snow, I was thinking of that sore and helpless feeling that comes from being stuck in the middle of who you are and who you wish you could be. How life is a daisy chain of moments where you have the chance to be better, but you fail at being selfless or honest or brave.

Like when someone comes to school and you know they no longer have a brother and you've spent the whole weekend obsessively imagining the empty place at their dinner table, not that you've ever even bothered to think much about that table since you went there for dinner about seven years ago on the way to a bowling party. And they turn up to class, that someone, and you've all just been told to Act Normal, and you just sort of whisper 'hi' into the ground when every bit of you wants to do and say and be more, to be everything, but you just can't bring yourself to look up and into their eyes.

Or when there's a guy on the edge of the road to your dad's office in the city, his knees pushing out his jeans and a bright-yellow sore on his knuckles, like a really bad new-shoe blister, his hair all greasy like he's been washing hot dishes all day except he hasn't because he doesn't have a job and he doesn't have a home and what he does have is a putrid smell like a baked cat-pee pie, and in spite of that, or maybe because, all you want to do is put money in his grimy, faded football cap but should you and can you because maybe he'll use it for something No Good, and don't you need the cash for the movies, and does that make you a terrible person, and what is the weight of that guy's life when you hold it in the palm of your hand? So you walk on by and you try to say 'Sorry' but it gets caught in your throat like a squeak.

It was Winter who pushed past the desks and chairs in the

classroom and, with the gentlest, truest hug, said, not even in a mumble, 'I'm so very, very sorry about your brother.'

It was Winter who was scared of that bright-yellow knuckle sore but shook that guy's hand anyway, and introduced herself like he was the boss of her work-experience placement, and gave him the Italian bread sticks and blackcurrant wine gums our dad's secretary had given us for movie snacks.

It had always been Winter. And I guess I've gone off topic just slightly here, but you get what I'm saying, and it isn't really about wine gums. Not even a bit.

Winter

The snow on the summit reminds me of Belarus at Christmas. We were there when I was seven, all wearing pompom hats. I had striped mittens. We were walking along, arms linked, in a line.

The streetlights made the snowdrifts glow golden. A sleigh went past with a powdery swish.

We had been singing rounds of Christmas carols. My mother sang the harmonies. Pops knew half the words in Latin.

'See those icicles hanging down from the tips of the trees?' my mother asked. 'There's a name for those. Clinkerbells. Isn't that pretty?' She closed her eyes and said it again.

'What colour is it, Mum?' I asked. 'Right now—right this second—what colour do you see?'

She paused, then she whispered with tears in her throat, 'What I see...What I see are the colours for Love.'

My father lay down, right in the snow. He stretched out his arms into glorious wings. He looked up at us. Stars shone out of his eyes.

'This is love,' he said. 'This right here. This is love. We are love.'

Taking Winter down the other side of the mountain, well, it shouldn't have been too tricky at all. She was so light by then, and so brutally tiny, that a whole flock of backlit angels could have flown down to pick her up, and it only would have taken one, medium-sized, to carry her home, wherever that was. But racing down a slope is so very much harder than climbing up, and if you're not Careful (capital C), you will tip on your ankles and jar your knees, and the stones will slip under you so that you get a fright like ice-water rushing to your feet, and there's so much clammy sweat it's like you're covered in glue.

But I did it, zigzagged down towards the settlement that I still couldn't quite believe was actually there, careful not to bump about too much because of that howling-dog pain that was living in Winter now. We got nearer to the lights and the square buildings with their flat-topped roofs and the empty roads that were hardly roads, and it struck me that this was a town—a real town. We passed a warehouse kind of building on the outskirts, and through the half-light I could read the sign—Rod's Roller Rink—and I had to try so hard not to start crying again, I almost bit a crater into my own tongue. All those years, we had been living across from a gosh-darn rollerskating rink, and shops, and probably a movie theatre that sold hot, buttered popcorn, and other children, other hearts, other stories that could have rescued us from the tight clamp of our little lives.

I started to whisper to Winter to distract myself from the full horror of that thought, and because, after all this time, the idea of interacting with another human was actually pretty terrifying, even for a Talker like me, and I felt like I needed to practise.

'Look at that moon,' I said. 'You wouldn't want to miss all those moons we've got coming. And the sunsets. It's worth staying just for those, isn't it? All peaches and orange and berry and plum.

'If I just keep talking and you just keep breathing, that's a fair deal, isn't it. In and out, just like that. You should be proud, how well you're doing. I'll be here. You just sleep.'

It wasn't hard to find it, a sign on a building with a cross in red. Someone opened the door below it, which I took as a very good omen. It was a lady, full-masked, everything covered and gloved, and only her eyes showing, but I could see straight away the 'sorry but no' on that tiny bit of face, even as she took in Winter's sad grey skin in the light that spilled from her doorway and automatically looked to her back for the rectangular slit that wasn't there, for the bloom of a bruise. She was gentle but firm in a way that made me want to tell her everything.

'We're not taking anyone, I'm afraid,' she said. 'We just can't. Our medical supplies here are virtually non-existent now. I'd love to help, but—'

'Not me,' I said. 'Just my sister.'

'She has…?'

'Yes,' I said. 'But look here.'

I lifted my knee and propped Winter up a little so I could reach, gently, gently, into the pouch around her neck. 'This here—see this vial? This is the cure for The Greying. My father was…He was captured, but he left this. He was the scientist who…He made it. Take it—there's enough for two doses. Give one to Winter and use the other one to make more. For everyone else. You can clone it, but promise me—*promise* me you will give one to my sister first.'

The lady's eyebrows frowned at the vial glowing green in my hand, so bright and merry against the gloom.

But she didn't take it.

She didn't believe me, I could tell, and suddenly Winter felt so heavy, so hot against my chest, that precious little bundle of bones.

My tears dripped down onto her hair and shimmered there like globs of mercury. After everything, it hurt so much to love her, but of course I couldn't help it.

I swallowed and licked the corners of my lips, wet and salty. I breathed as deep as I could. '*Please.* You might remember my mother. She was on the radio. Her name was Katherine King.'

The lady's hand flew up to her mouth, and there it was, that pain, that horror, even in the slim gap of her eyes through the mask. I knew what she'd seen.

'Oh, child, child,' she said. 'Oh, child.' She held out her arms then, and took Winter as if she were only cotton, and hugged her close. She said, 'And with your father gone, too. Oh, child, I'm so sorry. How did you survive out there so long?'

Our mother's books. Bartleby. Half a lifetime's worth of Bonne Maman. The silver fishhooks of our love.

'We had hazelnut praline,' I whispered. 'For a while.'

She took the vial between the thumb and forefinger of the hand that was cradling Winter's head. It looked so fragile there, and yet I knew she wouldn't drop it. This lady radiated strength. Like a lion. Like a bear.

'Is there anyone left?' I asked her. 'Out there? Is there anyone who cares?'

'You don't know?' she asked, her eyebrows raised.

I shook my head.

'Your mother,' she said, then paused. 'What they wrote on her chest...'

'Speak no more,' I whispered.

She nodded. She smiled. 'Well, believe you me, they're speaking now.'

Winter

Up on Our Mountain, I turned away from Summer.

'Come,' she had said. 'Come back to the cave with Doc and with me. Our bones will make crystals. They'll be there for always. Solidified light.'

But I already knew it, that story's sad end.

So I walked to the edge and I dropped right over. I blocked my ears from Summer's gasp.

Turns out Mama was the spark of something huge—a big old match on a haystack of hope. Apparently, people loved her even more fiercely once she was gone. Took to the streets in red reading glasses. Rose up and kicked back with her warm, kind words tattooed on their hearts. Formed chains of their own around the globe, lassoed it in a ring of light.

There was a branch right here in the settlement. They met at Rod's Roller Rink.

They'd been there the whole time.

Who knew if the world would start turning again—who ever really knows anything? But if it did, at least now there'd still be people to throw up their hats and cheer and fight on. And Winter would be one of them.

So that was it. My work was done.

'And not you? What about you?' said the lady in the mask. 'You could stay—we could find a place for you here. They would make an exception, I'm sure of it.'

I gazed down at Winter, who looked so like my mother when she slept. And suddenly I could see it all so clearly.

How she had moved a whole mountain, all on her own. How, when she was better, she would need space to run. How you can't put a butterfly back in a chrysalis.

'Oh, I'll be fine out there,' I said. 'I have strong mountaineering instincts. Please, please, just remember the vial. Please hurry.'

I kissed Winter's forehead, buried my face in her hair and breathed in.

She smelled the same as always, like sun after rain.

'Winter, it wasn't your fault,' I whispered next to her ear. 'They wouldn't want you to blame yourself. They forgive you, Mama and Pops—Walter, too. They never stopped loving you. Neither will I. Cross my gosh-darn heart.'

Winter

I crouched on a ledge, like Edward had showed me. He had showed me so many wonderful things. Whoever he was, whatever he was, couldn't change how I'd changed just being with him.

From there, I can see the tiny church my father built.

Saint Katherine's, it's called. After my mother.

I can see the shadow of our seaplane, sunk off the coast.

The forest where my father died.

The misty lights of another life.

The breeze is cool as the night falls slowly.

My stomach rumbles.

'Pops?' I whisper. 'Can you hear me?'

The whole world rustles.

I stand in the wind.

I smile. I feel pure.

I walked back up the mountain for who knows how long, because my mind felt like a big puff of fairy floss and I couldn't tell if an hour had passed or a hot second.

'Is this real?' I asked myself. 'Is anything real?'

And of course that made me think of *The Velveteen Rabbit*, who is basically the biggest sweetheart who ever was, and his conversation with the Skin Horse, which I guess is a horse with no hair, and that is not something I'd like to meet in a shady alley on a rainy Sunday, but the rest of it is A-plus.

The Skin Horse tells the Rabbit that being Real (capital R) isn't about how you start out. How it's what happens when a kid loves you—cuddles-you-to-death-a-bunch-of-times loves you. REALLY loves you. That's when you're finally Real.

And then the Rabbit asks if it hurts, which I think is a very good question, coming from a rabbit.

'Sometimes,' says the Skin Horse. But then he says that you don't mind being hurt if you're Real. It's kind of part of the package.

As I started climbing back up that mountain, all weary, I wondered, *Was I Real now? Had I become Real?*

Because every part of me hurt for Winter, Hurt (capital H), and yet somehow I didn't mind, not one bit, because now she was free.

'Is velveteen the same as velvet?' I once asked my mother.

'I think it's a velvet-sateen blend,' she said seriously, but I could hear the wink in her voice. 'I would advise a cold wash only for that kind of fabric hybrid.'

'You're tricking,' I said. 'You don't really know, do you?'

'Nope,' she said. 'First one to heaven gets to ask the author.'

As I hiked alone back the way we'd come, they bubbled up hard, those memories I'd pushed down these past years. Her reading glasses with the red frames. Crosswords at breakfast. Honey crumpets. Christmas-tree ornaments. Her palms on my cheeks. A brush through my hair.

It felt so nice to remember. Like leaning back onto the wind.

'Why did I do that?' I asked the stars. 'Why did I make myself forget?'

I was trying to get back to the cave, the cave with the ice crystals, but every now and then I stopped mid-step with the thought that it was a dream, that cave, or something from a book. I don't mean Doc and Peekay and *The Power of One*. I mean another story. Had Winter written it?

I felt her all around me, Winter; felt her in my breath and on my back. How it hurt from carrying her all that way, my back. How it ached tightly.

And then I was sitting on the ground, and because I couldn't remember how I got there, I laughed, and because I couldn't remember why I was laughing, boy, I laughed some more. And then I ate an apple, and that apple was the moon.

That was when Mikie came to the party, gliding on his belly through the snow, pulling up beside me with an impressive powdery swish.

'Hey, Summer,' he said gently, 'may I look at your skin?'

I went right up close to his big old eye, but he shook his head because my face was covered in frozen tears that made it hard for him to look me over properly. So I wriggled my arm out of the coat I wasn't wearing, but wasn't the light too gloomy to really tell what colour it was?

'Everything off,' he said.

So I pulled my clothes over my head. And though all around me was snow, my naked little self was in flames. I put up my arms and

266

wiggled my fingers, watching orange fire shooting out against the orange-purple sky.

'Look, Mikie!' I said, and turned a cartwheel. Over and over I turned, a burning tumbleweed against the plains of crinkly white.

And when I had finished, I sank to my knees. My dragon breath was tiny clouds.

I put my hands slowly up onto my back and that was where the fire was.

I gulped back the pain.

I felt the tender web of bruises there.

I stood up and walked over to that gorgeous whale. It took so much longer than cartwheeling. Was I ever weary.

'Mikie?' I whispered. 'I'm trying to get back to that cave.'

'Couldn't be easier, kid,' he said. 'Jump on my back.'

'I'm not wearing any clothes,' I said.

'Me neither,' said Mikie.

As I lay there, at the mouth of that big old crystal cave, I thought about Charlotte, the dear old spider in *Charlotte's Web*.

How, when her work is done, when she's weaved the magic that will save dear Wilbur the pig from being made into bacon, her time on earth is over.

And though it's Sad (capital S), perhaps that's the beauty of the world: to have lived, however long or short, and weaved some magic for someone else.

But what was the magic I'd weaved for Winter? My love? Her freedom? A future? Our past?

'Don't overthink it, kid,' was Mikie's advice from outside the opening.

'But isn't this the time to nail down the point of my existence?'

'Nah. Plenty of time for that where you're going.'

'Oh,' I said.

'Yup,' he said.

'Say, Mikie?' I asked. 'The ending isn't the story, is it.'

'Nope,' he agreed. 'There's so much more to it than that.'

'Mikie?' I said.

'Yes, Pretty?'

'I'm so tired.'

'It's okay, kid. Just scooch on over. Rest in me.'

Winter

From there I rolled and I slid and I scrambled.

I woke up with skinned knees not that far from the bottom.

The sky was navy, the blue mist had gone.

I started to run. Down the mountain, over rocks. I ran until there was nothing but me and my breath—no Edward, no Summer, no mother, no father, no Pete and no Walter. No future. No past.

Someone found me on a path. My feet had no soles. My heels bled trails of crimson dots.

They carried me, that someone. They said it wasn't hard. I was thin with the hurt that it took me to live.

I woke up. Time had passed. A drip in my arm. No part of me was still a child.

Not to get too whimsical about my demise, but I pretty much ended up just like Judy in *Seven Little Australians*.

We both slipped away just after sundown. And, sure, she had seen the sun that same day, whereas ours had been gone for a while by then. And yes, she had people all around her—all those little Australians kissing her lips and caressing her hair.

But I was not alone.

As I climbed into a floating hammock made of stars, Mikie was there. He swam alongside me—the whole way he was with me as I rose up and above and away. Boy, was that journey *long*. And arched above my head was a sign made of lights, flashing slowly, slowly, like a big old lighthouse: GOODBYE! I LOVE YOU! GOODBYE! I LOVE YOU!

When I got here, I yawned so deep I sucked in the whole sky and breathed it out again, but nobody seemed to mind.

And then, I'm not kidding, they gave me wings, *actual* wings, and I'm not exaggerating when I say that they are Huge (capital H). 'Proportionate to the love you gave on earth,' they told me when I asked about the sizing, and they sounded kind of bored with the question, truth be told. At the start I could hardly lift my arms but, hoo boy, you should see me now. Perhaps you already have.

Now I bet, I just bet you can't wait to hear what it's like, this place, and I don't blame you. Not one bit.

But lately I've realised there are some things that don't need to be crushed with all the world's words.

Which is why I like it here, where it's quiet and still and cool and white. Like winter.

Winter

I'm here now, and safe. The sheets are white. They feed me sugar water. I drift and grow bigger. I write all this down. At night time, the bed rails glow, silver as fish.

They talk about coping, survival, our choices. When they think I am sleeping, they read it, this journal. 'How real was Summer,' they ask, 'to you?'

Edward hasn't been. I still dream that he is coming.

And Summer isn't with me.

Perhaps she never was.

Summer

Now I have finished this story, I will go looking.

For my mother and my father—and for Ponyboy Curtis.

Perhaps I'll introduce them if the moment's right.

When I've found him, I will tell him, 'Just FYI, Ponyboy, if I were you I'd think about cutting your hair sometime in the next century. Because one day, some day, my sister is coming to meet you and she isn't into ponytails. But I kid you not, by the time she gets here she will have saved the world and, hoo boy, she is all you've ever ached for.'

Winter

Today I asked for a scone with jam.

The jam was bright peach, like the beat before sunrise.

I looked at that jam and I thought, *Yes, I will.*

As I ate that scone, my stomach was sore with the newness of it. I closed my eyes. My hands shook. I fought with my breath. But the end of the world wasn't bigger than love. At least, not for me.

So I chewed. And I turned my face to the stars. 'Thank you,' I whispered.

'You're welcome,' they replied in the voice of a man.

I opened my eyes. We looked at each other with wonder. With love.

'Walter?' I asked. 'Is that you? Are you real?'

'Are you?' he asked back with crinkled-up eyes.

I smiled. 'I guess. Hey—Walter?' I asked. 'How do I do this?'

He leaned across to the window, pulled open the curtain. Pink dawn spilled over the turning world. 'You just keep on living,' he said to me kindly. 'You just keep on living till you learn to live again.'

'In the midst of winter, I found there was, within me,
an invincible summer. And that makes me happy.
For it says that no matter how hard the world pushes
against me, within me, there's something stronger—
something better, pushing right back.'

Albert Camus

The Books in This Book

Alice in Wonderland by Lewis Carroll

Anne of Green Gables by Lucy Maud Montgomery

Bridge to Terabithia by Katherine Paterson

Catcher in the Rye by J. D. Salinger

Charlotte's Web by E. B. White

Diary of a Young Girl by Anne Frank

Extremely Loud and Incredibly Close by Jonathan Safran Foer

Forever by Judy Blume

Gone with the Wind by Margaret Mitchell

Little House in the Big Woods by Laura Ingalls Wilder

Little Women by Louisa May Alcott

Matilda by Roald Dahl

Moby-Dick by Herman Melville

Oliver Twist by Charles Dickens

Pride and Prejudice by Jane Austen

Seven Little Australians by Ethel Turner

The Graveyard Book by Neil Gaiman

The Great Gatsby by F. Scott Fitzgerald

The Harry Potter series by J. K. Rowling

The Lion, the Witch and the Wardrobe by C. S. Lewis

The Outsiders by S. E. Hinton

The Power of One by Bryce Courtenay

The Ramona series by Beverly Cleary

The Secret Garden by Frances Hodgson Burnett

The Velveteen Rabbit by Margery Williams

To Kill a Mockingbird by Harper Lee

With special Thanks (capital T)…

To the whole smart team at Text, and most especially to my talented and ever-patient editor, Alaina Gougoulis, for taking a gamble on this very strange book and making it the best it could possibly be. Alaina, what a gift it has been to work with you.

To Imogen Stubbs, Art Director and A-plus human, for dreaming up the miraculous cover, and to the illustrator, Kate Forrester, for pulling it off so beautifully.

To my agent, Pippa Masson, who watches over me with such loyal care.

To Helen Withycombe, my 1800PLOTFIX. It's always summer when we're together.

To dear Allison Colpoys, Jane Godwin, Katie Evans, Virginia Millen, Sally Rippin and Meg Whelan, whose enthusiasm for this book in various drafts kept it alive in my heart/mind.

To Edward and Peter Holmes, for workshopping this story in the back of a car and for making the world a better place.

To Suzie Brans, for her wise words and spare room, and for caring enough to know when I'd finished.

To the Scarlett Appreciation Society, for love and support over many writing seasons.

To Wendell Berry, for his poem 'The Peace of Wild Things', which is always there when winter falls.

To my sister and my brother, so smart and brave, for being with me through every chapter.

To my father—superfan and PR machine!—without whose sunny optimism, I would never have started this journey/novel.

And to my mother, dearest Vivienne, who fought to save the world in her own humble way.